THE HEIST

Jack Dillon Dublin Tale 14

Second Edition

THE HEIST

Jack Dillon Dublin Tale 14
Second Edition

Mike Faricy

Published by

MJF Publishing
https://www.mikefaricybooks.com

ACKNOWLEDGMENTS

I would like to thank the following people for their help & support: Special thanks to Nick, Roy, Julie, Mittie, and Toui for their hard work, cheerful patience and positive feedback. I would like to thank family and friends for their encouragement and unqualified support. Special thanks to Maggie, Jed, Schatz, Pat, Av, Emily and Pat, for not rolling their eyes, at least when I was there. Most of all, to my wife, Teresa, whose belief, support and inspiration has, from day one, never waned.

To Teresa
"It's all banjaxed . . ."

PROLOGUE

2001 - New Orleans

The Patrick Kincannon Abstract Art Museum was constructed in 1974 under the guidance of art collector Patrick Kincannon to house his personal art collection for the public to view. Kincannon died in 1987, leaving his substantial estate to the museum.

In the early hours of March 18th, 2001, two individuals, Martin Lane and Eddie McDonnell, dressed as police officers, parked at the side entrance to the museum.

They'd been sitting in the car for over two hours. It was almost 1:00 in the morning.

"Come on, Eddie, either we're going to do it tonight, or I'm going home. It was St. Paddy's Day, and I've missed the entire night of women too drunk to remember their own name. We've been sitting here twiddling our thumbs, and I've had it. So, either we go, or I'm driving you home, and I might still catch a pint at Cooper's and hopefully find some little dream who is too drunk to care."

"Jesus, will you ever calm down, Martin? I said we'd do it, and we will."

"Okay, fish or cut bait, man. I'm going. You with me?" Lane said as he opened the driver's door and stepped out of the car. He glanced at McDonnell, still looking unsure about what to do, and slammed the driver's door.

McDonnell shook his head and climbed out of the car. "You follow me," he said as he stormed past Lane. He headed toward the side door, the security entrance, pulling his police officer's hat on as he went. He gave three long rings to the security doorbell.

It took a couple of minutes before the light flicked on, and a man looked out the window. Seeing the two dressed as police officers, he gave a quick wave and opened the door. "Hi, guys. What's up?"

"We had a report of a silent alarm going off. Just want to check and make sure everything is okay," Lane said.

"Silent alarm? I don't even think we have one."

"Oh, yeah, you do. It alerted us about twelve minutes ago."

"It's not showing up on our screen."

"Yeah. It's designed not to do that. Mind if we just take a quick look?"

"No, no, that's not a problem. Come on in."

"Just procedure, but we need to check your ID as well, you know, just in case."

"Yeah, sure," the man said, pulling out his wallet and handing his driver's license to Lane.

"Thomas Fischer," Lane read. "And how long have you been working here?"

"This is my third year. I work the night shift. Live downstairs in the basement apartment."

"Anyone else on staff with you tonight, Thomas?"

"No, just me. Terry, he's the morning shift, comes in around 7:00. I sleep till noon and head over to Orleans U for classes in the afternoon."

"Let's take a look at your security system," Lane said as he handed the driver's license back to Fischer.

"Just back this way," Fischer said and headed down the hall to a U-shaped desk behind a floor-to-ceiling glass wall. Three computer screens were arranged on the desk. As they stepped into the office, McDonnell pulled out the roll of duct tape.

Lane pulled out his pistol and waved it at Fischer. "I think it would be a good idea if you got down on your knees."

"What the—Hey, wait a minute. I told you I'm the security guy. I work here. I—"

"On your knees, now."

"But I—"

"Now, damn it!"

As soon as Fischer knelt down, McDonnell pulled Fischer's arms behind his back and duct taped his wrists together. He lowered Fischer onto the floor, wrapped the tape over his eyes and his mouth, and then taped his ankles together.

"Check out these screens. Can you turn off the alarm systems?"

"I think so, give me a moment," McDonnell said. There was a Rolodex next to one of the computer screens, and he thumbed through it until he came to a card labeled Security Central. There were three passwords just below the 800 phone number. "Okay, here we go," he said and began typing on the keyboard. Two minutes later, the alarms had been disconnected. "We'll head up to the Abstract Expression room once we get the phone call."

It wasn't long before the phone rang. McDonnell lifted the receiver and said, "Kincannon Abstract Art Museum. Yes, not a problem. Something set off our alarm. Probably a mouse, but the police are here going through every room. Yes, just a moment," he said and pulled the Rolodex closer. "Our code is one-seven-seven-three-J-M-five-zero. Yes, thank you for checking. We should be back to normal within the next hour or so. Yes, sir. Thank you," he said and hung up.

"Let's go," Lane said as he wrapped duct tape around the leg of the U-shaped desk and then wrapped the tape around Fischer's ankles. Once that was completed, they headed into the front lobby and up the stairs to the second floor using their flashlights.

They both pulled out a box cutter armed with a razor blade. It took just seventeen minutes to cut eight Mark Rothko canvas paintings from their frames and roll them up. They placed four rubber bands around each rolled canvas and hurried back down the stairs. After checking on Fischer, still taped to the leg of the desk, they hurried out the door, into their car, and drove off.

ONE

Dillon heard the toilet flush and rolled over on his side. He opened his eyes and blinked a few times. The digital clock on the dresser read 5:55 AM. A moment later, he heard what sounded like the shower come on, and a few seconds after that, the shower door closed. He sat up and positioned his pillow against the powder blue upholstered headboard.

Nessa's bedroom, like the rest of her house, with the exception of Dillon's clothes on the floor, was neat and tidy. He debated getting dressed and leaving but decided that would cause an immediate end to the beginning relationship, so he waited patiently while reviewing the previous evening.

They'd had dinner at the Bald Eagle in Phibsboro with his partner Paddy Suel and a woman named Kira whom Dillon had never met. Try as he may, he couldn't recall Kira's last name. Not that it really mattered. Suel seemed to go through partners even faster than Dillon, and that was saying something. Although, given their jobs in Dublin's An Garda Síochána, Special Branch, it wasn't at all unusual. Still, Kira seemed like a nice enough woman, and Suel obviously fancied her, at least for the moment.

He thought about Nessa. They'd been an item for almost ninety days, which for Dillon was heading toward almost a record with an Irish woman. Of course, there was always Tara, his neighbor. He'd been in an on-again, off-again, physical relationship with her for a number of years, usually enhanced with a bottle or two of wine. She clearly had no interest in a long-term solo relationship with him, nor he with her. It was more a matter of convenience for both of them, and that was just fine.

"Your turn," Nessa said, stepping out of the steamy bathroom. A powder-blue towel was wrapped around her lovely figure, and a smaller white towel was wrapped around her hair. "Did you hear what I just said?"

"I think you said you wanted to crawl back into bed with me and—"

"Don't get your hopes up. Besides, we both have to get to work, and before you go, you've got to deal with your special friend Lucifer. Lord only knows what havoc he caused with you here for the night."

"I told you we could have gone to my place last night."

"And have him chew up another one of my thongs? I don't think so."

"How do you know that wasn't me?"

She glanced over and said, "Good point. Come on now, into the shower. I'll put the coffee on. Will you stay for breakfast?"

He shook his head. "No, you don't need to be cooking for me first thing in the morning. I'll grab a quick shower and get out of your way," he said as he climbed out of bed.

"Perfect. I'll have coffee ready for you when you come down," she said and gave him a peck on the cheek as he headed into the bathroom.

When he entered the kitchen, she was standing at the marble-topped kitchen counter, running the hairdryer over her shoulder-length blonde hair. She had traded the powder-blue bathroom towel for her powder-blue bathrobe. A mug of steaming coffee was on the opposite side of the kitchen counter, and a steaming mug of tea with about three drops of milk sat in front of Nessa.

Dillon knew it would be instant coffee, something he hated and an item that Irish tea drinkers were unable to comprehend. He took a quick sip, tried not to grimace, and said, "Busy day ahead?"

"We have a wretched zoom meeting at 10:00, a complete waste of thirty minutes, but better than sitting in the conference room for twice that amount of time. I'll never understand. They want everyone working, and then they insist we waste our time listening to nonsense on a zoom call. God save us."

Dillon took two more sips of instant coffee and said, "I'll leave you to it. With any luck, they'll cancel the meeting, and you can work through the morning."

"If only," she said and lifted her chin as he stepped around the counter to give her a kiss.

"Thanks again for last night. I don't like sharing you with other people, but it was a fun evening."

"Oh, the two of them, one crazier than the next. It was a fun night. Give me a call tomorrow, and we'll chat."

He gave her another kiss, and she pointed the hairdryer at him. "I'll call you tomorrow. Thanks again," he said as he stepped into the front entryway and out the front door. He closed the door behind him and checked to make sure it was locked. He climbed into his car and drove home. He let Lucifer out into the front garden and went upstairs to change.

TWO

Forty minutes later, he was in the Special Branch break room, sipping from a mug of coffee, when DI Paddy Suel walked in. "Well, nice to see you survived the evening, Dillon. Things are still going well with Nessa?"

"Yeah, so far. You look happy, which suggests Kira hasn't come to her senses yet."

"Lovely evening, nice dinner, and then some romance before I had to head home."

"Who knows, Paddy, it might be the two of us have finally lucked out and found the perfect women?"

"We'll see about that. I was just thinking that—"

"Dillon and Suel, if you wouldn't mind joining us in my office, please," DCI McCabe called from his office door.

"Oh, for the love of—Now what have you done, Dillon?"

"Don't look at me, Paddy. I'm sure this is about something you've managed to screw up." Dillon set his coffee mug on the counter and followed Suel into DCI McCabe's office.

"Gentlemen, if you wouldn't mind closing the door behind you," McCabe said as they entered. Two formal-looking men, one on the couch, the other in the wingback chair, studied Dillon and Suel.

It was the odd time that McCabe would be seated on the black leather couch instead of behind his desk, but that was where he was now. Next to him on the couch was a man Dillon guessed might be in his mid to late fifties. Neatly trimmed gray hair, with a sharp part on the left side. He wore a dark blue suit, a starched white shirt, and a red, white, and blue striped tie.

The man in the wingback chair looked to be twenty years younger. Black hair shaved on the sides and a crew cut on the top. Dillon's first thought was ex-military. He had a square jawline and wore dark gray trousers, a black sport coat, and a starched white shirt. His tie was black with some squiggly purple design.

McCabe stood and said, "US Marshal Jack Dillon, Detective Inspector Paddy Suel. This is US Senator Noel Brussard." McCabe nodded toward the gray-haired man who extended his hand but didn't bother to stand.

"Nice to meet you," Dillon said as he shook hands. Brussard had a strong grip. He gave Dillon's hand two shakes, released his grip, and gave Suel's hand two shakes.

"The senator's chief of staff, Wendell McCarthy," McCabe said as McCarthy stood and shook hands with Dillon and then Suel. "Have a seat, gentlemen," McCabe said.

Suel quickly slid into the other wingback chair, and Dillon pulled over one of the client chairs from in front of McCabe's desk, setting it between Suel and McCarthy.

Dillon immediately had the feeling something was about to be dumped on Suel and him. They'd both been through it too many times to count. Politicians who'd want a tour of, well, name it, Mountjoy Prison, the Docks area, or even the Irish Dance studios. No doubt they were in Dublin on a taxpayer-funded tour. They'd fly over in first class, stay in separate suites in a five-star hotel, have a chauffeur supplied by the American Embassy, eat at the best restaurants, and basically take a week-long vacation at taxpayer expense. Once back in DC, someone on the lower rungs of the ladder would be forced to write a lengthy report no one would ever read." To what do we owe the pleasure?" Dillon said.

McCarthy cleared his throat and said, "We're over here on a personal matter. The senator's daughter, Melanie, is attending Trinity University—"

"An art major," Brussard interjected.

McCarthy nodded and said, "There seems to be a bit of a problem. She was assaulted by—"

"Attempted assault," Brussard interjected

"By two individuals in Dublin's Temple Bar section."

"Could you be a little more specific as to the assault?" Dillon said.

"Sexually suggestive comments from two men. One of them grabbed her. Tried to force her into a car. She was able to break away, and the men fled," McCarthy said.

"Are you aware that we investigate murders and terrorist situations?" Suel growled, not hiding his anger.

"Which is exactly why I thought the two of you would be perfect for this situation. It's just a small step from what we might call a failed attempt to create an international incident. I'd like to nip any potential problem in the bud, and I'm sure you would as well," McCabe said in a tone that suggested *'You two are going to be dealing with this. So let's get on with it.'*

"Couldn't agree more, sir. Happy to look into this. Would there be a file available with the school or the local Garda station?" Suel said.

"Yes, we've given DCI McCabe a copy of our file, such as it is. As I'm sure you can understand, Melanie was hesitant about reporting this to the staff at Trinity. She was afraid they would confine her to campus or information on the incident would somehow end up in the newspapers."

"Is the school investigating?" Dillon asked.

"Actually, they've not been informed," Brussard said, "in the interest of keeping this private. The last thing we need is reporters and the media standing outside her dormitory or classroom. Good lord, it's one of the reasons we sent her over here for college, just so she could get away from the media, and now this."

"When did this happen?" Dillon asked.

"Just a few days after she arrived in August. Let me be honest. She is loving the fact that she is pretty much anonymous on campus. No one seems to know that her father is in congress. If news of this comes out, we may well have to find another school before the spring," Brussard said.

Suel cleared his throat and asked, "The incident is in your file?"

Both men nodded.

"Very well, we'll begin immediately," McCabe said and stood. "How long will you be in Dublin?"

"Three more days," McCarthy said. "I want to stress that Melanie is unaware of our being here, and we'd like to keep it that way."

"You're not going to be meeting with her?" Dillon said.

"No, it would only make her that much more upset," Brussard said.

"All right, hopefully, we can bring this to a close and quickly," McCabe said, shooting a glance at Dillon and Suel. Everyone shook hands, and McCabe led Brussard and McCarthy out of his office, through the Special Branch office, and into the hallway, directing them to the elevator down the hall.

"Lord love a duck," McCabe said, stepping back into the office and almost, but not quite, slamming the door closed. "And I thought dealing with our politicians was bad. God help the States if this is what they have running the country. All right, here's the *so-called file*," he said, emphasizing the last three words as he handed a thin file to Suel. "Check things out, keep it low-key, and get back to me. I haven't looked at this. Let me know what you think. Hopefully, all we're dealing with is a young woman who was acting stupid. Questions?"

"No, we'll be on this right away, sir. Thank you," Suel said.

"Happy to help, sir," Dillon lied.

McCabe saw them to the door, and once they stepped out, he said, "DI O'Toole and Kelly, a moment of your time, please."

THREE

Dillon groaned and said, "I need a coffee."

"I could use something a lot stronger than coffee," Suel said as they headed into the break room.

They were seated with the file, such as it was, scattered across the table, seven sheets of paper, two with photographs Dillon figured were from a high school yearbook. Against his better judgment, Dillon had finished his coffee and couldn't bear to deal with a second cup. "Anything stand out to you, Paddy? This seems to me like a lot more than a young woman having too much to drink. There's always something crazy happening down in Temple Bar, oftentimes alcohol-fueled, but still."

Suel shook his head. "I don't think we're going to learn anything until we actually talk to her. Even if she had too much to drink, trying to force her into a car? For Christ's sake."

"We'd better check the records. Logic tells me this has happened more than once. If these idiots were unsuccessful, what's to stop them from driving around the corner and abducting someone else?" Dillon seemed to think for a long moment. "I don't know. I get that they want to keep this quiet, but do you know anyone at Trinity, Paddy? I think we need to make them aware of this. We don't have to mention the girl's name. Just tell them we're investigating an incident near the school."

"Yeah, I think you're right. Meanwhile, O'Toole and Kelly just got called in to work that murder investigation down in Phibsboro, and we're going to be poking around Trinity College making sure—"

"Come on, man. Whoever it was apparently tried to force her into a car. Things go downhill from there awfully fast, and murder and or rape is one of the results."

"Yeah, I know. Where are they from anyway? They never mentioned it."

"Brussard? Louisiana, New Orleans, to be exact. I've caught him once or twice on the news. He's one of those politicians who seems to keep his head down. Votes whatever way the party tells him to vote."

"Yeah, and now those two are over here essentially on the sly, probably to the cost of about ten grand."

"I think you're probably on the low side. Politicians, you gotta wonder," Dillon said, shaking his head.

They went through the file twice, in just twenty-five minutes, and nothing seemed out of order, but then there was minimal information. There was a copy of an email from a boy, a student, saying Melanie had a nice figure and she must work out. Nothing really out of line. In fact, Dillon recalled himself at the same age making a similar, although more descriptive comment, which led to a meeting with a young lady's two older brothers.

Suel arranged the papers in front of him, handed them to Dillon, and said, "I'm afraid to ask what our next step is going to be."

"You know as well as I do. We need to head over to Trinity and talk to the girl. Then seek out the boy who sent the email, this Kevin Walsh from Cobh down in County Cork. The kid didn't do anything wrong. As a matter of fact, given some of the comments you and I have made to women, Paddy, I'd say the kid was down-right polite."

"Be nice if we could help move him toward some-one else, for his own damn good. Can you imagine, as a kid, let alone an adult, having a date with a woman, and suddenly you've got someone like one of us coming after you? I pity the lad and feel especially sorry for the girl. She's going to have a 'No go' sign hanging around her neck if she doesn't already. Might as well get it over with. I'll drive," Suel said.

It only took fifteen minutes, and they were headed over the O'Connell Street bridge just two blocks from Trinity College. Suel drove up Westmoreland Street, past the Edmund Burke Statute and the Irish Whiskey Museum. He pulled into a parking area labeled 'Staff Parking' and parked next to a white Audi A1.

Dillon opened the file and said, "According to her class schedule, she's in an art history class in the Creative Arts Building that gets out in fifteen minutes. Do you know where that building is?"

Suel nodded. "It's on the far side of the campus, about a ten-minute walk. Does it give a room number?"

Dillon read the number from the sheet in the file. "One-seventeen."

"Let's go. It can't be more than ten minutes from here," Suel said as he climbed out of the car.

Dillon had been on the campus countless times, attending concerts, interviewing staff, and working on different cases over the past few years. The campus was just as lovely as he remembered. There were at least as many tourists as students on the sidewalks. Of course, the Book of Kells, a major tourist attraction, was housed here in the Trinity College library. The library itself was a popular attraction.

Suel led them across campus to the Creative Arts Building with six minutes to spare. As they entered, an information office was located just to the right. They walked past and headed down the hall, took a left turn, and stopped outside of room 117. There was a window in the door, and Suel glanced in, looked for a long moment, and stepped back.

"She's in there. Not hard on the eyes. I'm amazed there's only one lad sending her email. She's a sight. We'll be able to talk to her as she steps out."

"Remember, we're not to mention the meeting with her father," Dillon said.

"So how are we going to explain our file and the fact that we've read copies of the emails sent to her?"

Dillon seemed to think for a moment and said, "Leave that to me. I've got an idea."

A moment later, a bell rang, various doors up and down the hall opened, and students stepped out. Dillon felt transported back to his college days for a second or two when suddenly Suel brought him back to the here and now by saying, "Excuse me, Miss Brussard? Melanie Brussard?"

Suel had been right. She wasn't hard on the eyes. In fact, she was downright gorgeous. Blonde, with an extremely nice figure. No wonder the boy from Cork sent her an email.

"Excuse me. Miss Brussard?" Suel repeated.

Her blue eyes seemed to flash for a second before she smiled and said, "Yes?"

"My name is Patrick Suel, and this is my partner, Jack Dillon. We're with An Garda Síochána, Ireland's National Police Force." Suel glanced over at Dillon, looking for help.

"We're actually with An Garda's Special Branch. As part of our service, we check in with American students and make sure everything is going okay. We'd like to give you our cards in the event you ever need any assistance, and we'd like to see if there's any way we might be of help."

"Oh, how nice of you," she said and smiled. "I'm just headed down to the art studio. Would you mind if we talked along the way?"

"That would be just fine. You'll have to lead the way," Dillon said.

They chatted for no more than ten minutes and were suddenly in the building's basement in front of a door labeled studio. Melanie Brussard never mentioned anything regarding an email or the assault incident in the Temple Bar area back in August. She led them into the art studio. There was the slight scent of turpentine and at least a dozen different easels lined up against the wall, all holding paintings in various stages. Landscapes, two portraits, a bowl of fruit, what appeared to be four people in a pub, and then down at the far end, a large canvas, four feet by five feet. The background was purple, and there were three rectangles, one on top of the other. The top one was a rust red color, and the bottom two were black.

Dillon was about to comment but bit his tongue just to play it safe. Good thing, Melanie Brousard strolled past the lovely works in progress and stopped in front of the three rectangles on the purple background.

"What do you think?" she said, then, fortunately, added, "I'm copying Mark Rothko's *Rust, Blacks on Plum*. He painted it back in 1962."

"An absolute work of genius," Suel said. "I recognized it but couldn't recall the artist's name, Mark Rocco."

"Rothko," Melanie corrected.

"Yeah, what did I say?"

"You said Rocco. Rothko was born in Latvia and moved to the US, Portland, actually, before moving to New York City where he painted."

"Latvia? Oh, I thought it was Russia, my mistake, I guess," Suel said.

"Oh, well, actually, you're right. He was born in 1903, and at that time, Latvia was part of Russia," she said.

"Marvelous work, absolutely marvelous. I'm trying to recall when he passed away."

"1970, took his own life, unfortunately."

"If I recall, his paintings increased in value following his death," Suel said.

"Yes, as so often is the case. They've gone for as much as sixty-three million, at least that's the highest I recall, but there certainly could be ones selling for more."

"Most interesting and very well done, I might add. Things are going well for you here? You're enjoying school, meeting new friends?" Dillon said, in an effort to get a word in edgewise.

"Oh, yeah, things are going very well. I've been quite busy copying the Rothko works. This will be my fourth Rothko work. I've four more to do after this one."

"Well, that will certainly keep you busy," Dillon said. "Want to thank you for your time. It's been wonderful to meet you." He handed her his business card, and Suel did the same, pulling his pen out and scribbling something on the back of his card. "I should mention that there have been two or three issues over in the Temple Bar area. Do you know the area?"

"I've been there once or twice," she said, suddenly avoiding eye contact.

"Best to be on guard. A couple of attempted abductions. Two thugs trying to force a woman into their car. Have you heard about them?"

"No, no, I'm not aware of anything like that."

"If you or a friend should see something like that, please give us a call. Of course, you know not to travel alone. Even if it's a short distance, it's best to have someone with you. My cell number is on the card, just in case you need some help. Very nice to meet you, Melanie. Should you need anything, feel free to call."

"Thank you, very nice to meet you both. Please stay in touch."

"Oh, we will. You do the same," Dillon said.

Suel gave a wave as they headed out the door and called, "See you later."

FOUR

Neither one spoke until they were out of the building. "Nice looking young woman," Suel said.

"I can't say I disagree. What the hell is going on? And that painting. Is that for real? She's supposed to be getting an Arts degree, and she painted that? The thing looks more like graffiti from a restroom in an abandoned building."

"I think her looks got her into that class. Odds are ten to one that the teacher is some horny old coot."

"I don't get that art style. Let's head back. I'm thinking I'll do some research and see if there were any other abduction incidents reported. Did you notice she avoided eye contact when I mentioned Temple Bar?"

"Yeah, makes me think she might be avoiding any mention of the incident altogether. You think we should bounce this off McCabe?" Suel asked.

"Let's hold off until we check and see if there have been other abduction attempts. If there have, it might be it's a couple of rookies, and they're in the learning stage. It'd be nice to nail their worthless asses before they're successful."

"God, I'd give anything to be investigating that murder in Phibsboro."

"That makes two of us. You're preaching to the choir on that note, Paddy."

They'd been back in the Special Branch office for fifteen minutes when Suel stepped over to Dillon's desk. "You find anything on other incidents?"

"Not yet. I wanted to check out the senator for a moment," Dillon said and turned his laptop toward Suel. There was an image of Senator Noel Brussard on the screen.

"I checked out that artist, Rothko. That painting of hers, those rectangles on the purple background, that's one of his paintings. It's called *Rust, Blacks on Plum*. It went for millions back in the nineties and was stolen from some museum in New Orleans."

"Stolen?"

"Yeah, pretty famous robbery, according to the stuff I read. A bunch of paintings were stolen. Thieves were dressed as cops and got into the museum in the middle of the night. Tied up your man supposedly running security. Made off with eight of the paintings, none of which have ever been recovered."

"And the senator's daughter is making a copy of one of them?"

"Apparently. They had a picture online of the thing. It looked just like the painting she was working on. Come on over to my desk. I've got it up on my computer."

Dillon stepped over to Suel's desk. The image took up most of the computer screen, and Suel was correct. It looked just like the painting Melanie Brussard was doing.

"What am I missing here? She didn't mention anything about the abduction attempt. She's making a copy of a painting that was stolen twenty years ago from a New Orleans museum. We're not supposed to mention that her father is in town. Does any of this make any sense?"

"Think we should talk to McCabe?" Suel said.

Dillon shook his head. "I got a better idea. I know we weren't supposed to mention the boy to her."

"Kevin Walsh from County Cork?" Suel said.

"Yeah. I'm thinking of looking him up and seeing what he has to say."

"Based on the email he sent, he seems like a nice kid. Oh, and by the way, that email was dated almost five weeks ago. Apparently, he hasn't sent anything since."

Dillon nodded. "He's probably lined up hot and heavy with some other girl. It would be nice to touch base with him all the same."

"We both don't need to go, do we?"

"No, I'll do it. In fact, if I head back over there now, I think his schedule said he had a class in the middle of the afternoon."

"Good luck," Suel said.

Dillon drove back to Trinity College and parked in the same spot Suel had parked in earlier. Kevin Walsh's class schedule listed a statistics class that ended at 3:00. Dillon was back on campus a good half-hour before the class ended. He took his time walking across the campus to the Hamilton Building. Walsh's classroom was on the second floor, in room 207.

Dillon glanced in through the glass panel next to the door. He counted sixteen students, each one looking more bored than the next. The class schedule for Kevin Walsh had his student ID image in the upper left corner. Dillon spotted him immediately, apparently fighting to keep his eyes open.

Ten minutes later, the bell rang. The professor, a rotund man who looked close to sixty, spoke for another minute or two and then dismissed the class. Everyone hurried out the door.

"Kevin, Kevin Walsh," Dillon called as sixteen young men hurried from the classroom.

Walsh gave a questioning look as he stepped over to Dillon. "I'm Kevin Walsh," he said.

"Hi, Kevin. I'm hoping to get a minute of your time. I'm Marshal Jack Dillon, assigned to An Garda Síochána, Special Branch."

"You're American?"

"Yes, I am. Just checking into a couple of things. You'd emailed Melanie Brussard a few weeks ago, and—"

"Yeah, and she told me not to contact her again, and I haven't. Is there some kind of problem? Is she okay?"

"Oh yeah, as far as we know, she's just fine. Her father is a United States Senator, and because he's in politics in the States, we just have to check things out. Standard security procedure is all."

"I can't even remember what the email said. Something like nice to see you or meet you or something. Haven't seen her or sent her an email since. I didn't want to date her if that's what you're thinking. I got a girlfriend back home."

"Melanie seemed all right?" Dillon asked.

"No, to tell you the truth, she seemed like a right pain in the arse. Told me not to contact her again, and I haven't. Life's too short to put up with that attitude. Pretty sure I haven't seen her since. Is she even still here at Trinity?"

Dillon nodded. "Yeah, still here. How long have you had the girlfriend?"

"How long? What is this? Did I do something wrong? Did someone report me for something?"

"No, it's one of the many things we do. Just checking to make sure everything is working out for you. Is there anything we can do to help you?"

"Yeah, you can stop with the questions and let me get to the library. I've got an exam tomorrow."

"Oh, well, don't let me hold you up. Good luck on that exam."

"Yeah, thanks," Walsh said, then headed down the hall. He looked back at Dillon twice. After the second time, he shook his head, walked down the hall a little faster, and disappeared behind a door marked 'Staircase.' Dillon waited a few more minutes to give Walsh plenty of time to disappear.

"How'd it go?" Suel asked when Dillon got back to the office.

Dillon shook his head. "The kid isn't stupid. He thought my questions were idiotic, and he's right. We chatted for all of thirty seconds, and he walked away shaking his head. Told me he thought the Brussard girl was a pain in the arse, and he hasn't contacted her since. Has a girlfriend back home and basically doesn't need the hassle. You check on any assaults in Temple Bar?"

Suel said, "No, haven't gotten to that point yet."

"I'll start in on it. You want to contact Trinity and ask if they've had any students assaulted? Obviously, they don't know about Melanie Brussard. It would be interesting if they're aware of any other incidents."

"Yeah, I'll give them a call."

"I'll get in touch with Pearce Street Garda Station and see what they have on Temple Bar assaults," Dillon said.

FIVE

Dillon called Pearce Street Station. It was just a five-minute walk from the Temple Bar area, and coincidentally, Trinity College was just across the street from the station. He gave his name and the reason for his call to the officer who answered.

"Let me connect you to DI Quinn," the officer said. Dillon heard three different clicks, and then the phone began ringing.

"Quinn," a gruff voice answered on the fourth ring.

"DI Quinn, my name is Marshal Jack Dillon. I'm with An Garda Síochána, Special Branch, and I'd—"

"You're that American, right? I can hear it in your voice."

"Yeah, that's me. We're looking into something over here, and I wondered what information your station has regarding assaults in the Temple Bar area. Specifically, assaults on women, possible attempted abductions."

"Mmm, off the top of my head, it's not unusual to have assaults, at least two or three on a weekly basis. Abductions—"

"And attempted abductions," Dillon said.

"Actually, few and far between. Hold on, I'm bringing it up on the screen as we talk. I will tell you this, assaults on women or men, for that matter, at no surprise, are usually alcohol-fueled. Abductions are a lot rarer, if for no other reason than the usual police presence on any given day and the crowds."

Dillon could hear him typing as he talked.

"Five assaults in the past seven, no, eight days. Resulting in three arrests. Three individuals were arrested, all male. Abductions or attempted abductions, hmmm, interesting, there were two, a woman on the twenty-eighth of August and another on the fourteenth of September. The August attempted abduction occurred at the Merchant's Arch, just opposite the Ha'penny Bridge. Two individuals, men, in a black vehicle. Approximate age thirty, one dark-haired, one blonde. Accent, middle European, possibly Russian. They were chased off by three men coming out of the Merchant's pub. Garda were called, and no arrest was made. The other attempted abduction was approximately two weeks later, just off the Wellington Quay. A woman, apparently over-served, had just come out of Fitzsimmons Pub. She was accosted by two individuals in a black vehicle. She managed to throw up on one of them. He assaulted her, punched her in the face, and they fled the scene leaving her on the sidewalk. Garda were called. She was interviewed, declined medical assistance, got in a cab, and left."

"That seem unusual to you?" Dillon said.

"Perhaps. It strikes me as strange that there would be two attempted abductions in that amount of time. It also strikes me as strange that, given the general description, both could have been conducted by the same two individuals."

"Can you send me what you have along with contact information for the victims?"

"Yeah, you're at Special Branch?"

"Yes, Jack Dillon, here's my ID number," Dillon said and read the number from his ID card.

"I'll send them your way in just a moment. Should you pick up anything else on this, please keep us informed. Just a first glance, but my sense is these two suspects aren't going to stop and may, in fact, quicken their pace. If I had to guess, I'd say they appear to be targeting women who've been over-served. No lack of them in Temple Bar."

"Be happy to keep you informed. What's your first name?"

"Seamus. Last name Quinn, double 'N' at the end."

"I'll look for your email," Dillon said and hung up.

Quinn's email arrived ten minutes later. He had sent two emails, actually. The first was a file labeled Ann Barry, and the second was a file labeled Mary Maher. Phone numbers and addresses were listed in each file. Dillon placed a call to Ann Barry first. Her attempted abduction had occurred back in August just opposite the Ha'penny Bridge. The phone rang three times, and then a recorded message said, "Hi, this is Ann. I can't take your call right now, but if you leave a message, I'll get back to you as soon as I can. Thanks, have a nice day."

"Hi, Ann. This is Marshal Jack Dillon. I'm with An Garda Síochána, Special Branch. I'm calling regarding the incident you were involved in back in August. If you would give me a call, please. Thank you," Dillon said and then left his phone number.

He opened the second file labeled Mary Maher and called the number. He was just about ready to leave a message when a woman answered, "Yeah."

"Oh, hi. I'm calling for Mary Maher."

"That's me. Look, if you're selling something, you're wasting your time. I—"

"Actually, I'm not selling anything. My name is Marshal Jack Dillon, and I'm with An Garda Síochána, Special Branch. If you have a moment, I'd like to talk to you regarding the incident you were involved in back on September fourteenth. An attempted—"

"There was nothing attempted about it. Those two gobshite's grabbed me and tried to drag me into their car. One of them punched me in the face and knocked me on my arse. I hurled on the bastard, and they took off. Wish I would have done it in their car."

"Can you describe them to me?"

"The two of them? One had dark hair and needed a shave. Your other was blonde, short hair with a part, you know."

"Anything that would distinguish them? Tattoos, scars, or even a limp."

"Your one, the blonde, he'd a tattoo on his left hand, on the fingers actually. You know, like they were rings, only they were tattoos. Shitty looking if you ask me, faded and blurry."

"What about the other guy, the one with the dark hair?"

"I don't recall anything about him. Well, except he was the driver. When I hurled on the blonde piece of shite, your dark-haired bastard laughed, ran around the front of the car, and got behind the wheel. They never turned the car off. Just pulled over, got out, and said they were going to give me a ride."

"What did they sound like?"

"They weren't from around here, that's for sure. In fact, I was on the piss and said something like, 'What'd you's say?' Because I couldn't understand your man. Then he tells me to get my arse in the car, the blonde one, and he grabs both me knockers and pulls me. That's when I hurled on him. So the bastard punched me in the face, and they took off."

"You remember their car?"

"Only that it was black, and it had Republic license plates, but like I said, I was on the piss, so even if I saw the numbers, I wouldn't remember them. You asking all these questions, did you arrest the bastards?"

"No, unfortunately. We think there might have been another incident with them, possibly two, but the women were able to get away."

"Well, your one thought he'd get a free feel, and that didn't work out too well for him. Oh, he had some kind of accent. Not Irish. I don't know where it was from, but he was hard to understand. Probably a good thing. Like I said, I was on the piss, and if they'd asked nice, I might have gotten in the car."

"You think they may have been watching you and followed you out of the pub? Where were you, by the way?"

"Met up with some bitches at Fitzsimmons. We'd a table out on the patio. All of us were over-served. One of our friends just got engaged, and we had a girls' night out. I lost count of the pints of Guinness. Then there was champagne. Some shots of tequila. I know it was after midnight, but I don't know how late it was. I'd just made my way out onto the quay and was gonna grab a taxi when these two pulled up. Your blonde one, he put the window down and said something. I remember that. Then, next thing I know, they're out of the car, and like I said, your blonde one grabs me with both hands. I hurl, and he knocks me on my arse."

"You see anyone since that might have been them?"

"Only if it's been on the telly. I haven't been out anywhere. Cut back on the drink, too. Right now, I must be the most boring woman in town."

"Well, just glad you're safe, Mary. Let me give you my phone number. If you think of anything else, feel free to call me. You got a pen so you can write this down?"

"Yeah, go ahead. I'm puttin' it on the back of an envelope."

"Okay, my name is Jack Dillon, and here's my number," Dillon said and gave her the number. He asked her to read the number back to him, and she did. "Thanks for your time, Mary. It's been nice talking with you."

"Hope you get those wankers," she said and disconnected.

SIX

Dillon hung up as Suel walked over and asked, "You talk to Pearce Street Station?"

"Yeah, DI Seamus Quinn. You know him?"

Suel shook his head. "Not really. I know of him but never met him. He's got a good reputation. What'd he have to say?"

"Two attempted abductions in Temple Bar. One in August, late August, and the other a couple of weeks after that on September fourteenth. Add to that the Brussard Abduction around the middle of August, and suddenly, we've got three failed abductions approximately two weeks apart. Does that mean the idiots doing this gave up? By the way, the woman they tried to grab in September was definitely over-served and threw up on one of the guys when he grabbed her."

"Perfect," Suel said and chuckled.

"It sounds like the same two guys in all three incidents. I haven't spoken with the woman in the late August attempt, but what this other one told me matches up with the information in the Brussard file. Two guys, one with dark hair and a blonde with an accent, driving a black vehicle."

"And she threw up on one of them?"

"Yeah, then he punched her, knocked her to the ground, and they took off. She'd been out with girl-friends at Fitzsimmons, just off Wellington Quay. Definitely over-served, and she walks out on the quay sometime after midnight to hail a cab. The guys stop, say something she can't understand, and then get out of the car. Interestingly, she told me she hasn't really been out anywhere since. So the assault really had an effect on her."

"It would be nice to hear Melanie Brussard's version firsthand. Hearing it from her old man and reading the bit they had in their file is little to no help. You learned more from this woman who was pissed to the gills."

Dillon nodded. "Yeah, I left a message for the other woman. Hopefully, she'll call back. Once I talk to her, I was thinking about touching base with Melanie Brussard again and getting her story firsthand."

"You thinking of calling or seeing her in person?"

"I'm thinking of giving her a call, might just offer to buy her lunch or something. If nothing else, I'd like to mention the fact that there are two other instances that we know of, and she should travel with a couple of friends. How many times have you seen a woman out late at night trying to catch a taxi?"

"Oh yeah, God, you'd lose count on any given night."

"You aren't kidding. What'd you learn from the folks at Trinity?"

"Nothing out of the ordinary. In other words, no one attempting to abduct a student. That said, there's a report of something just about every night and more on the weekends. Just about all of it is alcohol-fueled, and that's from the woman I spoke with."

"Gee, unlike the two of us at the same age. Of course, we were busy saying our prayers and doing homework."

"You may have been," Suel said just as Dillon's phone rang. "I'll let you get that."

"Marshal Jack Dillon, Special Branch," Dillon said, answering after the second ring.

"Hi, my name is Ann Barry, and I'm returning a call you left for me. Were you able to arrest those two criminals?"

"Unfortunately, no. At least not yet, Ann, and thank you for returning my call. I'm working with my partner, and we're looking into the attempted abduction you suffered. I've read the file, but I wanted to talk to you and hear exactly what you have to say."

"So, they're still out there?"

"Yes, I'm afraid they are."

"Well, it happened almost six weeks ago, and other than work and the grocery store, I haven't really been anywhere since."

"That's pretty standard, and I don't blame you one bit. Would you mind if I asked you a few questions?"

"If it will help to lock up those two plonkers, go ahead."

"Okay, thanks. The first thing is, did you regularly go down to Temple Bar?"

"Regularly, you mean like every night?"

"Or on weekends, how often were you there?"

"Well, not as often as back a year or two. To tell you the truth it's a lot, working full time, taking the bus to city center and a taxi home, plus paying for drinks. I suppose over the past year, I was probably down there a half-dozen times. I never went down there alone. I was always meeting up with friends. A couple of times, I met up with some workmates, but I was usually home by, say, 10:00. It wasn't ever a late night if I was with workmates. The friends, well, that was a little different. You know, catching up on who is doing what to whom, of course, that usually led to a late night then grabbing a taxi home. Frankly, it got to be expensive. Of course, the other thing is, or was, there's five of us. Two of the girls are married now and have little babies, so even if they can join us, they can't stay very late, and they're not going to get pissed."

"So you said you haven't been out, but have your girlfriends been down to Temple Bar since your incident?"

"No, and I don't think any of us will be going back there, ever. I told them all about it the following day. The next time we get together, it's going to be here, at my place."

"Makes perfect sense. So, tell me about that night. Where were you, and what exactly happened?"

"We were at a couple of places. We met at Temple Bar Square and then went into the actual Temple Bar, but it was so full of tourists that we didn't even order. We left and went to La Caverna. Do you know it?"

"I think I do. It's a wine bar, isn't it?"

"Yeah, that's right. We stayed there for close to two hours, then the mams had to leave, so we walked them to the bus stop on Dame Street. Three of us stopped in for a glass of wine at the Foggy Dew. That turned into three glasses because we all bought a round. Then we stopped at the Quays bar and then one more for the road at the Old Mill. We split up, and I walked out on Crown Alley, through the Merchant's Arch, and was trying to hail a cab right across from the Ha'penny Bridge. Suddenly, this car stopped. It was a black car, and there were two guys in it. The guy in the passenger seat opened the door and said, 'Get in, Baby, and we'll give you a ride.' As soon as he called me baby, I knew that wasn't a good idea. I said, 'No thanks,' and he was suddenly out of the car. He opened the rear door and said something like, 'Get your ass in here.' He grabbed me, and I hit him and screamed. Fortunately, three guys were just coming out of the Merchant's, and one of them yelled something. He let go of me, hopped in the passenger seat, and they took off. The three guys stayed with me until the Garda arrived. That was only a couple of minutes. They gave statements, and I gave one too, and then the Garda drove me home. They were really nice."

"Can you describe the two guys in the car?"

"A little; one had dark hair. He was the driver, and I didn't really get a good look at him. The other one, the guy who got out, opened the door and told me to get in, he was blonde, and his hair wasn't long, but it was combed over, you know, with a part on the left side. He had the kind of part that's cut in, so it looks really sharp."

"Can you guess their age?"

"Mmm-mmm, looked like late twenties, early thirties. I'm twenty-eight, and they could have been a year or two older than me, but I don't think they were thirty-five."

"What about size? Was this blonde person tall? Slender?"

"He wasn't unattractive. He might have been six feet or there about. Oh, and the few words he said, he had a heavy accent. Not French or German. Could have been Polish or Russian, I would guess definitely Eastern European."

"Any tattoos or scars on him?"

"Oh, yeah, on the fingers of his left hand, he had a tattoo on each finger. You know, like they were supposed to look like rings. To tell you the truth, they didn't look like they were professionally done. More amateur-looking, faded blue, and blurry. I don't know, the tattoos and his yelling, well, plus, I had no idea who in God's name he was. There was no way I wanted anything to do with him. All I can say is thank God for those guys coming out of the Merchant's pub."

"And they took off as soon as one of the guys yelled?"

"Yes, thank God. Then like I said, the Guards were kind enough to take me home. I'm afraid it will be a cold day in hell before I'm down in Temple Bar again. If I am, I'll be drinking fizzy water."

"Ann, thank you for calling me back. If you have any concerns or something else comes to mind, please give me a call."

"Thanks, I'll be sure to do that, and thank you for listening. I didn't mean to go on like that."

"Oh, listen, you've helped immensely. You take care now."

"You do the same, Officer Dillon. Thank you for listening," she said and disconnected.

SEVEN

S uel called over from his desk, "You up for a pint?" It was after 5:00, and besides Dillon and Suel, there were only two other people at their desks. DCI McCabe had left two hours earlier.

"I'd love to, but I've got to meet up with someone tonight."

"Meet up with someone? Does that mean you're going to Nessa's, or is she coming over to your place?"

"She's coming over to my place for dinner, which reminds me, I'd better call and place an order."

"Enjoy your evening," Suel said and headed toward the door.

"I intend to," Dillon said, then picked up the phone and called Apache Pizza over on Glasnevin Avenue, next to the Autobahn Pub and a couple of blocks from his home.

Someone answered on the third ring, "Pizza."

"Yeah, I want to order a large pizza with sausage, onion, and red peppers. Oh, and extra cheese."

"Anything else with that?"

"No, that'll do, and I'll pick it up."

"Should be ready in twenty minutes. Your name?"

He gave his name, said, "Thank you," and disconnected. Against his better judgment, he placed the Ann Barry and Mary Maher files in his briefcase, cleared off his desk, locked it, and headed out of the office. He drove home. Lucifer met him at the door. Dillon let him out into the front garden. Lucifer jumped off the front step and then assumed the position next to the driver's door facing Dillon and did his duty. Dillon walked into the kitchen, set his briefcase on the counter, took a biscuit from the cookie jar, and tossed it to Lucifer, just now lifting his leg against the front tire on the driver's side of the car.

Other people might have been upset, but Dillon figured since Lucifer hadn't destroyed the house, he was actually ahead of the game. He placed his briefcase next to the backdoor, set the table for two, placed two wine glasses on the kitchen counter, set a box of crackers and a package of Brie cheese next to the wine glasses, and hurried upstairs to change. He slipped on blue jeans, applied deodorant, and got a reasonably clean shirt from the closet. He let Lucifer back in the house and then drove over to Apache Pizza.

He was back home ten minutes later. He parked his car in the drive, parking over Lucifer's recent deposit, so Nessa wouldn't notice it, and Dillon wouldn't have to clean it up tonight.

He set the oven on warm, placed the pizza on a cookie sheet, and ran the pizza box out to the trash bin. He'd just let Lucifer back in the house when he spotted

Nessa's car coming down the lane. He turned the oven off, set the pizza in the oven, and filled the wine glasses with chilled white wine, one of three bottles in the refrigerator, just in case Nessa needed that much to get in the mood. A moment later, the doorbell rang.

"Well, right on time," Dillon said as he opened the door and handed a wine glass to Nessa.

"Mmm-mmm, thank you. Trying to get me in the mood?"

"No, just a thank you for coming over. I feel like it's been a week since I've seen you."

"Oh, that's sweet," she said, gave him a peck on the cheek, and took another sip of wine. "Say it smells delicious. Don't tell me you actually made dinner."

"I did. Left the office early and thought you might enjoy a homemade pizza, sausage, cheese, peppers, and a few onions. I've got it in the oven, just warming," he said as he led the way into the kitchen.

She walked over to the stove and looked in through the oven door window. "Oh, wow, you made that?"

"Yeah," he lied. "Don't look so surprised."

"Well, it's just that I thought you couldn't cook. We're always going out to eat. Not a complaint, by the way. I'm sure I'll enjoy this."

"Let's just say I'm a man of many hidden talents."

"And you made that pizza?"

"Yeah, I hope you like it. More wine?" Dillon asked, noticing her glass was almost half empty.

She nodded and pushed her glass toward him. "You know, Jack, as a man of many hidden talents, you should probably hide this receipt from Apache Pizza," she said and pushed the sales receipt across the kitchen counter.

"Oh, well, umm, I was—"

"Save whatever you were going to say and top up my glass. You want to go to bed before or after the pizza?"

"I was thinking both."

"I think I can handle that. Lead the way."

Dillon glanced at the digital clock on his dresser. 4:00 AM. Nessa was sound asleep, no surprise given the two bottles of wine they'd had. He made sure all night that her glass was never empty. He climbed out of bed, slipped into the pair of boxers lying on the floor, and headed downstairs. At least what was left of the pizza was in the refrigerator, and the wine glasses were in the sink. He grabbed his briefcase next to the backdoor, placed it on the kitchen table, pulled out the two files on the attempted abductions, and started going through them.

Two hours later, he heard the alarm going off in his bedroom and hurried upstairs. Nessa was lying on her stomach with both pillows over her head. Once he turned off the alarm, she seemed to take a deep breath and then didn't move. He walked over to her side of the bed, sat down, and began to rub her back. After a minute or two, she slowly rolled over and pulled the pillows away from her head.

"Is it really time to get up?"

"Afraid so. Do you want to climb in the shower, and I'll—"

"No, I should probably get dressed and get cleaned up at home. Thanks for the most wonderful evening, and the pizza was delicious, even if you didn't make it."

"Thanks, I'll get a tea ready for you downstairs."

"Let me put the milk in," she said.

"See you in the kitchen," Dillon said. He grabbed his jeans off the chair in the corner and headed downstairs. Nessa came down fifteen minutes later. When he heard her on the stairs, he turned the tea kettle back on. She insisted her tea be made the moment the kettle turned off.

"God, you're beautiful. You can go right into work."

"I don't think so. Thanks again for the wonderful evening. Just what I needed."

"Yeah, me too." The kettle turned off, and Dillon poured the boiling water over the tea bag in the mug.

"I'll do the milk," Nessa said. "I just need three drops."

"I'm prepared. Give me a chance here."

"You always add too much milk, and I can't stand to drink it when you do that."

"Hold on," he said and took a measuring cup from the kitchen drawer. He poured milk into the measuring cup.

"See, that's way too much. You never—"

"Please," he said, holding up his hand. "I'm not finished." He pulled the kitchen drawer open again and took out an eye dropper. Put it in the cup of milk, filled the eye dropper, and then placed exactly three drops of milk into Nessa's tea mug. "How's that?"

"Oh. My. God. I don't believe it. That is perfect. Who knew you can be trained?" She grabbed a spoon, took the tea bag out of the mug, stirred the tea mixing the three drops of milk, and then took a sip. "Mmm-mmm, excellent."

"Good. Do you want to dump that tea in a travel mug?"

"And ruin it? No, I'm going to enjoy this right here."

Ten minutes later, she set the empty mug on the counter, kissed him goodbye at the front door, and hurried to her car.

EIGHT

illon was in the office well before Paddy Suel. As Suel headed to his desk, he shot Dillon a look and said, "I thought you were meeting up with Nessa last night. Did she tell you not to come over?"

"No, she ended up at my place. We took a break, had some pizza, and she left early this morning."

"So, she'd finally had enough of you."

"I think she figured, if she didn't leave, she'd end up staying the entire day and begging me not to go to work."

"Yeah, sure, you keep thinking that."

"I spent some time early this morning going over the two files from Pearce Street on the attempted abductions."

"And what did you learn?"

"We've got an uphill situation on our hands. A very steep uphill situation. I've got the names and phone numbers of the three guys who scared these two knackers off. Ann Barry was the target, and I spoke to her yesterday. She's the one by the Ha'penny Bridge. The guys were coming out of Merchant's Pub and yelled at the lowlifes in the black car, and they took off. I want to talk to those guys, and then I'm thinking of going back and chatting up Melanie Brussard."

"Weren't we instructed not to mention the incident to her?"

"We were, and I'm of the opinion that these two idiots aren't going to stop. We've got next to nothing to go on, and sooner or later, these clowns are going to be successful, make off with some woman, and once they're finished, they'll probably kill the poor victim."

"You want to clear it with the powers that be," Suel said and nodded toward McCabe's open office door.

"We can, but if we get a negative response, if he tells us no, I'm still going to talk to her."

Suel seemed to think about that for a long moment and then slowly nodded. "I'm with you on that. You want to call the Brussard woman and set up an appointment? You said yesterday you might offer to take her to lunch."

Dillon shook his head. "No, I think we can track her down at the school. She'll probably be painting more rectangles."

"Gee, I can hardly wait," Suel said. "Let's hold off for a bit. I think she had a 10:00 class. We could catch her at 11:00 as she leaves the room."

"That will give me a chance to call these three guys, see if they can add anything," Dillon said and opened the Ann Barry file. He left a message on the first two calls. The third guy answered Dillon's call after the first ring.

"Mitch Crowley."

"Hi, Mitch. Thank you for taking my call. My name is Marshal Jack Dillon. I'm with An Garda Síochána, Special Branch. I'm calling regarding an incident in Temple Bar last August. You—"

"You referring to those two knackers who were trying to force that woman into their car?"

"Yes."

"How's she doing?"

"About like you'd expect. Doesn't go out much and certainly not alone. I'd say it will be a long time before she has any desire to head back into the Temple Bar area."

"Too bad, she seemed like a nice lady. I stopped for a pint with two pals at the Merchant's. You know how it goes, suddenly, we'd been there for a couple of hours. We were coming out of the place when we heard her scream and saw her fighting with your man. I shouted at him, and we hurried down the steps. He took one look at the three of us and jumped back in the car. They sped down the Wellington Quay. She was pretty upset, as you can understand. We stayed with her until the Guards came. That was just a couple of minutes."

"You get a look at the car?"

"It was black, a 2020 Kia. Unfortunately, that's all I can remember from the license plate."

"A Kia, any idea of the model?"

"No, sorry, it was probably there for less than five seconds. When I yelled, your man looked over at the three of us coming toward him, he jumped back in the car, and it took off down the quay. I was more focused on the woman. She was crying with her arms wrapped around her, literally shaking. The Guards were nice enough to give her a ride home. So, you didn't catch these bastards?"

"No, we haven't yet. But there have been two more incidents. Can you describe these guys?"

"I can only describe the one. He was the putz trying to grab the woman. He had blonde hair, neatly trimmed. Average height. Not fat, but he wasn't some muscular prick either."

"Did you hear him say anything?"

"No, we were too far away to start, and as soon as he saw us, he was in the car. I mean, it couldn't have been more than five seconds total that he was out there, probably even less than that when we yelled, and he jumped into the front seat, and they took off."

"How was he dressed?"

"He was dressed casually. You know, like everyone. I think he was wearing jeans, black jeans, and black shoes, not runners. His shirt had short sleeves, you know, with just the two or three buttons."

"A sport's shirt?" Dillon said.

"Yeah, I think dark blue, but it could have been black. The shirt had horizontal white stripes running across the shoulders."

"Did he wear glasses?"

"Glasses? No. He didn't have glasses."

"A tattoo or any scars?"

"Not that I could see, but I'm afraid it all happened so fast, and I was too far away to catch any of that."

"Anything else you can think of?"

"No, wish I could be more help, but like I said, I saw him for just a few seconds, and then he jumped back in the car, and they took off."

"Well, your info on the 2020 Kia was news. That was nowhere in the reports I read."

"Really? God, I know I told Guards that. In fact, it was a detective, guy name of Teflon, or Tevlon, something like that."

"I've read two reports on attempted abductions. The fact they were driving a Kia was never mentioned. Let me give you my number. If anything should come to mind, I'd appreciate a call."

"I've got your number on my phone. You said your name was Jack Dolan?"

"Close, Jack Dillon, with Special Branch."

"If I think of anything else, I'll give you a call."

"Thank you, Mitch. A pleasure talking with you," Dillon said, but Crowley had already disconnected.

He placed a call to the NVDF, the National Vehicle and Driver File. After dealing with two different recordings and someone who was unable to help, he finally spoke to a woman named Kathleen Toolen. "Hi, thanks for taking my call, Miss Toolen."

"Thank you for surviving our recordings."

"No comment," Dillon said, and they both laughed.

"You said you were with An Garda Síochána?"

"Yes, Special Branch. We're looking into what appears to be a pattern of attempted abductions in the Temple Bar area. The information we have is that the suspects are driving a black 2020 Kia. Is there a way you could get me a list of the owners of such a vehicle?"

"A black 2020 Kia. Would this be just for Dublin County?"

"Yes, at least I would hope so."

"It will take some time, but I could probably have that for you in the next twenty-four hours."

"That would be excellent."

"All right, before I begin, I'm going to need a few things from you, starting with your An Garda Síochána ID number."

By the time Dillon finally finished providing information, Suel wasn't at his desk. Dillon checked the break room and the men's room but didn't find him, so he left a note.

'Paddy, heading over to Trinity to talk with Melanie Brussard. Talked to one of the guys who chased off the knackers attempting to abduct Ann Barry by the Ha'penny Bridge. He said the car was a black 2020 Kia. I've got a call into the National Vehicle and Driver File, and they'll hopefully be sending a list over of black 2020 Kias registered in Dublin County. Dillon'

It was later than he thought. He taped the note to Suel's desk phone and hurried out to his car. He groaned through road construction along the Inns Quay, took the O'Donovan Rossa Bridge across the Liffey, drove up to

Castle Street, merged onto Dame Street, and wound his way to Nassau Street, where he pulled into the staff parking lot at Trinity College. He hurried to the Creative Arts Building and room 203, where Melanie Brussard's class was held, only to glance at his watch and realize he was five minutes late, which was why the classroom was empty.

On a whim, he headed down to the basement level and the art studio.

NINE

Dillon opened the door to the art studio. He spotted Melanie Brussard in the far back of the room. She was the only person in the studio and was wearing shorts and a long sleeve, paint-splattered top. The easel with the *Rust, Blacks on Plum* painting stood on a drop cloth, and she was making small jabs at the canvas with a brush.

"Melanie," Dillon called, not wanting to surprise her. She turned and stared for a moment and then smiled. "Oh, it's Marshal? Right?"

"Yeah, but feel free to call me Jack or Dillon, or Marshal's fine too. Whatever you're comfortable with."

"Is there a problem?" she asked.

"No, quite the contrary, everything's fine. Just meeting with another student for a few minutes, thought about your painting, and wondered how you were doing," Dillon lied.

"Oh, well, just finishing up, actually. But it seems like every time I'm ready to declare the work finished, there's something else I see, and suddenly, I've been at it for another four hours."

"I know how that goes. I checked out your man Rothko and read up on him. Quite the artist. Very interesting."

"Some of his paintings were even larger than this one," she said and dabbed her small brush in the corner of the canvas. "Probably the most popular was Number seven, Dark over light, which was nearly eight feet high. I think he painted that in 1954," she said, as she applied another small amount of the plum color to an edge of the painting. Her paintbrush was very small and looked more like something a kid would use to paint a model car or a toy soldier.

"Have you seen any of his paintings in person?"

She nodded. "Oh, yes. At the National Gallery of Art in Washington. The East Building Tower One gallery features a rotating series of paintings by Mark Rothko. I was there four times last year to view the different works. I loved to just sit in the gallery and stare for hours. Of course, I can only do that if my father isn't there. He's not really into art, and he certainly doesn't like abstract art."

"Then, how did you get so involved if your father doesn't like it?"

"You know, I'm not sure. It started when I was just around ten or eleven. My father dragged me to the gallery for photo op pictures for an upcoming election. It was my first time there, and I just fell in love with the paintings. Of course, since my father didn't like any of it, that made me just that much more attracted to them.

Then I think four years later, I was a senior in high school, and the Gallery had just acquired a number of Rothko works. I took one look and knew that was what I wanted to do for the rest of my life. And, well, here I am."

"And your father supports your work."

She laughed, "That might be too strong a term. But at the end of the day, he's paying for me to study here. I mean, I was awarded a scholarship, but there's still a high cost, and he's paying for it. That makes me a happy girl."

"Fascinating, hey, I was thinking about grabbing a bite to eat. You interested in joining me? My treat. I'd love to hear more about your work. You could even advise me on the best galleries."

"You have any place in mind for lunch?"

"I was thinking about the Red Torch. It's a Thai place, really good food."

"I've heard of it but never been there."

"Have you seen the statue of Molly Malone? The Dubs refer to her as the Tart with the Cart."

She smiled at that and nodded. "Yeah, I think I saw it my second day here. I remember the statute is all dark except for her breasts, which are all shiny from people rubbing them."

"Yeah, lots of folks, tourists, line up to have their picture taken there."

"That's exactly what I did."

"Well, the Red Torch is just around the corner from there. Like I said, it's really good food."

She seemed to think for about two seconds and then nodded. "Yeah, that sounds good. Give me about ten minutes to clean up, and we can go."

"Great, take your time. I'll just look around the studio if that's okay."

"Help yourself," she said and proceeded to set her paint pallet on a counter against the far wall. She actually had three brushes, and she placed them in a jar of what Dillon presumed was turpentine. He busied himself looking at a number of paintings on easels and others leaning against a wall. It took more like fifteen minutes, but she finally hung her painting smock on a hook, exposing the light blue sports shirt she had on underneath.

"Okay, all set?" Dillon asked.

"Lead the way," she said.

It was a nice ten-minute walk. The sidewalks were filled with locals and tourists. Fortunately, Dillon knew the way and pointed out a few things as they walked. If Melanie Brussard already knew about them, she was gracious enough not to mention it. They passed the Molly Malone statute, and sure enough, there were two couples standing in front of it having their picture taken.

The Red Torch was almost half full. Dillon recognized the hostess but couldn't remember her name.

"Good to see you again," she said in her Thai accent.

"Nice to see you again. How have you been? It's just the two of us today."

"Certainly, I have a special table just for you," she said, making him sound like a regular, although he knew she said the same thing to almost everyone. She led them to a table and placed a menu in front of both of them.

"Apparently, you come here often," Melanie said once they were seated.

"Oh, well, I really enjoy the food and, not knocking the pubs, but it's nice to relax in a quiet atmosphere. You ever go to the pubs and listen to the session music?"

"I've been once or twice to a couple of places. That's where people just show up to play music, right?"

"Yeah, and at least in my experience, they're all very good musicians."

A waiter set down two glasses of water and said, "Something from the bar?"

"Melanie?" Dillon asked.

"Are you going to have something?"

"I'm just going to have tea but get a glass of wine if you want."

"You sure?"

"Yeah, not a problem."

"Okay, umm, I'll have a glass of whatever your house white is."

"I'll be back in a bit with your drinks, and you can order," the waiter said.

They ended up ordering curry for lunch. Dillon ordered the mild version, and Melanie Brussard ordered the spicy. They were halfway through their meals, Dillon taking the occasional sip of tea and Melanie close to finishing her glass of wine.

"So, when you're not studying or working on a painting, have you had many opportunities to see Dublin or anywhere in Ireland?" Dillon asked.

She shook her head. "Not as much as I'd hoped. I've seen some of the sights in the city. When I first arrived, I went with four other students, and we took the Hop On, Hop Off bus. Are you familiar with it? It goes to all the tourist sites and museums."

Dillon nodded and swallowed his mouthful of mild curry. "I've been on it a number of times. I have to say, every time I take it, I see something different. Not that I'm getting off at different places, but you know the driver is telling you about different sites and mentioning historic events, and there's always something new I pick up on. If I have friends from the States coming over, I always recommend they take the tour. It's really good."

She nodded and smiled.

"You know, another similar tour is the Haunted Dublin. It's a nighttime tour. You see all sorts of supposedly haunted places. When they stop at one of the cemeteries, there are two people dressed like zombies who suddenly appear. One of them has a pair of manacles around his ankle. They stop at the Gravediggers pub for a beverage. It's fun."

"I don't get out that much now. Kind of busy with all the schoolwork, and I don't want to spend night after night in a pub, drinking."

"That's not the worst idea, not going to pubs every night. I mean, they're fun, but you've got a busy schedule. Obviously, you take your classes and your painting very seriously. If you get into partying every night, that's not the best plan for doing well on the things that count."

"You're with the police here, right?" she said and scooped up the last of the curry from her bowl.

"Yeah, in Irish, they're called An Garda Síochána. I'm assigned to the Special Branch. We investigate all sorts of things, and we check with students," Dillon said and nodded at Brussard. "Sometimes we're involved in a case that may be outside of Dublin, down in, say, County Cork or up in Donegal. On a couple of rare occasions, we've dealt with the police up in Northern Ireland and once or twice with a department in Spain or France."

She nodded and said, "Are you familiar with the Temple Bar area?"

"More wine or tea?" the waiter suddenly asked.

Brussard looked at Dillon. "Sure, why not? Go ahead," Dillon said, and Brussard nodded at the waiter as he gathered up their bowls.

"How about a dessert?"

Both Brussard and Dillon shook their heads.

TEN

Dillon Said, "So, you asked about Temple Bar. Yes, I'm familiar with it, very familiar. We've had a number of cases in the area. That's not surprising given it's so popular and a big tourist area. Most of the everyday sorts of incidents are handled by the Pearce Street Station. They're right across from Trinity if you ever need help. But you can always call me, and I'll get on it right away."

The waiter returned with the glass of wine. Melanie took a big sip, followed up with another, and then asked, "Are you aware of any attacks on women in the Temple Bar area?"

Dillon nodded. "We're looking at two situations right now, although I fear there are more. One occurred at the end of August and the other about two weeks later in the middle of September."

"What happened? Was anyone ever arrested?"

Dillon shook his head. "No one was arrested, or a better response would be, no one has been arrested yet. But slowly, we're getting more information on the suspects."

"Can you tell me about them, I mean the cases?" she said and took another healthy swallow of wine.

"Yes, in both cases, two men attempted to abduct a woman late at night on the quays along the Liffey River. It's just along the edge of the Temple Bar area, so you know where I'm talking about. Neither attempt was successful. In one instance, three guys were coming out of the Merchant's pub, which is next to the Merchant's Arch right by the Ha'penny Bridge."

Melanie nodded.

"They walked out of the pub just as a car stopped, and a guy got out and told a woman to get in the car. She ended up fighting him off and screamed just as these three guys started down the stairs. They yelled at the idiot, and he hopped back in the car and drove off."

"But he didn't take the woman, did he?"

"No, the guys called the Guards, Pearce Street Station, and they were there in minutes. Took down the information, and then they drove her home. That was at the end of August. In the other case, about two weeks later, a woman was hailing a cab further down on the Wellington Quay sometime after midnight. A car stopped, and a guy tried to force her into the backseat. He grabbed her breasts, and she immediately threw up on him. He hurried back to the car, and it drove off. The Guards were called, and when they were finished, she took a taxi home."

"So those are the only two you know about?"

"Those are the two cases that have been reported. Each time someone reports a case, we garner a little more information. Right now, we know there are two men involved. One has dark hair and is the driver. The guy who attempts to force the woman into the car is blonde, probably in his late twenties, no more than thirty. His hair is shorter, and he has a sharp part cut in. He has tattoos on the fingers of his left hand that appear to be homemade rather than professional. Both men have accents, not French or German, but possibly Polish or even Russian. We also just got a lead that they may be driving a black 2020 Kia. I hope to have information on that license later today or tomorrow."

"So you'll be able to arrest them?"

"Not exactly. There are over a half million cars in Dublin County alone. Even cutting it down to black 2020 Kias, we're probably looking at a lot more than one or two. Still, that's better than nothing, and the more information we get, the better our chances of finding these two guys are and locking them up."

"It would be hard to report that, plus if you waited for a bit before reporting, I'm guessing the police wouldn't be too happy about it," she said and drained her glass.

Dillon caught the waiter's attention and nodded toward Melanie. "Actually, you're wrong on that note. Just to get the information, any information, is so important in gradually closing the net around these guys. Only this morning, I was talking to one of the guys that broke up that attempt on the woman near the Ha'penny Bridge. He mentioned the car being a Kia, and the license plate said the car was a 2020. Suddenly from over half a million cars, we can narrow it down to, I don't know, a thousand, or even less. Then we'll eliminate women and elderly owners. Now suddenly, we're down to a hundred names. The only thing that will help is if we get the information."

The waiter set a very full wine glass in front of Melanie and picked up the empty. She immediately took two large swallows, then said, "I might know something."

"Melanie, anything you could tell us would really help. Believe me. And we would keep it very private."

She took another big gulp of wine. "I don't want my name out there. My father warned me about reporting this, said it could affect his standing, and there could be all sorts of ads on the internet saying I was trying to get into their car or things along that line. He's afraid it might cause a problem in his next election."

"I'll keep a tight lid on it. In fact, if you have information, I'll take it, but I won't file a report, so it will just be between you and me. No one has to know where it came from."

"You promise?"

"Scout's honor," Dillon said and raised his right hand. "If it's okay, I'll just take some notes, and I won't make an official report. I won't include your name."

"Okay, but you have to promise you won't mention my name. I really mean it."

"And I meant what I just said," Dillon said, taking a notebook from his pocket. "Your name will not be anywhere in this."

She seemed to think about that for a minute, took another swallow of wine, and said, "So it was, I think my fourth, yeah, my fourth day here, the tenth of August. I was finally getting used to the time change that's five hours ahead of DC. Four other girls and I go into the Temple Bar area. We start going into pubs, and before we know it, we're all drunk and having a really good time. We end up in a pub with what sounds like a really good band, but as drunk as we were, who really knows? We were just dancing and doing shots. Guys were buying us drinks. Kelsey, she's this girl from Cleveland, she starts feeling sick, and one of the girls, I think her name is Julie, gets her into the bathroom, and they're in there for like twenty minutes. Kelsey was throwing up the entire time. Julie and another girl decided to walk her back to the dorm. The other girl and I stay at the pub. We stopped drinking after Kelsey left. But we're dancing and stuff, you know. We end up getting separated. I can't find her. I look for her, and eventually, they're doing that last call thingy, you know, where they're getting ready to close. So, I leave the pub and head back to Trinity."

She took another sip of wine, but this time only a sip.

"Anyway, I somehow got turned around, and I'm going the wrong way on that road along the river."

"You're probably on the Wellington Quay at that point," Dillon said.

"Whatever. Anyway, I'm walking, and this car slows down. It's a black car, and this nice-looking guy lowers his window and says something. Only the first word he says sounds like 'privet,' and that means hello in Russian. Then he says, 'You all right?' and he calls me baby. He had a heavy accent, and it wasn't Irish.

"I asked him, 'Can you tell me where Trinity is?' He steps out of the car and opens the rear door, and says, 'Get your gorgeous ass in there, baby,' and then he grabs my ass and tries to push me into the car. He had blonde hair, and his left hand had those tattoos you mentioned on each finger. I backed up, and he grabbed my arm and tried to pull me into the back seat. I kneed him and ran back the way I'd come and just stayed in a crowd of people walking the other way. About five minutes later, that black car drove past, but I don't think they saw me because they never stopped. Then all of a sudden, I saw the O'Connell Street Bridge, and I knew how to get back on campus from there."

"So you made it home safe?"

"Yeah, but I haven't been back there, or for that matter, I haven't been off campus since, well, except for today because I have an armed escort. I gotta tell you. I'd kill that guy in an instant if I had the chance. I'd kill both of them."

"I can't blame you. You said he had blonde hair?"

"Yeah, under other circumstances, I would have said he was nice looking. Umm, blue eyes, oh, and he had this scar just next to his left eye, not too big. It was in the shape of a backward letter 'C.' And it was just below the edge of his left eye, on his cheekbone. Might have been sexy under a different circumstance."

"What about clothes?"

"Mmm-mmm, he was wearing jeans and a short sleeve button-down shirt, light blue. Oh, and he had this belt. I think the buckle was brass."

"Was there a design on the buckle?"

"Not that I recall."

"The girl you couldn't find, did she get back to campus okay?"

"Yeah, she went back to the dorm with another student, a guy she knew, and just left me on my own. I saw her the next morning but didn't tell her about the guy grabbing me and trying to force me into the car. The next day, I was online listening to different languages and how they say hello. That jackass sounded exactly like the Russian version on Google."

"You get a look at the guy driving?"

"Only from the back, dark hair and a beard that would give you whisker burn on your thighs. You know, a stubbly two-day beard."

Dillon nodded.

"What about the interior of the car?"

"The interior? Umm, black seats, I couldn't tell you if they were cloth or leather. I mean, the whole thing from the time they stopped until I kneed that prick in his balls, it wasn't even fifteen seconds. I ran back across the street and into the crowd. I looked over my shoulder, and the car was gone."

"Anything else you can think of?" Dillon asked.

She shook her head and drained her wine glass.

"How 'bout I walk you back to the art studio?"

"Better make it to my dorm. After three glasses of wine, I'd better not pick up a brush."

"Fair enough," Dillon said. "Thank you, Melanie. You've given me more information, and this will really help. I promise to keep your name out of it."

"Thank you. I meant what I said. If I ever got the chance, I would gladly shoot those guys. I don't go any-where, I'm turning antisocial, and it's all because of them."

"We'll see if we can't get them off the street for a decade or two."

ELEVEN

When Dillon returned to the office, Suel walked over to his desk. "Hey, got your note. Sorry I missed you. Did you see the Brussard girl?"

"Yeah, in fact, we had lunch together, and after the better part of three glasses of wine, she described her assault. It's the same two guys. The dark-haired driver and the blonde jerk. The blonde guy grabbed her by the ass and tried to force her into the car. She did have a couple of interesting bits."

"Such as?" Suel said.

"He said some foreign word to her initially. She was drinking with new friends, feeling no pain. The girl she was with, another student, headed back to Trinity with a guy and never told Brussard. She leaves the pub at closing time alone, goes out onto the quay, and heads in the wrong direction. This black car slows down, and the blonde idiot gets out of the car, says the Russian word 'privet' to her, which I guess means hello, and then asks if she's all right. She asks for directions to Trinity, and he grabs her ass and tries to force her into the car. She knees him in the balls, runs across the street, and hides in a crowd of people walking along the sidewalk. She sees the black car again, but they don't stop, and, eventually, she finds her way back to campus. She told me she pretty much hasn't left the campus since then."

"Back up for a second. She speaks Russian?"

"No, he said the word to her, and apparently, you can listen to it on Google. That's what she did the next morning. Looked up the word 'hello' in Russian and listened to it."

"She never reported the incident?"

"No, in large part due to pressure from her old man. As we talked, she was adamant that her name not be mentioned. Her father told her it might hurt his reelection chances."

"There you go, typical. Your daughter gets assaulted, and your big concern is if you'll be able to get your worthless ass reelected. Not surprising."

"Yeah, well, she only told me this because I promised I wouldn't mention her name. She also said the blonde guy had a little scar, just below the corner of his eye on his left cheekbone. Said it looked like a backward letter 'C.'"

"Interesting. It would probably be a good idea to send this information to Pearce Street."

"Yeah, along with the car being a black 2020 Kia. But I'm going to keep Melanie Brussard's name out of it, so please don't mention her to anyone."

"Relax, my lips are sealed."

"You know, I spoke with Mitch Crowley this morning. He was one of the three guys coming out of the Merchant's, and he told me he spoke with a detective, mentioned that the car was a black 2020 Kia. But that's not mentioned anywhere in the reports."

Suel shook his head. "Yeah, more than a little strange. A key piece of information. I'm guessing they're short-handed, like most stations, and it just got overlooked."

"Yeah, that could be, but it's key to nailing these two idiots."

"Speaking of which, your note said you were getting a list from the NVDF."

"Supposedly. The woman I spoke with thought she could probably send it over by the end of the day tomorrow."

"The list is all computerized. Doesn't she just have to push a couple of buttons, and it's sent to you?"

"After having to listen to two different recordings and a person who was absolutely no help at all, I got a nice woman who said she would have it to me by late tomorrow. That's better than I expected, and I'm not going to hassle her."

"Surprisingly, that seems to make sense."

Dillon was typing up his notes from Melanie Brussard when his phone rang. "Marshal Dillon, Special Branch."

"Hey, this is Colin Byrne, returning your call from earlier this morning. You said you were investigating the guy that assaulted the Barry girl last August outside of the Merchant's Pub."

"Yes, Colin, thank you for returning my call. I spoke to Mitch Crowley earlier this morning. I'd like to hear anything you can recall from the incident."

"Well, your man, actually there were two of them, one driving and the other one trying to push her into the car, they both got away. But I'm guessing you probably already knew that."

"Yeah, we're aware of two additional instances that seem to involve the same two individuals. In both of those cases, the women were able to escape and—"

"Escape? You mean these two took them somewhere and then raped them?"

"No, fortunately. Just like the incident you witnessed, they couldn't force the woman into the car, and she was able to get away. Any information you have would help our investigation. Including the woman you guys helped, Ann Barry, there are at least three instances that we know of, and I have a hard time believing those two guys stopped at three."

"Well, Mitch probably told you it all happened pretty fast. One minute we heard the woman scream. Mitch yelled at the plonker. I think he just yelled, 'Hey, what the feck you doing?' And your man is back in the car, and it's speeding off down the quay. We stayed with her until the Guards arrived, but that was just a couple of minutes. It kind of put a lid on the crazy night we were planning to have. You got any idea who these knackers are?"

"We've got some general information, general descriptions. You wouldn't happen to have a license number, would you?"

"Oh, I wish. I'd find 'em meself and give 'em what for."

"Any description of the man trying to force her into the car?"

"Well, he was a blonde bloke. I'd say in his late twenties, not older than thirty. If you saw him at the bar or in a shop, you wouldn't look twice. Nothing stands out that I can remember. He certainly wasn't fat, but I wouldn't call him muscular. You know, he just looked average. Then again, I only saw him for a second or two. I was more focused on your woman. She was nice looking and at the time looked like she had the bloody hell scared out of her."

"You remember anything about the car?"

"Mmm-mmm, about all I can recall is that it was black. When they took off, they must have floored it because it was gone in just a couple of seconds. Good thing the light on the bridge was red and there weren't any cars coming. Wish I could tell you more, but that's about it."

"Thank you for calling me back, Colin. If anything else comes to mind, please give me a call."

"Yeah, thanks, I'll do that. Hope you catch these bastards."

"Me too," Dillon said, and they hung up.

Dillon finished typing his updates based on his conversations with the three women plus Crowley and Byrne. It wasn't much, but he now knew a little more than when they'd started. He read through his notes and double-checked to make sure no mention of Melanie Brussard appeared. He did not mention his phone conversation with Kathleen Toolen at the National Vehicle and Drivers File, thinking there was no point in doing so until after he had received the list and gone through it. Plus, that would give him the opportunity to send a second email which would at least give the appearance that something was happening. He was going to send the email but decided to wait until tomorrow.

TWELVE

Dillon was getting ready to leave for the day when his phone rang. "Dillon, Special Branch."

"Hi, Jack," Nessa said.

"Hey, how's your day going?"

"Oh, other than almost falling asleep at my desk a few times, it went okay."

"Amazing, and you were so energetic last night."

"I was trying to keep up with you, darling. Hey, just wanted to give you a quick call. I'll be in bed and sleeping by about 8:00 tonight, and then I'm out with girlfriends tomorrow night."

"Oh, where you going tomorrow?"

"We've tickets to the Abbey Theatre. We're going to see A Whistle in the Dark, a play written by Tom Murphy."

"Oh, that should be fun. I know how much you love the theatre."

"Yeah, and I know how much you don't like live productions."

"That's because I'm a crabby guy."

"Well, I'm doing my best to work on that."

Dillon chuckled and said, "And you're doing a good job."

"Just wanted to keep you updated. Thanks again for a wonderful evening, an exhausting night, and a great wake-up in the middle of the night."

"Believe me, it was all my pleasure."

"Mine too. Talk to you later," she said and hung up.

"You got time for a pint?" Suel called from his desk.

"Where are you thinking?"

"I'm thinking the Autobahn. That will give you a chance to go home, let your little devil out, and—"

"You mean Lucifer?"

"Do you have another little devil? You can survey whatever damage he's done today and then meet me up at the Autobahn for a pint."

"Sounds like a great idea," Dillon said.

Fifteen minutes later, he was in his car heading home. It was rush hour, and the traffic was heavy. There was no point in trying to speed things up or take a shortcut that would most likely be even worse. He had dialed in a radio station that he liked and started to relax. He let Lucifer out when he arrived home, coaxed him back inside with a biscuit ten minutes later, and headed up to the Autobahn bar and restaurant. He saw Suel's car on Collins Road, and he pulled to the curb and parked three cars behind.

Suel was seated at a table in the bar area, chatting up a waitress. He gave Dillon a wave, and by the time Dillon made it over to the table, the waitress had left.

"Were you just lying about your age and telling that waitress you were independently wealthy?" Dillon said.

"No, if you must know, I was ordering you a pint."

"Oh, perfect timing on my part."

"Did you send your updated information to Seamus Quinn at Pearce Street Station?" Suel asked as he gave a friendly nod to a couple walking past.

Dillon shook his head. "I decided to wait until tomorrow morning. It still bothers me that the 2020 Kia wasn't listed in the information Quinn sent to us. The one guy, Crowley, was adamant he told a detective it was a black 2020 Kia. At this stage, it's one of, if not *the* major fact in identifying these guys."

"I know it sounds crazy, but what if whoever typed up that information missed that part? Wouldn't be the first time."

"Yeah, I guess. You learn anything?"

"Yes and no. There are a few reports of guys pulling over and chatting some women up, and it ended in an argument and, in one case, an assault. That one was the woman assaulting the guy, actually spraying him with pepper spray. If I had to guess, I'd say most of the incidents were arguments over what the price for service was going to be." Suel glanced up as the waitress returned with two pint glasses of Guinness and set them on the table. "Will you be ordering dinner?" she asked.

Suel looked over, and Dillon shook his head.

"You change your mind, let me know, and I'll bring you the menus," she said.

Dillon raised his glass in a toast, and they each took a sip.

"So, as I was saying, I couldn't find anything that resembles the three incidents we've been looking at," Suel said.

Dillon nodded. "You know, the other thing I find interesting is that after the first failed attempt with Melanie Brussard, these two idiots still returned to the Temple Bar area and tried two more times that we know of, could be even more. Your woman Melanie knees the blonde jackass. Three guys chase him off two weeks later when he goes after Ann Barry. Two weeks after that, Mary Maher throws up on him. Given all that, at what point do you start to think things aren't working out for you in Temple Bar?"

"Might be that's why it's been almost three weeks, and we haven't had a report of them trying to abduct someone else."

"Yeah, I suppose," Dillon said.

"Not to worry, bastards like these two never seem to cop on," Suel said and took a healthy sip. They had one more pint and went their separate ways. Since Apache Pizza was right next door to the Autobahn, Dillon got a pizza to go and headed home. He let Lucifer out into the front garden and set the pizza on the kitchen counter. He thought about calling Nessa and then remembered she was exhausted after their action last night, so he took the pizza into the den and turned on the TV. Thirty minutes later, there was just one piece left in the pizza box, and

Dillon was debating whether or not to eat it when he heard Lucifer barking at the front door.

He let him inside and did a quick look around. Nothing appeared to have caused him to bark, so he must have just wanted to come back inside. He headed back into the den, looking forward to the final piece of pizza, only to find Lucifer licking his lips and the pizza box empty. Dillon made him watch the news, and then they headed up to bed.

THIRTEEN

Dillon was back in Special Branch early the following morning. He reread his update on the facts regarding the attempted abductions. He triple-checked to make sure Melanie Brussard's name wasn't mentioned and then sent copies to DCI McCabe, DI Seamus Quinn at Pearce Street Station, and Paddy Suel.

Forty-five minutes later, Suel was sipping a tea, and Dillon was grimacing as he swallowed his coffee. DCI McCabe suddenly stepped out of his office and said, "Dillon, Suel, a moment of your time, please."

Suel set his tea mug on Dillon's desk, and they headed into McCabe's office.

"Grab a seat, gentlemen," McCabe said as they entered. He turned in his desk chair and pulled pages from his printer. "Thank you for the update on the Temple Bar assaults, Dillon," McCabe said. He proceeded to take two pages from the stack he'd just printed off, stapled them together, and handed them to Suel. He repeated the process and handed the copy to Dillon. "Unfortunately, there's been an update. A woman was abducted late last night, assaulted, and raped. From initial reports," he nodded at the pages he'd just handed them, "it sounds an awful lot like the two individuals involved in the attempts you mentioned."

"Was this in Temple Bar?" Dillon asked.

"No, but the victim had been in Temple Bar and was in the process of returning to her hotel. It's all there in that report. She was intoxicated, accepted a ride, was assaulted, and raped. She's currently in James's Hospital, where an officer is assigned to guard her room. She is expected to be released sometime this afternoon. I'd like the two of you to interview her prior to her release. I want these individuals off the streets and behind bars. Any questions?"

"She's identified in the report?" Suel asked.

"Yes, if you'd read it," McCabe said. "Any other questions?"

Dillon and Suel shook their heads.

"Don't let me hold you up. Go through that report and then interview her. I presume Pearce Street Station will be sending someone to do the same. I want you two to interview as well. Any questions?"

They both shook their heads, stood, and headed out of McCabe's office.

"I'll drive," Suel said back at Dillon's desk. He took a sip of his tea and made a face. "Damn, already cold. Let me dump this, and we'll head over to James's if you can fit it into your schedule."

"So much for my updated information," Dillon said as they headed out to Suel's car. He climbed into the passenger seat with the two-page report McCabe printed off for them.

St. James's Hospital was on the opposite side of the Liffey River, and Suel drove down to the Wolfe Tone Quay. He drove past the Frank Sherwin Bridge since it was one way, going the wrong way across the Liffey. He turned onto the Rory O'More Bridge, crossed the river, and drove up to James Street, where he took a right and, a few blocks later, turned left and entered the St. James's grounds. He parked near the Famine Memorial and placed a letter-sized sheet of paper on the dash identifying the car as An Garda Síochána, Special Branch, complete with a department logo.

Along the way, Dillon had read out loud the report on the abduction, assault, and rape of the woman. Her name was Kathleen Cullen. She was from County Wicklow. She had arrived in Dublin the day before, searching for a wedding dress. Last night, she headed into the Temple Bar section and ended up in a pub, The Quays, listening to a band. Two men bought her a drink and offered to give her a ride back to her room at the Arlington Hotel. She passed out in the back seat of their car, a black vehicle, and when she woke, she was lying in a field in the process of being raped. Her blouse was tied around her mouth so she couldn't scream. She put up a fight, which resulted in a broken right arm, a number of contusions, and a lost tooth, not to mention anal and vaginal injuries.

"So, in other words, they raped her and beat the shit out of her," Suel said as he pulled to the curb and parked.

"Yeah, but they didn't kill her, which is surprising. She was in Killinardin Park and—"

"Killinardin? She was down in Tallaght?" Suel asked.

"Yeah, they left her out there with a thong around her ankle. She somehow found her jeans twenty feet away. Her blouse was torn in half and had been wrapped around her head. She thinks she passed out again. Eventually, she made her way to a home at 14 Knockmore Park and rang the doorbell. Fortunately, someone answered and called the Guards. Jesus Christ, she's lucky to even be alive."

"If she passed out, I wonder if those two bastards thought she was dead?"

"Could be. She's in a private room, number 326," Dillon said as they entered St. James's Hospital.

They took the elevator up to the third floor, then made their way through a series of winding hallways until they came to a nurses' station. There were eight rooms behind the nurses' station, and Dillon could see number 326 with a uniformed officer seated in a chair next to the entrance to the room. Just now, he appeared to be reading something on his cellphone.

"May I help you?" a nurse seated behind the counter asked. She had a stack of what looked like a half-dozen files in front of her.

"An Garda Síochána, Special Branch," Suel said. "We're here to interview," he glanced at Dillon.

"We're here to interview Kathleen Cullen. She was brought in earlier this morning," Dillon said.

"There have already been two officers here this morning taking her statements," the nurse said, not sounding very happy.

"Yes, and we're going to follow up and attempt to learn about the individuals who attacked her. It's our job," Suel said.

"Would you happen to have her file handy so we can review her injuries," Dillon said. "It would go a long way in making our interview less difficult for her. We realize she's been through an awful experience. But we have to talk with her, so we have a chance of arresting the individuals responsible."

The nurse seemed to think for a moment and then quickly sorted through the half-dozen files in front of her. She pulled the second file from the bottom and handed it to Dillon, and then shot a look at Suel.

"Mind if we just sit over there?" Dillon said and nodded at three blue plastic chairs lined up against the far wall.

She nodded and said, "Fine." Still not sounding happy. She refocused on the open file in front of her as Dillon and Suel stepped over to the plastic chairs.

"Jesus Christ," Suel said under his breath as they sat down.

Dillon opened the file and placed it on his lap. There were three black and white images of Kathleen Cullen. In the first image, both her eyes were black and swollen. Her nose had been broken, and there was a gauze bandage with a splint taped over it. Her lips were swollen and clearly split in three different places. Her forehead, cheeks, and chin were bruised.

The second image showed both bruised arms. The right arm was at an odd angle with a fiberglass cast wrapped around it. Her chest and shoulders were bruised, along with bruised or possibly even broken ribs on her right side. Her breasts were black and blue. There was a vicious scratch mark from fingernails running down her left side.

The third image was of her lower region, again more bruising. What appeared to be bite marks were along her thighs.

"I'd say whoever did this literally kicked the hell out of her," Dillon said.

"Yeah, and check this out," Suel said and pointed to the word 'Rohypnol' typed on the report with a question mark behind it.

"Roofies, that makes sense," Dillon said. "They buy her a drink or two, slip the drug in. In thirty minutes, she has no idea what's happening. She can't fight them off, can't call for help. They put her in the car, and by the time she's in the park, they can do whatever they want to her, and she probably can't remember much of any-thing."

"You ready to see her?" Dillon asked.

"Yeah, but then I want to find these two bastards and deal with them. See how they like what I have in mind," Suel said.

Dillon stepped over to the nurses' counter and handed the file back to the nurse. She actually flashed a quick smile.

"Thank you, would it be possible to get a copy of that file? I fear we may be running into additional victims, and it would help to check for similarities."

She seemed to think about that for a moment and said, "Let me check with our supervisor."

"Thank you. In the meantime, we'll interview Miss Cullen," Dillon said. "I want her to know we will find these two and deal with them."

FOURTEEN

Dillon and Suel showed their IDs to the officer seated in front of the door to Kathleen Cullen's room. "Has she had any visitors?" Suel asked him.

"Detectives first thing this morning, asking the usual questions. From what I could hear, she didn't remember much. Had the hell beat out of her, broke her arm. Her face looks like she went ten rounds with a pro. She has to call a nurse in to help her get to the bathroom, poor thing."

Suel looked at Dillon and said, "Well, let's interrupt her morning."

"Good luck. Oh, she apparently goes by Kate."

"Thanks," Dillon said. He knocked softly on the door as he opened it. "Good morning, Kate. I'm Jack Dillon with Special Branch." He had to raise his voice to be heard over whatever was playing on the TV.

"And I'm Paddy Suel. We wanted to check in with you. See how you're doing."

Kate Cullen looked as bad, if not worse, in person. The hospital bed was raised, so she was sitting up, clothed in a light blue hospital gown. Both eyes were swollen and black. The gauze on her nose was gone, and it was now covered with a green metal splint. Raw areas were on both swollen cheeks. Her right arm was wrapped in a dark blue fiberglass cast from her shoulder down to and around her wrist. Using her bruised left arm, she picked up a TV remote from the rollover table in front of her and turned the TV off.

"Sorry, couldn't hear. Tell me your names again," she said, speaking with a lisp.

"Jack Dillon, and this is my partner, Paddy Suel. We're with An Garda Síochána, Special Branch."

"So you came all the way from America to track down the bastards who did this?" she said and then attempted a smile with swollen, bruised, and split lips. Dillon immediately noticed the missing front tooth. Her voice sounded as if her nose was plugged.

"Not exactly. I was already here, which saves us a day in travel. So we can find these two just that much faster."

"Well, when you find the feckers, just shoot both of them and send 'em straight to hell."

"Be happy to do that," Suel said.

"We read your medical report. Based on all you went through, it's a good thing you're a strong woman, and you're here. Now, it's going to be our turn to deliver some payback. Do you mind if we ask you a few questions?"

"I'll tell you just what I told the other two earlier this morning. I came up to Dublin yesterday afternoon. I was supposed to do final fittings today on a wedding dress. You can see how well that's working out. I checked into the Arlington Hotel. Grabbed a burger at the McDonald's over on Grafton Street, looked in some shops, and then went to listen to a band at the Quays Bar. I wasn't doing anything crazy. I was drinking a half-glass of Guinness. Two guys came up next to me. They ordered pints and offered to buy me another half-glass. They looked nice enough, a blonde and a dark-haired guy. The Guinness came. We toasted and listened to the band. They didn't say much. Asked if I was a Dub, and then everything gets kind of foggy. Next thing I know, I'm in a field or someplace, no clothes, and trying to fight them off. You can see how well that went."

"Do you recall, were they Irish?" Suel asked

She started to shake her head, grimaced, and said, "If they told me where they were from, I can't remember. Everything gets real hazy. But there was an accent with one of them."

"Did the Guinness they bought you taste different?"

"Different? No, it was a good Guinness. It wasn't my first time in Quays Bar. If I'm in Dublin with friends, we usually end up there. Always nice music, nice crowd, and close to the hotel where we always stay, the Arlington."

"Do you stay in the hotel or the hostel?" Dillon asked.

"The hotel."

"Your medical report mentioned they may have put Rohypnol in your drink."

"They put something in there. They had to. Everything just got so hazy. I was listening to music in the pub, and the next thing I remember, I was on the ground with one of them on top of me and the other one grabbing me. I couldn't get your man off me. I started to hit him, and he rose up and was going to hit me. Next thing I know, I woke up. I was alone and didn't know where I was…" She seemed to take a deep breath and, after a long moment, said, "Sorry, I can't remember more. I don't know. That just might be a blessing in disguise."

"Can you describe how they looked in the bar?"

"How they looked?" She seemed to think for a moment. "Well, the dark-haired one, he had what looked like a two-day beard, you know. His hair was nice. Brown eyes. Your blonde one, he had shorter hair, combed over. Oh, and he had blue eyes. To tell you the truth, they looked like nice guys and didn't say much. It's not like they were all over me in the bar or anything. They just bought the Guinness and listened to the music. I remember at the end of a song, the dark-haired one, he leaned over and said, 'That was good,' and we started clapping."

"Do you remember what their vehicle was like?" Suel asked.

She shook her head slightly. "I think it might have been black. I can't really remember leaving the pub. I just remember waking up and trying to push your one off me, and they started to hit and kick me. Oh, and they were laughing. One of them said something, but I couldn't understand whatever it was he said."

"Did they take your purse or credit cards?"

"I didn't carry a purse, and I'm not sure. I think my jeans are in the cabinet over there." She nodded at the wardrobe against the far wall. "My phone should be in there too if you'd check."

Suel stepped over and opened the cabinet door. A pair of muddied and grass-stained blue jeans hung on a hook. A torn, muddied, and blood-stained blouse, white with a design of black safety pins across it, was draped over a hanger. He reached for the jeans and pulled out a small, pocket-sized green leather card holder with a flap that snapped close. He set it on the rollover table, then checked the back pockets on the jeans and pulled out a cellphone. The screen on the phone was shattered.

"Oh, no. My phone. God, I just got it last month. Now look." She pressed a button on the side of the phone a number of times, but nothing happened, and she tossed the phone onto the rollover table. It slid across the table and onto the bed. "Damn it. Those two worthless bastards."

Suel reached for the cardholder, pulled the flap open, and handed it to her. "Check to see if all your credit cards are in there."

She set the cardholder on her lap and held it open with the fingers of her left hand. She nodded and looked up. "Yeah, all my cards are here. But the damn phone.

Jesus Christ. Honest to God, if I ever get my hands on those two bastards . . .”

“Is there anyone we can contact for you?” Dillon asked.

She seemed to think for a moment and slowly shook her head. “No, my parents are on the way up. My boy-friend, fiancé, actually, is on his way, too. I had to have a nurse dial the phone,” she said and glanced over at the phone on the bedside cabinet. “I just don’t know—Oh God, I’m an absolute fucking mess. He won’t want to marry me,” she said and began to sob.

Fortunately, the nurse who’d been seated behind the counter had just stepped into the room and hurried over to the bed. She shot a look at Dillon and Suel. “Kate, honey. Kate, you’re okay, darling. You’re okay.” She shot another look at Dillon and Suel and indicated the door with a vicious nod of her head.

“Thank you, Kate, we’ll leave you to—”

“Go,” the nurse half-shouted, and if looks could kill

. . .

“How’d it go?” the officer seated outside the room said as Suel closed the door behind them. They could still hear Kate Cullen crying.

“About like you’d expect,” Dillon said. “Anyone besides the officers earlier this morning and us been in to see her?”

“No, just you and the earlier pair.”

“She mentioned her fiancé and her parents were on their way.”

"I'll be right here," he said.

FIFTEEN

They climbed into the car. Suel removed the An Garda Síochána sign from the dash and slipped it back into the storage console. "What do you think?"

Dillon shook his head. "I think she's lucky to be alive. Those two bastards probably left her for dead. You got time to make another stop?"

"Depends on what you're thinking."

"I'd like to talk to the person who called the Guards." Dillon opened the two-page report on Kate Cullen's assault. The address was listed as 14 Knockmore Park, with no name of the resident. He read the address to Suel.

"I think that's a good idea. Let's check it out," Suel said and input the address into his GPS.

"While you're driving, I'll make a call and get the name of whoever lives there. Hopefully, they're home."

Suel pulled away from the curb and headed back to James Street.

Dillon pulled out his phone and a moment later said, "Yeah, Andy. It's Dillon. I'm with Suel, and we're heading to an address at 14 Knockmore Park in Tallaght. Can you look up the address and get the name of whoever lives there? What? Yeah. No, Suel's driving. I know. That's why I'm wearing a crash helmet, and I've got pillows wrapped all around me. Yes, Terrence Greely, thanks, got it," Dillon said and disconnected.

"That's the owner, Terrence Greely?" Suel said.

"Yeah."

"Amazing you could hear him with that crash helmet on."

Dillon wrote the name at the top of the two-page report and then studied the report again. "God, I can't imagine what that Cullen woman is going through. Afraid her boyfriend won't marry her now. Did you catch her missing front tooth?"

"Yeah, how fecked up do you have to be to do that to someone, a woman no less. We gotta find these bastards, Dillon, and when we do . . ."

They drove on in silence for ten minutes, and then the GPS directed Suel to turn right onto Knockmore Park. They drove past a length of eight attached houses on both sides of the street, all of the same design. A stucco exterior, a front door with a large sitting room window next to it on the ground floor, and two windows above on the second floor. They crossed a street and drove past another length of attached housing units, this time only six. Number 14 was at the end next to a six-foot concrete block wall with Killinardin Park on the other side. There was a standard metal gate entrance to the park. You'd have to push the gate open and then make a right-hand turn for two or three steps to actually enter the park.

Suel pulled to the curb in front of number 14 and parked. They climbed out of the car, walked over to the entrance gate, and looked into the park. A large grass field ran in either direction as far as they could see. Directly across and about a hundred yards away was a line of trees. Just then, a woman was walking a dog along what appeared to be a paved path just in front of the trees.

"Well, let's see if your man Greely is home," Dillon said.

"Looks like it," Suel said. "At least there's a car parked in front.

Dillon glanced at the older model Toyota Camry parked in what used to be the front garden. The car was backed in, and the area that originally had grass and possibly flowers was now completely covered with concrete. A six-foot-high wooden gate with a rounded top led to a sidewalk running between the side of the house and the wall along the park.

They walked up to the front door, pushed the doorbell, and then pulled their IDs from their pockets. A moment later, a gray-haired woman opened the door. She wasn't much taller than five feet, if that, and perhaps ninety-five pounds.

"Garda?" she asked.

"Yes, Marshal Jack Dillon, and this is DI Paddy Suel. We're with Special Branch," Dillon said and held out his ID.

She nodded her head and said, "We spoke with someone earlier. Come in, please. We're just about to have a tea. Terry's in the kitchen. Dreadful, absolutely dreadful what happened to that poor girl last night. You just have to wonder. Please join us," she said and held the door open.

Dillon and Suel stepped into the house. Suel closed the door behind them, and they followed her down a narrow hall with large orange tiles on the floor. A staircase on the right side led up to the second floor. Dillon knew the layout. A bathroom and two bedrooms along with a smaller room would be upstairs. A sitting room with a fireplace would be off to the left, with a kitchen and dining area in the back of the house.

"Terry, more officers from the Guards. They'll be joining us for tea," the woman said as she entered the dining area.

Terry Greely was seated at the dining table. A plate with two muffins, one of which had a bite taken out of it, sat on a plate. The sound of the tea kettle coming to a boil was in the background.

Terry rose to his feet as they entered. He was a gray-haired man with flashing blue eyes. Dillon placed him at mid-seventies. He was probably six feet tall at one time but was now stooping forward, probably from sixty-plus years of labor.

"Marshal Dillon, Special Branch," Dillon said and shook hands. Greely had a strong, firm grip.

"Paddy Suel, nice to meet you, sir," Suel said and shook hands.

"Suel? You wouldn't be related to a Finbar Suel, would you? Worked at the docks some years back."

Suel grinned. "Finn was my grandfather's brother. My grandfather was the oldest in that family, Aidan. A right gang they were, ten boys."

Greely nodded and said, "Yes, and a lot of fun, too. Do you remember that wedding, Cara?"

"Terry, no, now not another word about that evening," she said and placed the kettle beneath the faucet and added more water.

Greely glanced at his wife. She was facing the sink with her back to them. He smiled at Dillon and Suel and mouthed the word 'pregnant.' His wife turned the kettle on and stepped over to the table, looked at the plate with the muffins, and focused on the one with the bite out of it. "Really, Terry?"

"One of the Guards did it, honey. They heard how good your baking is, and they couldn't wait."

She shot him a look and then turned to Dillon and Suel. "I may ask you to take him with when you leave."

"We're not equipped to deal with that, ma'am," Suel said, and everyone laughed.

They were seated around the table, sipping tea and eating a muffin. Cara had served the tea mugs and then returned with a plate of four muffins, none with a bite out of them, and sat down at the table.

Greely was in the midst of telling their story from the past night.

"I'd slept through the doorbell, but it kept ringing, and Cara woke me."

"He would have slept right through, leaving the poor girl out there ringing the doorbell and crying for help."

"I slipped my robe on and hurried downstairs. I left the light off and looked out the window but didn't see a car."

"All the while, the doorbell is ringing, and I can hear the poor thing crying," Cara said and shook her head.

"I opened the door, and she stumbled in. She collapsed right on the hallway floor. At first, I thought she was drunk, but then all the dirt and the blood. She'd had the hell beat out of her."

"Terry!"

"Well, she did. The bastard what done that to her. I called Cara and—"

"I could hear her crying. I pulled my robe on and hurried downstairs. I took one look at her and—"

"I just said, Cara, call the Guards."

"I hurried out to the kitchen and called the guards. I got an ice pack from the freezer, ran warm water on two washcloths, and came back out to the hallway."

"I held her on the floor, kept telling her she was safe, and Cara was trying to calm her down, dabbing at the blood and the mud on her face. It seemed like hours, but the Guards were here in just a few minutes. The ambulance came a minute or two later and—" A tear rolled down Greely's cheek, and his wife squeezed his hand. "Who the hell would do that to a woman? God help me if I ever see them."

Dillon waited a long moment to let the couple collect themselves. "Probably the best thing that could have happened was Kate Cullen came to your house. God was looking out for her, and the two of you are saviors. You saved her life. There are no two ways about it. Were you aware of anyone out front looking at the park that day or some days before?"

They both shook their heads. "People go in and out of the park gate all the time. Almost always, they're locals. Unless you lived in the immediate area, you wouldn't really know the gate was even there."

They chatted on for a bit, but other than letting Kate Cullen in the door in the middle of the night and calling the Guards, they didn't know much. Dillon brought the conversation to a close. They both left their cards with the Greely's, thanked them again for saving Kate Cullen's life, and left.

"God bless the two of them," Suel said as they drove back to Special Branch.

"I'm determined to find these bastards," Dillon said.

"That makes two of us," Suel replied.

Sixteen

They headed back to Garda Headquarters and the Special Branch office. Once Suel had parked, they walked over to the four food trucks lined up on North Road. Dillon bought two tacos, and Suel got an Irish stew. They headed back to Special Branch and settled in at a table in the break room.

"What's your takeaway from this morning?" Suel asked as he tore the plastic lid off his stew.

"I think our boys, and I believe it's the same two bastards, have upped their game. After a number of failed attempts at dragging some woman off the street and into the car, they're smiling, acting nice and polite, and slipping drugs into some innocent woman's drink. This Kate Cullen is the perfect one. She's alone. They're apparently a nice-looking pair, polite, and they buy her a half-pint of Guinness along with their pints. They don't talk much other than to say a couple of funny things as they're watching the band. Next thing you know, she can't remember her name, and nice guys that they are, they're helping her out of the pub and into their car after she's apparently been over-served."

"After lunch, we need to check the security tape at The Quays pub," Suel said.

"Yeah, God forbid we'd get these two on tape. I find it interesting that despite the three failed attempts we know of, they're still operating in the Temple Bar area."

"Yeah, and this last one was successful. Makes me wonder if they'll up their game."

Dillon nodded. "I'm a little surprised they don't have somewhere they could keep a woman locked up. You know, hang on to her for a couple of days, keep her drugged, then when they finally get tired of her, they get rid of her."

"Man, you are one warped plonker. Are you—"

"Dillon, Suel, a moment of your time, please," DCI McCabe called from the door of his office.

"I didn't know he was here. The door was closed, and the blinds were drawn in his office," Dillon said.

"Oh God, this doesn't sound good. No doubt my stew will be cold by the time we're finished. He probably wants an update on the rape."

"Should have been smart like me and gotten these tacos," Dillon said, cramming the remaining half into his mouth. He squirted red sauce onto his shirt in the process.

Suel shook his head and said, "The last thing I want to do is be like you."

They headed into DCI McCabe's office. Next to him on the couch was a younger-looking man, Dillon thought perhaps mid-thirties. He had long black hair pulled back in a ponytail, a thin beard on the base of his chin, and looked to weigh no more than a hundred and forty pounds. Both arms, from what Dillon could tell through the long sleeve shirt, appeared to be heavily tattooed.

"Gentlemen, please take a seat," McCabe said, pointing to the two wingback chairs opposite the coffee table in front of the couch. "I'd like to introduce FBI agent Dennis DaVanni."

"DI Paddy Suel, nice to meet you."

"US Marshal, Jack Dillon," Dillon said as he nodded.

"Agent DaVanni is here from Boston," McCabe said as he turned toward DaVanni. "Perhaps you'd like to explain your visit here."

"Happy to," DaVanni said. "First, let me begin by saying I read about you, Dillon. Your incident at the Dublin airport a few years back. Glad it worked out in your favor."

Dillon nodded.

"The FBI established ATCT, the Art Theft Crime Team, almost twenty years ago back in 2004, beginning with the looting of the Bagdad Museum. Since then, we've been involved in local and international cases and recoveries amounting to over three hundred and twenty-four million dollars. I'm one of thirteen agents on the Art Theft Crime Team."

"So, what brings you to Dublin?" Dillon asked.

"Back in 2001, eight paintings by an abstract artist named Mark Rothko were stolen from the Kincannon

Abstract Art Museum down in New Orleans. At the time, the paintings amounted to a total of fifteen million dollars. That value has now increased to ten times the original, bringing it to one hundred and fifty million dollars."

At the mention of Rothko's name, Dillon and Suel looked at one another.

"A hundred and fifteen million dollars for a painting?" Suel said.

"That's for eight Rothko paintings. As I mentioned, the paintings were stolen from a museum back in 2001. Two suspects were later arrested and identified by the security guard working that evening, but the arrest didn't hold up. The paintings were never recovered. One of the suspects, a man by the name of Edward McDonnell, died in 2007 under suspicious circumstances."

"Define suspicious circumstances," Suel said.

"What was left of his body was found in the Jean Lafitte swamp just outside of New Orleans. No way he could have gotten to that point without a boat. He'd been eaten by alligators, and a boat was never found."

"Jesus," Suel said.

"Jesus played no part in his death," DaVanni replied. "In 2020, the second suspect, a man by the name of Martin Lane, was found dead in his bed. The New Orleans Medical Examiner determined that Lane had died of natural causes. Interestingly, there was a portion of his bedroom wall that had been torn open, and in it, tiny bits of paint that matched the paints used by the artist Mark Rothko were discovered. What we don't know is whether the wall was torn open before or after Lane's passing. We're more or less convinced that some, if not all, of the stolen Rothko paintings were hidden in the bedroom wall at some point."

"So, what does this have to do with Dublin?" Dillon said.

"Does the name Aidan Phalen ring a bell?"

Dillon and Suel looked at one another and shook their heads simultaneously.

"Aidan Phalen is Irish and a known art thief. He served four years in France, two years in Italy, and is a suspect in a half-dozen unsolved cases. He flew to the United States and spent a week visiting Martin Lane. He left the country just thirty-six hours before Lane's body was discovered."

"You want to extradite him?" Dillon said.

"That would be ideal, but actually, we can't. Believe me, we've tried. Unfortunately, the fact that he merely visited is not grounds for extradition. That, coupled with Lane's death listed as due to natural causes, provides no opportunity to invoke extradition. Phalen, on the advice of his solicitor, has refused to be interviewed."

"So why do you think he stole the paintings? And even if he did, how in God's name would he get them out of the United States?" McCabe said.

"Let me answer your second question first. We don't know how, or even if, he somehow got the paintings out of the United States. When they were first stolen, they were cut from their wooden frames and rolled up. The fact they were rolled up, in part, explains the scattering of paint bits found in the Lane residence. That said, we've watched the TSA video of Aidan Phalen passing through security to board his flight to Ireland, and he clearly is not carrying a canvas painting, let alone eight of them. To answer your first question, a gentleman by the name of Royce Farley is an expert on Mark Rothko, and he legitimately owns not one, but two Rothko paintings. Both insured for over a million dollars, or Euros as the case may be."

"Does he live in Ireland?" Suel said.

"He lives on the south side of Dublin, in an area called Castleknock, about eight kilometers west of the city center."

"We know where it is," Suel said. "Is he in an apartment?"

"No, he owns what is referred to as an unattached home. Are you familiar with Tower Road?"

"Yes. Phoenix Park is just outside our building, and at the far end of the park is the Knockmaroon Gates. Tower Road is just outside the gates, no more than a hundred and fifty meters or so," Suel said.

"Royce Farley happens to be an acquaintance, if not a close friend, of Aidan Phalen."

"So, with all due respect, you've really nothing but suspicion for us to go on," Dillon said. "Certainly nothing that would allow us to get a warrant and search this Farley person's house. What exactly do you want us to do?"

"I understand, and unfortunately, I have to agree with what you're saying. All I'm really doing is introducing myself and hoping I could review any files and information you might have on Royce Farley and Aidan Phalen. My sense is Farley is not in possession of the paintings, at least for the moment. But I have to believe he eventually will be, and I'm hoping that he will attempt to gain possession sooner rather than later."

"We'll do whatever we can to help you. But, in all honesty, it seems like a long shot. Are you thinking he'll have them shipped over from the States? That just seems—"

"No, not at all. I'm thinking someone, possibly a number of individuals, are going to bring the paintings to him. I think there's a good chance these people will have no idea what they are carrying. They may already be en route. Perhaps they're going to travel from France or the UK and into Ireland. At this stage, we don't know."

"They could enter some small fishing village on a boat," Suel said and laughed.

"Well, anything is possible. I just want you to know that I'm here for a while, and if you should hear of anything or something pops into your head, please let me know."

A few minutes later, Dillon and Suel shook hands with DaVanni, nodded toward McCabe, and left the office, closing the door behind them. "What the hell was that about?" Dillon said.

"Does it strike you as strange that these paintings were done by the same artist that Melanie Brussard is copying?" Suel said.

SEVENTEEN

Dillon ate his second taco, and Suel warmed his stew in the microwave. Once they finished, Dillon drove them over to the Temple Bar area and parked on Wellington Quay. They walked down Fownes Street Lower and entered the Quays pub. Five minutes later, they were in the manager's office reviewing a security tape from the previous evening.

The manager, a middle-aged man, named Thomas Brennan, was speeding backward through the tape. It took ten minutes, but they eventually saw Kate Cullen seated on a stool at the bar.

"Wait a minute. I think that's her," Dillon said.

Brennan stopped the tape and then enlarged the image of Kate Cullen. It became a little blurry, but there was no mistaking the fact that it was her. Her white blouse with the black safety-pin design appeared pressed instead of torn and covered with mud. She was seated on a bar stool, leaning with her back against the bar. The time on the digital clock in the upper left corner of the screen read 21:21 (9:21 pm). Hard to believe the smiling woman in the image would have a broken arm, get the hell beaten out of her, and be raped in the next few hours.

"Move forward at a normal pace," Dillon said. The images were jerking, a new image appeared every four or five seconds, but Kate Cullen seemed to be alone and would occasionally sip from her glass resting on the bar. Two men appeared alongside her. One was blonde with shorter hair parted on the side. The man with him had dark hair, shaved on the sides, and combed back.

"That's gotta be them," Suel said.

The man with dark hair said something to Cullen, and she seemed to nod. They placed an order with the bartender, and three glasses were delivered four and a half minutes later, two full pints and a half-glass, apparently all Guinness. The blonde man appeared to line up the three glasses. When he handed a pint to his dark-haired friend, the tattoos on his fingers were apparent. He lingered over the half-pint glass before he handed it to Kate Cullen.

"Can you play that back and slow it down? The guy lining up the glasses," Dillon said.

The manager reversed the tape and ran it at half-speed.

"There, stop," Dillon said. "Right there. See, he's spiking her glass."

The blonde man had powder in his left hand, between his thumb and two fingers, scattering it into the half-glass. Cullen seemed focused on whatever was happening on the stage, not paying attention to her drink still on the bar. He seemed to swirl the half-glass before handing it to her. She smiled, said something, and in the next image, she was taking a healthy drink.

The dark-haired man made a total of three comments to Kate Cullen over the course of the next twenty minutes. At about the thirty-minute mark, Cullen began to have difficulty sitting. Her head began to sway. She had a strange look on her face and looked as though she was unable to focus. Five minutes later, they each took hold of her arm and led her toward the door. A few people seemed to glance over as she was led out of the pub. They appeared on an outside camera for three frames. The blonde man seemed to be laughing and had his hand down the back of her shorts. They disappeared from sight a moment later.

"Mr. Brennan, can you make us a copy of that tape?"

"I can. It'll be a digital copy."

Dillon pulled out a business card and said, "If you would email it to me, that would be great."

"I can do that. Have it to you later this afternoon."

"Thank you. If you could make it from the first view of her seated alone at the bar until the three of them disappear from view, that would be perfect."

"Not a problem."

"Thank you, very much appreciated," Suel said.

"I just hope you get these two. The last thing we need is a reputation for drinks being drugged. I'm going to show this to our staff, have them keep an eye out for those two eejits."

Back in the car, Dillon turned the engine on and said, "You mind if we hop over to Trinity? I'd like to find the Brussard girl and see why she's copying those Rothko paintings."

"Not a problem. As a matter of fact, I was going to suggest the same thing. We're no more than five minutes away. It's been nagging me in the back of my mind ever since. What's his name, your FBI agent?"

"DaVanni, Dennis DaVanni."

"Yeah, it's been bugging me ever since he mentioned Rothko. And the price, fifteen million. Can you believe it?"

"That was the old price, Paddy. Now they're worth a hundred and fifty million. Ten times the original price."

"Oh yeah, crazy. We're in the wrong business, Dillon. The two of us should make a couple of dozen of those things on a Saturday night with a case of beer, and we could retire for the rest of our lives."

Dillon pulled into the Trinity Staff parking lot on Nassau Street. They headed over to the Creative Arts Building and went down to the art studio. Melanie Brussard was in the studio wearing her smock and working on a new canvas, more rectangles, this time on a black background. Two other students were painting. A woman was painting the proverbial bowl of fruit, and a young man with a half-dozen piercings in his right ear was dripping red paint from a jar onto his canvas lying on the floor.

Suel stared for a long moment, then started to talk to the guy dripping the red paint from the jar.

"Hi Melanie," Dillon said.

Brussard turned and said, "Oh, Marshal. Umm, hello. What are you doing here?"

"Just in the neighborhood and thought we'd stop by. Everything going okay with you?"

"Yeah, as you can see, I've finished one painting, and I'm starting on the next one."

"Another Rothko?" Dillon said, looking at the rectangles sketched out in pencil on the canvas. At the moment, she was painting a narrow blue rectangle above a larger reddish-orange rectangle.

"Yes, this work was entitled *Blue Over Red*."

"And you're always doing Rothko's work?"

"Yes, I'm in the process of recreating the eight paintings stolen from the Patrick Kincannon Abstract Art Museum in New Orleans. I've only seen pictures of them, and they're actually what got me interested in art to begin with. Well, that, and the fact that my father didn't like them, and what could be more engaging to a young girl than doing something her parents don't like?"

Dillon chuckled at that. "Do you remember the paintings being stolen?"

"That was before my time. But it was the talk of the town for quite a while, with my parents and their friends, years after it happened. It still is. And that's saying a lot, coming from New Orleans where something crazy is happening every day."

"Very nice," Dillon said. "Have you been to any of the local Dublin museums? You know you've got a half-dozen very nearby you could walk to."

"Which, if you'll remember, is exactly what I don't want to do. I told you that the other day when we had lunch. I'm very uncomfortable leaving the campus, which is why, with the exception of our lunch, I don't go anywhere. I'm the most boring student at Trinity. I hope to make a copy of each stolen painting and give them to the Kincannon Abstract Art Museum in New Orleans.

"I don't think that makes you boring," Dillon said.

"Well, thanks, but I'm afraid it's true."

"No one who paints Mark Rothko's work is boring. I'm here to tell you."

"Thanks," she said and proceeded to place a number of blue strokes onto the canvas.

"Well, I'll let you get back to work. We were just in the neighborhood and hoped we might be able to catch you working."

"I'm here eternally," she said but then turned toward Dillon. "I'm okay with that. Thanks for stopping in."

"My pleasure. You keep up the good work."

"I'll try," she said and turned back to the painting. Dillon walked back to Suel, who was laughing with the young man who had been pouring the red paint on the canvas.

"Oh, Dillon, this is Conrad. If you can believe it, he saw this being done in a movie. A naked woman strung up from the ceiling, and she sails over the canvas, splashing paint onto it."

"The Big Lebowski, with Jeff Bridges?"

"Yeah, you know it?" Conrad said.

"I'm an American. We've all seen it a half-dozen times at least."

"See, there you go. I told you it was popular," Conrad said to Suel.

"I get the naked woman part. But splashing paint on a canvas?"

"She was an artist, Paddy," Dillon said.

Conrad extended his arm and fist-bumped Dillon.

"What'd you learn from your woman?" Suel said once they were back in the car. Dillon turned the key and headed out of the Trinity Staff parking lot.

"Not much. I didn't really expect her to say anything. She mentioned making copies of the paintings stolen in New Orleans and hopes to donate them to the museum. I don't know. I'm thinking it's more coincidental than anything else. If you had hold of eight paintings worth over a hundred million bucks, would you seek out the help of a college kid? The daughter of a politician no less?"

"Good point," Suel said. "I'll have to check out that movie. What was it called?"

"The Big Lebowski. It was very popular, Jeff Bridges, John Goodman, and a number of other big names. It's a good laugh."

EIGHTEEN

Back in the office, Dillon logged onto his computer and checked his email. The first thing he saw was the email from Kathleen Toolen at the NVDF, the National Vehicle and Driver File. He opened the email and read the sentence from Toolen.

"Here's the file of 2020 Kia's listed in Dublin County. Hope this helps."

Dillon clicked on the Excel file, and it opened. One-hundred-and-fifty-eight Kia's, nine different models, were sold in Dublin County in 2020. He quickly looked up the model names and then listed the number of each particular model sold during the year. He isolated the top six most expensive models and then added up the number of those models sold in 2020, a total of 12 vehicles. Of those, three were licensed to women, and two were licensed to men sixty-five or older. He eliminated those five vehicles from his list, leaving seven possibilities. Of the seven remaining vehicles, a Kia Sorento stood out for two reasons. First, it was one of the more expensive Kias at thirty-seven thousand euros. More importantly, it was apparently purchased by an Irish man by the name of Dessie Phalen.

Dillon called over to Suel, "Hey, Paddy, come over here and check this out."

"What is it, a picture of women on the beach?"

"Very funny, not. No, I got the list of Kia's sold in Dublin County in 2020 from the NVDF. I broke the list down to the twelve most expensive vehicles and eliminated the names of two guys over sixty-five and three women. That left seven. The most expensive one was a Kia Sorento. But check this out," Dillon said and turned his computer screen toward Suel.

"Dessie Phalen? Okay, sorry, but that name isn't ringing a bell. What am I missing?"

"DaVanni, the FBI agent in McCabe's office earlier. He mentioned Aidan Phalen, the art thief who served time in France and Italy and was over in the States visiting the guy who died, Martin Lane, in New Orleans."

"Well, first off, Phalen is not an uncommon name. And, I hasten to point out that this individual isn't named Aidan. His name is Dessie."

"Yeah, and his age is listed at twenty-five, and he's paying thirty-seven grand for a new car."

"Okay, and the driver of the car and his pal have both been described by multiple people as having eastern European accents, either Polish or possibly Russian. Oh, and, as far as I can recall, no one has described them as being art collectors or art thieves."

"It just strikes me as an interesting coincidence."

"Is there an address listed on the registration? Check it out and see who owns the property. If it's listed to Aidan Phalen, you just might be on to something. You might want to send a picture of that Kia model to the potential victims and the witnesses we've spoken to and see if it rings any bells."

"Good idea. I'll send an email before I drive out to," Dillon glanced at the Phalen address listed on the NVDF document, "Malahide."

"Let me know what you find out," Suel said and wandered back to his desk.

Dillon sent individual emails to Melanie Brussard, Ann Barry, Mary Maher, Seamus Quinn, Mitch Crowley, and Colin Byrne. The email had three images of the two suspects with Kate Cullen at Quays Pub along with a stock photo of a black 2020 Kia Sorento. He did not send an email to Kate Cullen since she had stated she had no memory of being in the vehicle, let alone what make or model the car was.

No sooner had Dillon finished sending his emails when his phone rang. "Marshal Jack Dillon," he answered.

"Dillon, this is DI Tevlin, Pearce Street Station. I just got your email."

"Oh, sorry about that. I don't know what went wrong. I meant to send that to Seamus Quinn. We've been communicating back and forth on the attempted abductions in the Temple Bar area and—"

"Yeah, I'm aware of that. Seamus is out on medical leave. He passed the info over to me. I'm taking charge of the case on this end. From what I've read, the common denominator seems to be women who are acting like they might deliver a favor or two if a lad buys them a drink, and they're upset when he wants to get what he paid for."

"What? I don't know where you're coming up with that information, but we've spoken to a number of women who were assaulted in an attempt to get them into a car. Always the same two men. In fact, we viewed a security tape from the Quays pub just this morning that had the two suspects adding a drug to a woman's drink that later turned out to be identified as Rohypnol in her medical report. They beat the hell out of the woman, raped her, and left her for dead."

"And you've got a tape of this."

"I just sent a copy of security tape images to some of the victims and witnesses. The suspects supposedly have accents. They've been labeled as Eastern European by a number of victims and witnesses."

"I'd like to see that. Can you send me a copy?"

"Yeah, be happy to. Give me your email address," Dillon said and wrote it down. He read the address back to Tevlin just to make sure he'd written it down correctly.

"Yeah, that's right. I'll be looking for that tape. Nice talkin' with yas," Tevlin said and hung up.

Dillon stared at his phone for a long moment and thought, *What the hell?*

An email alert suddenly pinged on his computer. Ann Barry. Dillon clicked on the site and opened the email.

Oh my God, those are the same two monsters who assaulted me back in August. I'm sure of it, and that looks like the car they were driving. Did you arrest them?

Dillon was thinking of a response when another email came across, this one from Mary Maher.

I don't know about the one guy drinking the pint. But the one who handed the half-glass to the woman is definitely the fecker I threw up on. Looks like he put something in her drink before he gave it to her. Did you see that? I think that's the car.

Dillon walked over to Suel's desk. "I just sent off some images from the Quays pub security tape and a stock photo of a Kia Sorento. Got two responses after just a couple of minutes. Both said the car looks like the one the two were driving, and it's definitely them on the security tape."

"Finally, some progress," Suel said.

"The stock photo of the car was a Kia Sorento. There was only one sold in Dublin County in 2020, and it was sold to Dessie Phalen," Dillon said.

"And you said he lives out in Malahide?"

"Yeah, at least that's the address listed on the NVDF list."

"The bad news would seem to be that may mean the car was purchased in another county."

"Yeah, possibly, but there was only one Kia Sorento sold in all of Dublin County in 2020. That would seem to increase the odds that this is the car."

"Okay, except explain to me how someone named Dessie Phalen has a Russian or Eastern European accent."

"Perhaps he's friends with those two?"

"Sounds like you're trying to link this up with that FBI American."

"Which reminds me, do you know a DI from Pearce Street named Tevlin?"

"Oh, God. Horace Tevlin? Horace the Whore? Keep your distance from that bastard. No good will come from dealing with the likes of him. How in the hell did you ever get in touch with him?"

Dillon told him the story of Seamus Quinn being out on medical leave.

"Well, I never liked Tevlin, and I can't think of anyone who does. There's just the sense of a lot of under-the-table activity where Horace the Whore is involved. Keep your distance is all I can say."

"Yeah, I can't quite put my finger on it, but I immediately had the same feeling."

"Trust your instincts."

Rather than drive up to Malahide at the end of the day and park across the street from Dessie Phalen's home, Dillon did some research on the address online.

Dessie Phalen was listed as the owner of a home in Malahide. The estimated sale price, not that it was for sale, was currently one point four million euros. Not bad for someone twenty-five years old.

NINETEEN

D illon looked at the clock. It was just after 5:00. He took out his cell and called Nessa. She answered on the second ring.

"Jack? Oh, I was beginning to wonder."

"Beginning to wonder? You were in bed by 8:00 the other night, and—"

"I was exhausted and, by the way, not complaining after spending the previous night with you."

"Well, thank you. That works both ways. Last night weren't you at the Abbey Theatre with girlfriends watching that Tom Murphy play?"

"Yes, A Whistle in the Dark. It was lovely. We had a great time."

"Would it be possible to talk you into dinner tonight? Or are you planning to go to bed again at 8:00?"

"I could do dinner again. Would you be interested in joining me later as well? Dinner beforehand sounds good."

"And then perhaps you for dessert," Dillon said.

"That sounds even better. Where can I meet you?"

"I'd be happy to pick you up."

"You sure?"

"Absolutely, you tell me when, and then you choose a restaurant. Somewhere you want to go."

"Oh, I've just the place, great crowd, food, casual, and very nearby. I'll make a reservation for half-past seven if that works for you. We can have a glass of wine at my place beforehand."

"That sounds perfect," Dillon said, and they disconnected.

"You thinking of a Friday night pint?" Suel called over from his desk a few minutes later.

"I'd love to, but I was able to get a dinner date, so I'm afraid I'll have to take a pass."

"Don't tell me, Nessa?"

"Yeah, if you can believe it. She continues to put up with me."

"Gosh, and I had her figured out for such a smart woman. Well, there you go. I guess even the smart ones make a mistake from time to time."

"Don't remind her," Dillon said and began shutting down his computer and locking up his desk. "You still seeing Kira?"

"Yeah, at least I think so. I mean, she hasn't formally kicked me to the curb yet."

"Hopefully, she won't come to her senses," Dillon said as he walked out of the office with Suel.

As soon as he arrived home, Dillon let Lucifer out into the front garden. Once again, he was pleasantly surprised there wasn't a mess to clean up. He headed upstairs, showered, and changed into a nicer set of casual clothes. He topped up Lucifer's water dish, coaxed him inside with a biscuit, and set up the coffee pot and the tea kettle for tomorrow morning. He parked in front of Nessa's home on Lindsay Road. She lived in a gorgeous two-story red brick home with a slate roof. The structure, one of six attached residences, was built in 1910. Like every home along the street, each unit had a wrought iron fence across the front of the property. The ceilings were ten feet high. The woodwork was oak. The fireplaces, four in each unit, were marble, and the door between the dining room and the sitting room slid into the wall.

Dillon opened the wrought iron gate and entered the front garden. He walked up to the front door and rang the bell. Nessa answered a moment later. She was dressed in a short black skirt and white top that left nothing to the imagination. "Oh, Jack. Perfect timing. Please come in. I made a 7:30 reservation, so we have plenty of time for a glass of wine."

"Can I just say you look absolutely gorgeous," he said and kissed her on the cheek.

"Thank you. All things considered, you don't look half-bad yourself."

He laughed and said, "I'll take that as a compliment," and followed her back into the kitchen. Two glasses of chilled white wine sat on the kitchen counter. A wooden platter with a wedge of creamy cheese and ten crackers was next to the wine.

Dillon raised his wine glass and said, "To the most beautiful lady."

"Oh, thank you, Jack, but we're going out to dinner first, so don't think you can talk me into bed just yet."

"Can't blame me for trying," he said. "Where did you want to have dinner?"

"I made a reservation just around the corner at the Bald Eagle. Informal, nice crowd, great food, and it's a five-minute walk."

"Absolutely perfect," he said.

They chatted over the glass of wine along with the crackers and cheese. Nessa ate two crackers. Dillon ate five. At twenty-five minutes after seven, they stepped out of the door and headed around the corner to the Bald Eagle. Along the way, they crossed over the Royal Canal. They stood for a half-minute watching a pair of swans and then entered the Bald Eagle.

They were seated in a rear booth, which was perfect. Dillon's back was against the wall, and he could watch all the activity in the dining area. Nessa ordered a bottle of wine, and they chatted while sipping wine and reading the menu. She ordered a second bottle of wine halfway through dinner, and Dillon debated on dessert.

"I thought you said I was going to be dessert," Nessa said when Dillon suggested they request the dessert menu. They were back at Nessa's ten minutes later.

Once Dillon closed the door behind them, Nessa was on him, pushing him up against the door, kissing and nibbling his ear. From there, it was just three feet to the brown leather couch where they helped each other out of their clothes, dropping them on the floor and the coffee table. Thirty minutes later, they were in the bedroom, both apparently on a more exploratory mission.

Nessa woke Dillon just after midnight, and Dillon woke her just before sunrise. They had a leisurely breakfast of tea, coffee, and caramel rolls in bed. Dillon made his way home just after 10:00 AM.

Lucifer met him at the front door. As Dillon opened the front door, Lucifer leaped off the front stoop and assumed the position. Dillon wandered into the kitchen and was amazed there was nothing he had to clean up. He filled Lucifer's food and water dishes and, fifteen minutes later, coaxed him back inside with a biscuit.

Even though it was Saturday, Dillon drove over to Garda Headquarters and the Special Branch office. He checked his email messages, scanned the previous night's reports to see if there had been any abductions or attempted abductions, and last but not least, he opened the email from DI Horace Tevlin at Pearce Street Station.

Marshal Dillon. You seem to have forgotten to include me in the recent email you sent out. The one with the three images of your suspects, along with the picture of a black 2020 Kia Sorento. Fortunately, I was able to access DI Quinn's computer and was able to view the file. In future, please add my name to your list of recipients.

Tevlin

Pearce Street Station

Not that it created a problem. After all, Tevlin was covering for Seamus Quinn. But the tone of the response and the fact that he even viewed the email sent to DI Quinn bothered Dillon a lot.

He decided it would be best not to respond and began reading the half-dozen other emails that had come in overnight. The first email was from the department insurance company reminding Dillon he had an annual physical scheduled for next month. He already had the appointment on his calendar, so he deleted the email. The second email was from someone asking for donations to a retirement celebration for a person Dillon had never heard of. He deleted that email as well.

The third email was from FBI agent Dennis DaVanni.

Dillon, nice to meet you earlier in DCI McCabe's office. Please give me a call on Monday. I'd like to schedule a lunch or dinner with you. Get your take on the city and any thoughts you may have on the stolen paintings and my suspicions regarding Aidan Phalen. Thank you, Dennis DaVanni.

A phone number was listed just below the message. Dillon thought for half a moment and then called the number from his desk phone. DaVanni answered after the first ring.

"DaVanni."

"Yeah, Agent DaVanni, Jack Dillon with An Garda Síochána, Special Branch. Just read your email."

"Oh, I didn't think you'd be working the weekend, and—"

"I'm working all the time. It makes me the most boring guy in Dublin. You're looking to get together sometime next week?"

"Yeah, nothing formal. I just want to get the lay of the land. I got the sense from yesterday's meeting that no one was familiar with Royce Farley or, for that matter, Aidan Phalen."

"That's correct, but in Farley's case, owning a couple of paintings and being a successful businessperson are not grounds for an investigation. Aidan Phalen apparently served time in France and Italy, but he's currently not suspected of anything here. We've received no mention of him other than your casual reference that he may be involved in something that, up to this point, is nowhere on our radar."

"I get that, and that's vintage Phalen. He keeps a very low profile. Despite having served some time, he's very successful."

"Are you aware of his son, Dessie?"

"Dessie? No, not really. I was unaware he even had a son."

"He does. But I'll be honest, I just learned of this yesterday. An initial perusal brought up some more questions. I'm wondering if you might have time to meet this weekend?"

"Let me check my calendar," DaVanni said and laughed. "Just joking, I don't have anything scheduled. I could meet you somewhere for dinner tonight. You pick the spot, and I'll meet you. I'm working at getting used to driving on the wrong side of the road."

"Are you going to rent a car?"

"Already have."

"The first thing I'd recommend is getting one with an automatic transmission. Shifting with your left hand on strange roads is just one more complication you don't need, and I've —."

"Got that advice from my boss. You have some place in mind for tonight?"

"What hotel are you staying in?"

"I'm in a, umm, private home. In a house on Havelock Square. You know it?"

"Yeah, somewhat. Havelock Square, are you behind the Aviva Stadium?

"I think so, I mean, there's a stadium a few blocks away, but I don't know the name of it."

"It's probably the Aviva. Why don't we meet at a place called Roly's Bistro? It's a nice place, and we can chat. Wear something decent, doesn't have to be a suit but a nice shirt and slacks if you have them."

"Half-past five okay for you?"

"Yeah, that works."

"I'll see you there. Can you give me the spelling of that place? I'll put it in my GPS."

Dillon spelled out the name and finished up with, "It's right by the American Embassy."

"Oh, I've been there. Had to deal with some folks and introduce myself."

"I'm sure they approved. I'll see you at half-past five. Looking forward to getting to know you, Dennis."

TWENTY

Dillon arrived at Roly's Bistro fifteen minutes early. It was a two-story red brick building with a terrace off the dining room. All the tables on the terrace were set for four guests. The terrace had large windows on three sides that looked out onto a garden with vines along the wrought iron fence. The wood trim inside was painted a light green, and the tables had white tablecloths. Two candles and a small vase of flowers were on every table. Dillon left DaVanni's name with the maître d'. He sipped water while he waited for DaVanni to arrive.

Dennis DaVanni arrived at 5:40.

"Hi, Dillon. Thanks for making the time," DaVanni said, then glanced at the table for four. "You expecting someone else?"

Dillon shook his head and said, "No, just the two of us. But I brought my laptop. Sooner or later, we'll end up talking business, and I've got a couple of things to show you. I'll be interested in your feedback."

DaVanni nodded. "Sounds good. Officially, I'm off duty. Can I talk you into a glass of wine, or are you hooked on Guinness? Oh, and I've got this on my expense account, so no pressure on you tonight."

"Wine would be just fine, and thank you," Dillon said.

They ordered dinner, and DaVanni ordered a bottle of wine. Once their glasses had been filled, he raised his in a toast to Dillon. "Thanks for meeting up with me. I don't mean this to sound negative on your department, but I have to keep a very low profile. We deal with people who have a number of different sources of information, and just the nature of what the Art Theft Team does leads folks to mention us and pass information around. Unintentionally, I might add, but the information still gets out there. I'm guessing you find the same thing as a US Marshal assigned to An Garda Síochána."

"To a degree," Dillon said. "Most of my work involves unfortunate situations that Americans get involved in over here. But nothing on the level of your work. What number did you mention yesterday?" Dillon glanced around and then said, "A hundred and fifty million?"

Their dinners suddenly arrived, and DaVanni waited until the server departed.

"Yeah, for the Rothko paintings. Of course, as you alluded to, that's if the items arrive here. I happen to think they will. There are two individuals on our team who are convinced they won't and, in fact, believe that they may have been destroyed."

"Destroyed, something of that value? Whoever has them could sell them at a ninety-nine percent discount and still live very comfortably and never have to work for the rest of their life."

"Yeah, but you're saying that as a man with experience. In the initial robbery, the paintings were cut from the frames. Right there points to individuals who are out of their element. Security at the museum was virtually nonexistent. The primary suspects, Martin Lane and Eddie McDonnell, or whoever it was, had all the time in the world. They could have removed the paintings from the picture frames, kept them on the canvas frames, and still gotten away with them.

"The two team members who don't believe the items will show up here are convinced the paintings were destroyed a year or two after the robbery. The fact that bits of paint chips were found in the wall in Lane's bedroom did nothing but convince them Lane and McDonnell had no way to move the items and probably destroyed them before the police showed up to arrest them."

"Did the New Orleans police finger them for the robbery?"

DaVanni shook his head. "They were initially suspects, identified by the security guard, but both claimed to have alibis. Oh, and they had cash receipts from the bars they were supposedly in. Remember, the robbery was in the early hours of March eighteenth, the day after

St. Patrick's Day. They claimed to be out partying all night."

"The only real evidence we ever had was the paint chips twenty years later in Lane's house and the fact that Aidan Phalen was with him for the better part of a week before he died. But all of that was after the fact."

"Back up for a minute," Dillon said and reached over to the chair next to him. He pulled open his computer bag and set his laptop on the table. "I want to show you something," he said, quickly running his fingers across the keyboard. "Yeah, here we go. Take a look at this," he said and turned the laptop toward DaVanni.

"You took this picture?" DaVanni said, studying the image of Melanie Brussard copying the Mark Rothko painting, *Rust, Blacks on Plum*.

"Yeah, about a week, no more than a week and a half ago."

"So it's local?"

"Trinity College. She's an American student there. Working on a degree in art or art science or something. Here's the deal. She finished that painting and is starting another Rothko painting. She's originally from New Orleans. In fact, her father is a US Senator. Currently, the family is living in Washington, DC. She arrived here in Ireland in August."

"And she's painting Mark Rothko paintings?"

"Yeah, and I have to say, no offense, but I'm really not into that style. That said, she seems to know what she's doing. She wants to make a copy of each painting

that was stolen from the museum in New Orleans and—
"

"The Patrick Kincannon Abstract Art Museum," DaVanni said.

"Yeah, she said she's going to make a copy of those eight paintings and donate them to the museum."

"Well, just looking at this image, it appears to be very good. I'd like to see it in person. Would there be a chance you could line me up with her or even introduce me to her? I'd be very interested in meeting her."

"I think we can work that out. Actually, this is just the beginning of what I have to show you. After the email you sent, it all of a sudden began to click. I might have found a connection. It's tenuous at best but better than the nothing we currently have." Dillon looked around. "I'm thinking a restaurant may not be the best place to launch into this."

"So, in other words, this picture of her painting the Rothko is really just you trying to get me hooked?"

Dillon nodded and said, "Yeah, something like that."

"I'd say it worked. Let's go back to my place, and we—"

"How about we finish our dinner first and then head over?"

"Oh, yeah, sure, good idea," DaVanni said and began shoveling food into his mouth as if he was in an all-you-can-eat contest.

"Take your time, Dennis. We've got all night," Dillon said.

TWENTY-ONE

They left Roly's Bistro, and Dillon followed DaVanni back to his place on Havelock Square. As he suspected, it was located just behind the Aviva Stadium. All the homes around the square were single-story, attached brick structures that had been built in the late 1800s. DaVanni's place happened to be painted white and had a bright pink door. The three-foot wide front garden was filled with pebbles, and if you stood on the public footpath, you could reach over the wrought iron fence and touch the front wall of the house. There was a window next to the pink front door, and Dillon guessed the entire unit couldn't be more than sixteen feet wide.

DaVanni pulled into the only parking space in front of the place. Dillon parked three units further down the road. He grabbed his computer bag and walked back to DaVanni, standing next to his blue Volkswagen Golf.

"Nice job driving," Dillon said. "You like this car?"

"It's okay. One of the more popular cars in Dublin, so theoretically, it helps me blend in."

"Your pink door isn't hard to miss," Dillon said, glancing toward DaVanni's unit.

"Yeah, well, I didn't have anything to do with that. You gotta take what they give you. Come on in," he said and opened the front gate. The narrow gate missed hitting the front step by no more than half an inch. Dillon took hold of the gate and closed it as DaVanni stood on the step and unlocked the pink door.

They stepped into a narrow hallway that led to a room in the back. Off to the left was a small sitting room. Dillon's first thought was he'd been in larger bathrooms. A small fireplace about eighteen inches wide was positioned in the middle of the wall. A worn couch with a stained pillow crumpled up at one end was opposite the fireplace. The room looked to be about eight by ten feet.

Dillon followed DaVanni down the narrow hallway past a closed door and into a small kitchen. There was a two-burner stove, a small, three-foot-tall refrigerator, and a small sink. Next to the sink was an open door to what served as the bathroom, clearly an addition from back in the 1930s or 40s.

"Get you something to drink?" DaVanni said.

"You got any bottled water?"

"Yeah, in fact, that's what I'm going for, too." He reached into a cabinet and pulled out two plastic bottles of water.

Dillon pulled out his laptop and set it on the small kitchen table that had a red Formica top. Fortunately, there were two wooden chairs, and he pulled one out from the table and sat down. The chair creaked but held together. DaVanni settled into the other chair and twisted the top off his water bottle. Dillon turned on the computer, and DaVanni gave him the password to hook up to the internet.

"They, ah, didn't seem to worry too much about your accommodations," Dillon said, looking around.

DaVanni smiled. "If I'm here for about a week, I'll probably be the longest resident in the past ten years. Usually, it's someone coming in for a day or two. It's close to the Embassy. Despite the pink door, it's low-key and on a quiet street. There's a small safe room and a crawl space if you need a rear escape hatch. Hopefully, my stay won't come to that. You said you were involved in another case that may have some ties to the Rothko paintings. Does it have anything to do with the art student?"

"Yes and no," Dillon said. "Let me give you the long version. I first met her because someone, actually two guys, had attempted to abduct her in the Temple Bar area."

"Temple Bar? I've heard of it, but that's all I know."

"It's a large area in the city center. Mostly foot traffic, lots of pubs and restaurants. It's a major destination for tourists as well as local folks, although the locals would tend to be under forty years old. Last August, the art student was in Temple Bar with some new friends, all young women. It was her third day in Dublin. They were going from pub to pub. One of the girls had too much to drink and ended up in the ladies' room, getting sick. Two of the girls escorted her back to campus. The art student remained with another girl who ultimately disappeared. She found out later the girl went back to campus with a boy.”

“No surprise,” DaVanni said and laughed.

“Yeah, except when the art student heads back to campus, she gets turned around and heads the wrong way. A car stops. We now know it was a black Kia Sorento. A guy asks if she needs a ride and gets out of the car. Push comes to shove, she fights him off, and he hops back in the car, and the driver takes off. There are two of them in the car. Her father, the US Senator, came to our office, and my partner and I met with him. Her assault was not reported to the police. We reviewed police reports and discovered two similar attempted abductions in the Temple Bar area. Descriptions from the witnesses and victims were similar to the art student’s incident.

“We met the art student. She was working on that Rothko painting at the time. I had lunch with her a few days later, and her descriptions of the attempted abduction matched the others.

“One of the witnesses to a later abduction gave us the car make and a partial license plate number. Irish license plates list the year of the vehicle, the county it was purchased in, and the purchased vehicle number.”

“What’s the purchased vehicle number?” DaVanni asked.

“So if your car is the one thousand and tenth car sold in the county that year, your license number would be the year, plus a letter identifying the county, and in that case the number 1010, for the one thousand and tenth car sold."

"And that works?"

"Actually, for a small country with a population of just over five million, yeah, it actually works pretty well. Anyway, with the partial license number, the make, and color of the car, I contacted the National Vehicle and Drive File. They sent me a list of all the Kia vehicles sold in Dublin County. Turns out to be a Kia Sorento, by the way. I sent a stock photo of a black Kia Sorento to the victims and the witnesses. All but one identified the vehicle as the one the assailants were driving. The one woman who couldn't identify it said she was too drunk to remember. I checked the Dublin County records that were sent to me, and there was only one black Kia Sorento sold in the county in 2020."

"So you got the guy?"

"Not quite, but we're closer. Here's the deal. There are two abductors, and here are their images from a bar security tape," Dillon said and brought up the three images of the two men buying a half-glass of Guinness for Kate Cullen. "You'll note they're in the process of lacing the woman's glass with Rohypnol, roofies. She was hospitalized after having the shit beat out of her and getting raped."

"All very interesting, but other than attempting to abduct the art student, I'm not seeing the link here, Dillon."

"Here's the link. By the way, one and possibly both these abductors speak with a Polish or Russian accent. My money is on a Russian accent. That said, the only black Kia Sorento sold in Dublin County was purchased by Dessie Phalen, son of Aidan Phalen. Dessie, age twenty-five, apparently purchased the car for thirty-five grand. He also, at the age of twenty-five, is listed on the property records as owning a home in Malahide worth one point four million."

"Where's Malahide?"

"Just north of Dublin. Aidan Phalen's kid's name is on the deed for the house, and two thugs are driving around town in his car, drugging and raping women. Could be it's just coincidental," Dillon said.

DaVanni slowly shook his head. "This is so perfect. Vintage Aidan Phalen, except for the screw-up with the rapists. You have someone keeping a tab on these idiots?"

"I just started to put it together. Other than my partner, Paddy Suel, you are the only other person I've told about it. You think it's viable? That the paintings would end up in their possession?"

DaVanni nodded. "It's textbook. Aidan Phalen isn't leaving a trail. My guess is the Russians are somehow involved in transporting the paintings into Ireland. Meanwhile, Phalen could be cooking up some sort of deal with Royce Farley."

"I'm unaware of any link to Farley."

"Thus far," DaVanni said and grinned. "Farley is the reason those paintings are coming into the country. I'm sure of it."

"You have anything scheduled for later this evening?" Dillon said.

"No. Why? What are you thinking?"

"I'm thinking it would be interesting to drive up to Malahide in your Volkswagen Golf and have a look at the Phalen home."

"I'd love to," DaVanni said.

TWENTY-TWO

Dillon gave DaVanni the address of the Phalen home. He input it into his GPS, and they headed north into the city center, across the Liffey, past Fairview Park, through Donnycarney, Coolock, and then onto Malahide Road. The GPS eventually led them to a street called The Sycamores. Number 11 turned out to be near the end of the short, dead-end street.

DaVanni slowed as they drove past the unattached, two-story, white stucco and brick house. The wall in front of the house was built of dressed stone with a flowering vine growing along the top. A paved brick driveway led up past an extensive grass front lawn to a parking area with three vehicles. A garage with the door closed was attached to the left side of the house. Halfway along the driveway, a lamp post illuminated the area and the curve leading to the parking area with the three cars.

One of the vehicles in the parking area appeared to be the Black Kia Sorento. Lights showed through the draperies in what Dillon guessed was the sitting room. DaVanni drove past and turned around one house later at the dead-end.

"Let me out here," Dillon said.

"What are you going to do?"

"I want to get a photo of those license plates."

"You sure that's a good idea?"

"It will just take a minute. The drapes are pulled on the front windows. Drive back, turn at the corner, and wait for me."

"Okay," Davanni said, not sounding all that happy.

Dillon climbed out of the car and waited for DaVanni to turn around, drive back down the street, and disappear around the corner. Once the Volkswagen was out of sight, Dillon walked back toward the Phalen house. The dressed stone wall was four feet high. Dillon placed both hands on the wall and hopped over, walking along a holly hedge as he headed toward the parked cars. A white concrete wall ran along what was most likely the property line behind the holly hedge. He moved slowly and kept an eye on the window curtains and the front door.

He crouched down and waited a long moment once he was in front of the cars. He pulled his phone out and quickly took a photo of each license plate. He ignored the urge to slit tires and hurried back along the holly hedge and over the front wall. He didn't run to the Volkswagen, but he didn't waste any time either.

"Everything go okay?" DaVanni asked as Dillon slipped into the passenger seat. He pulled away from the curb before Dillon could respond.

"Yeah, not a bother. Lovely looking place. I can't imagine what sort of job a twenty-five-year-old would have that allows him to buy a house for a million-four euros." DaVanni gave him a quick look. "Just joking, Dennis. I'm absolutely convinced that Kia Sorento is the same car used in the assault and abductions. I wonder if the two Russians are staying in the house."

"Try this on for size," DaVanni said. "What if they're collateral for the paintings? Someone's son or brother is there under the watchful eye of Phalen, guaranteeing the paintings will ultimately be delivered."

"Yeah, good up until the point where they're allowed to go out and abduct women. Not the sort of attention you'd want and certainly not the type of attention Phalen would want. But now that you mention it, perhaps he doesn't know, or possibly one of them is the son, Dessie."

"I thought you said they were both Russian?"

"That's what we've been thinking, but now I'm wondering if the only one who ever spoke was the passenger. The one who tried to force the women into the car. What if Dessie is the dark-haired driver? He'd certainly know his way around the city. I'll have to check. They've apparently changed their routine. The last woman we know of was drugged, and the dark-haired guy spoke to her three different times over the course of twenty-five or thirty minutes. That could be Dessie Phalen. I'll have to check the driver's records and see."

"You ready to head back to my place?" DaVanni said.

"Yeah, hey, thanks for driving, by the way. What do you have planned for tomorrow?"

"You really want to know?"

"Yeah, or I wouldn't have asked."

"I've got to figure a way to keep an eye on Phalen. I can feel it. These paintings are en route. He's going to get them and disappear. It's what he does, and he's very good at it."

"What do you think the odds are of the paintings being delivered to the house."

DaVanni shook his head. "No, too obvious. They'll be delivered somewhere no one thinks of, a warehouse, a pub, a boat offshore, or it could be to a car parked on a gravel road out in the country."

"Do you think the paintings would be exchanged for the Russian guy we have pictures of?"

"The guy trying to force the women into the car? It's possible, it even makes a lot of sense."

"If we could find out his name, that might tie in with whoever is transporting the paintings. Could be someone flying into Dublin. Of course, he could be coming from anywhere, the States, France, the UK. The list goes on and on."

"We need to get the name of the guy here. We need to see if the driver of that car is Phalen's son. This is going to happen soon. I can feel it," DaVanni said.

"When we get back to your place, let me make a couple of calls on those license plates. We can run the images of the two guys through facial recognition programs. Hopefully, someone will be in the Tech Lab tomorrow."

"You know, a tracking device on those cars would be helpful. Find out who owns them and where they might be during the day. That could save a lot of hassle."

"Good idea," Dillon said as DaVanni took the Talbot Memorial Bridge across the Liffey and ten minutes later pulled in front of his place on Havelock Square. Dillon followed him into the house, and they headed back to the kitchen.

Dillon fired up his computer and shook his head.

"What's wrong?" DaVanni said.

"I should have sent these images of the guys to the Tech lab when I first got them. It just never occurred to me before I came over that they could be related to the Rothko painting robbery from twenty years ago down in New Orleans."

"Better late than never," DaVanni said.

Dillon placed the three images of the two guys in The Quays pub lacing Kate Cullen's drink with Rohypnol into an email and addressed it to Emily in the Tech Lab.

Emily, Security camera images of these two lacing the woman's drink with Rohypnol. Hoping you can run a facial recognition. The blonde guy is suspected Russian or Polish. The dark-haired guy may be Irish by the name of Dessie Phalen.

Please let me know you received this.

Thanks,

Dillon

"All right, there we go," Dillon said, hitting the send button. A moment later, the laptop made a swishing sound signaling the message had been sent.

"Can I talk you into a glass of Jameson?" DaVanni asked.

Dillon thought for a moment and said, "Yeah, why not?"

TWENTY-THREE

Dillon was home just after 9:30. He debated calling Nessa and quickly decided it was too late. He let Lucifer out and made a list of the things he had to do in the morning, starting with getting the names of whoever owned the other two cars parked next to the Kia Sorento registered to Dessie Phalen. He listed the tracking device, although he thought that would probably require a warrant. If that was the case, DaVanni might have a way around that. Although, the thoughts on Aidan Phalen, his son Dessie, and the tie-in to the abductors were still a matter of speculation.

What if Aidan Phalen wasn't involved in any way with the stolen art? What if Dessie Phalen's car was borrowed by the two abductors, and he thought he was just being a nice guy? What if Melanie Brussard didn't want anything to do with Dennis DaVanni, and she complained to her father, the congressman? What if Nessa was checking her cellphone in the hope that Dillon would call and come over?

He let Lucifer in and watched the late evening news, after which he caught one of the 'Vera' episodes on the Brit Box cable station. When he woke, the episode was over, and he went upstairs to bed. Lucifer was stretched out on the bed, and Dillon didn't have the heart to move him.

He was up early Sunday morning. He sent an email to Dennis DaVanni, thanking him for dinner last night and suggesting Sunday might be a good day to meet with Melanie Brussard if DaVanni had the time. He received a reply from DaVanni fifteen minutes later, who said a meeting would be wonderful.

Dillon phoned Melanie Brussard. She answered just before he was dumped into voicemail, and from the sound of her voice, it was clear she had been asleep.

"Hell?" She managed to say in a raspy, froggy voice and then proceeded to clear her throat. "Hell, Hello?"

"Hi, Melanie. Jack Dillon with An Garda Síochána, Special Branch. Say, I've got a guy who is a bit of a Mark Rothko fanatic. He's in town for just a day or so, and I told him about your work. Now, I didn't mention your name because I know you'd like to keep this very private. But, I wondered if you'd like to talk to him and show him your work. Hello? Hello? Melanie, are you there?"

"Mmm, yeah, I'm here. Sorry, there was a party on our floor last night that went kind of late. So, what time were you thinking?"

"Well, it's Sunday. Were you planning to be in the studio anytime today?"

"Yeah, I guess after lunch. How about 1:30?"

"Okay, we'll see you there this afternoon, 1:30."

"What's this dude's name?"

"DaVanni. Dennis DaVanni."

"See you then." Click

He emailed DaVanni. *I'll pick you up at 1:15. I told her you were in town for just a day. I did not mention the Bureau. Dillon*

He scrambled three eggs and ate some toast with blackberry jam. After breakfast, he clipped the leash onto Lucifer's collar, and they did three laps around St. Albert's park. Dillon pulled in front of the house with the pink door five minutes early. DaVanni was already out in front, waiting for him.

"Hope you weren't waiting out there very long," Dillon said as DaVanni climbed into the passenger seat.

"No, just a couple of minutes. I really haven't had the time to look around the neighborhood. It's nice and quiet. A couple with a stroller walked past and gave me a nod."

"That's the Irish way of giving you the finger," Dillon said.

"What? You're kidding, right?"

"Yeah, I'm kidding. So, I spoke to Melanie Brussard on the phone this morning. Clearly woke her up after some get-together on her dormitory floor. I'm sure she fell back asleep once she got me off the line."

"Well, she is a college kid."

"Anyway, we'll meet her in the studio. I told her you knew all about Rothko's work and were interested in her effort. I didn't mention the Bureau, and I—"

"Told her that I was in town for just the day. Yeah, I know. I read your email."

"Just making sure, Dennis."

Once again, Dillon pulled into the Trinity Staff parking lot just off Nassau Street. Today being Sunday, there were only two other cars in the lot.

"This is where the Book of Kells is, right?" DaVanni said.

"Yeah, if you want, once we're done talking to Melanie, we can go in and take a look."

"Yeah, I'd like that."

Dillon led the way to the Creative Arts building and then downstairs to the art studio. The lights in the studio were off, and the door was locked.

"Oh, God, don't tell me she forgot," Dillon said.

"Give her a few minutes, Dillon. She's the creative type. They're almost never on time."

They waited ten minutes, and Dillon had his phone out, ready to call Brussard, when they heard footsteps hurrying down the stairs.

"Oh, hi, sorry I'm late," she said and quickly input a code onto the keypad next to the door. There was a loud buzz, and she opened the door, stepped inside, and turned on the lights. Just like before, her current work rested on a large easel at the far end of the studio.

"Oh my, well done. *Blue over Red*," DaVanni said and made his way to the painting. Brussard followed him, leaving Dillon to catch up.

DaVanni stopped and examined the painting for a long moment. He stepped closer and studied it from a distance of about three inches and then stepped back. "You did this using a book image or a photograph?"

"Both," Melanie said. "I have a number of photos from The Patrick Kincannon Abstract Art Museum in New Orleans along with a book on Rothko with full-page color images. The book also gives the dimensions, so the painting size is accurate to the original."

"I'm impressed, very impressed. Where did you learn to paint?"

"Mmm, classes over the course of a number of summers, reading, and just self-taught, I guess."

"It's good, very good."

They talked for the better part of forty-five minutes. Dillon wandered around the studio, looking at various paintings. He saw the bowl of fruit the girl had been painting the last time he was here and the blotchy image the boy had been pouring red paint on. Eventually, he sat down in a chair at the opposite end of the room and pulled out his cell phone, checking for messages. There weren't any.

DaVanni was talking to Brussard, explaining something with his hands, and Brussard was nodding. She took him over to a cabinet and pulled out her *Rust, Blacks on Plum* painting, which apparently began a whole new conversation. It was close to ninety minutes later when they wandered over to Dillon.

Brussard's eyes seemed to sparkle as she said, "Oh, this has been so wonderful, Dennis. It's been so nice to meet you."

"The same here, Melanie. If I can be of any help regarding your Kincannon Museum work, please don't hesitate to let me know. I'm sorry I don't have any of my business cards, but I've got your email address. Please, let's stay in touch."

"Oh, I'd love it, and you'll email me those contacts?"

"I'll send them to you tonight," DaVanni said. They shook hands, and she led them out of the studio. The door locked behind them. Once outside, Brussard headed in the direction of her dormitory. Dillon and DaVanni headed toward the Book of Kells in the Grand Library.

There was a line waiting to get into the library, but it was only fifteen minutes before they were inside. DaVanni paid, despite Dillon's objections, and they looked at the images of the Book of Kells and toured the Grand Library. It was almost 5:00 when they climbed back into Dillon's car.

"I have to thank you, Dillon, for an absolutely wonderful afternoon. Marvelous, absolutely marvelous."

"Glad you enjoyed it. What did you think of her paintings?"

"She is one talented person. I meant what I said. I'll help her in any way I can. She's not some hack. I'm sure you look at those images of Rothko's paintings and wonder what the hell? But she really knows what she's do-ing. Impressive, very impressive. I'll stay in touch with her, and not to worry, I won't mention the Bureau. I promise."

"I have to ask. If she's so good at recreating his work, do you think she may be involved in the stolen paintings?"

"What? No, not in the least. Absolutely not. Of course, now that you mention it, I can understand why you might consider that, but no. I'm fairly confident she's clean."

TWENTY-FOUR

Dillon was in the office early the following morning. He made a coffee in the break room, took a sip, shuddered, and dumped the rest down the sink. He headed back to his desk and, on a whim, phoned the Tech Lab.

"Tech Lab, Emily."

"Oh wow. I didn't think you'd be in this early."

"Which makes me just as boring as you. Good morning, Dillon. I got your email. I'll be running both images through the facial recognition programs this morning. Keep your fingers crossed. I had to enlarge the images, and they're blurry. Not sure how that is going to work, but I'll give it a try."

"Thanks, Emily. I'll say a prayer. Give me a call one way or the other."

"Will do."

Dillon disconnected and turned on his computer. He uploaded the three license plate images he took last night and then did a search on the plates. The first image, the Kia Sorento, at no surprise, came up as Dessie Phalen with The Sycamores eleven address in Malahide and

Dessie's picture. The second image, a black BMW 8 Series Gran Coupe M Sport, came up as registered to someone named Pavel Krupin. The picture showed a man who appeared to be in his late forties or early fifties. He had dark eyes, a low forehead, and a square chin. It was a name that Dillon didn't recognize. He did a quick search and couldn't find anything on Krupin, although money didn't seem to be a problem since the BMW was listed at ninety-eight thousand euros. Dillon copied Krupin's address located in Tallaght.

The third license was on a red 2015 Nissan Note registered to Horace Tevlin. Dillon double-checked the registration. Horace Tevlin's name appeared again. Tevlin, the Detective from Pearce Street Station covering for DI Seamus Quinn. The same person Suel referred to as 'Horace the Whore.' He was at Phalen's house with some Russian guy named Krupin and probably Aidan Phalen.

Dillon phoned Dennis DaVanni.

"Dillon?" was how he answered.

"Hi Dennis, just got done doing a search on those license plates last night."

"I'm guessing you found something if you're calling me first thing this morning."

"A couple of things. The Kia Sorento belongs to Phalen's son Dessie, no surprise there. The second car, a sporty-looking BMW, belongs to a gentleman by the name of Pavel Krupin. I did a quick search and didn't find anything on him except that he lives over in Tallaght. Given the name, my guess would be that he's Russian. Here's the big news. The third car, a red 2015 Nissan Note, belongs to Horace Tevlin."

Dillon waited for a moment before DaVanni said, "That name isn't ringing a bell with me."

"I didn't think it would. He's a detective at the Pearce Street Station. My partner, Paddy Suel, refers to him as Horace the Whore. Apparently not very well liked in the department."

"You've dealt with him?" DaVanni said.

"Not really. I was sending information, actually the images you saw yesterday, and an update to someone else at Pearce Street Station, and Tevlin phoned and said he was covering for a guy out on medical leave. Anyway, he joked about the women who were assaulted, said they were probably looking for it, or some stupid comment along that line. But now, all of a sudden, he's at Phalen's house last night."

"Odds are he's their contact or certainly one of them within the department."

"But my only interaction with him is on the phone, once, and an email. How would he know anything about the Rothko Paintings?"

"My guess is you'll hear from him again the moment he learns we met in McCabe's office."

"I'll talk to Suel, and we'll keep it buttoned up. I've got the Tech Lab attempting to do facial recognition on those guys putting the roofie into the woman's Guinness.

They had to enlarge the image, and it might be too blurry to work."

"Keep me posted. Anything else?"

"Yeah. I've got the addresses on all three of these vehicles from last night. Any chance you might have access to a tracking device we could attach to the cars?"

"You can't get a tracking device?" DaVanni said.

"Not without a lot of legal back and forth, starting with a warrant."

"Let me see what I can do."

"You need anything else, Dennis?"

"Not at present. Send me the info on that Pavel Krupin person. He's not ringing a bell in my one-watt mind, but I can do some checking."

"Sending it your way in just a minute," Dillon said and disconnected.

He copied the little info he had on Krupin and emailed it along with the guy's photo to DaVanni just as Suel stepped into the office and headed for his desk. He gave Dillon a wave and said, "Early bird."

Dillon picked up his coffee mug and nodded toward the break room.

"How'd your weekend go?" Suel asked. He opened the water kettle, peeked inside, filled it, and turned it on. "Any action?" he asked as he placed a teabag in his mug.

"Yeah, but not the kind you're thinking about. I ended up spending a good deal of time with Dennis Da-Vanni."

"DaVanni? The FBI guy we met in McCabe's office Friday?"

"Yeah, we talked about the paintings. I took him over to Trinity yesterday, and he had a long chat with Melanie Brussard. I showed him the images we got off the security tape and told him about the assaults and attempted abductions."

"I thought he was here looking for those stolen paintings."

"Yeah, he is, and we think there might be a link between the abductions and the paintings."

"What? You think these idiots attacking women are into fancy painting?" Suel said as the kettle clicked off, and he poured boiling water over his tea bag.

"Not exactly, but I did a search on the Kia Sorento and looked up the license on the only one sold in Dublin County."

"Yeah, you told me that."

Dillon went on to tell him about driving past the Phalen house in Malahide, taking photos of the license plates, and getting the owner's names.

"So, who'd you come up with?"

"Along with Aidan Phalen's son, I got the name of a Russian guy driving a BMW that goes for close to a hundred grand and one other name."

Suel took a sip of his tea, made a face, and said, "So are you going to keep me in suspense? Who owned the third car?"

"Your close personal friend, Horace the Whore."

"What? Get the hell out of here. The third car belonged to Horace Tevlin? That plonker?"

Dillon nodded. "Yeah, looks like he just may be the inside information source for the two guys assaulting and raping women and just might be the inside source on any information regarding what we know about those paintings."

"That worthless, fat arsed bastard," Suel said, shaking his head. "I knew it. I knew he was always up to no good. Did you tell McCabe?"

"No, not yet. DaVanni thinks this painting thing is going to go down pretty soon. It would be nice to be in on it. We tell McCabe, and word might get out. I want to keep it quiet and wait and see what's going to happen."

"You're trusting this FBI knacker? Dillon, they have us do all the heavy lifting, and they take all the credit. We've both been through it before."

"DaVanni seems to be on the level. He's not asking me to do anything. In fact, I'm asking him."

"Asking him? What are you asking him about?"

"I want to get some tracking devices and place them on those cars."

"First of all, you're going to need a warrant, and unless I'm mistaken, you don't have any proof that would stand up in a court."

"Which is exactly why I want DaVanni to get the tracking devices. A tracking device that lasts more than forty-eight hours."

"And he's going to do this?"

"He's going to try. I sent him what little information I had on the Russian guy who owned the BMW, a guy named Pavel Krupin."

"Krupin? Never heard of him."

"Me either. I looked him up, and other than finding an address in Tallaght, nothing else was available. But the FBI might have a little more in-depth information. It doesn't hurt to ask."

Suel shook his head. "I think you're pissing in the wind."

"Could be, time will tell, I guess. I did most of this on my own time, so if it doesn't work out, then Special Branch isn't out anything. But just the fact that Horace the Whore is meeting up with these people suggests something's about to go down."

TWENTY-FIVE

It was just after the noon hour when Dillon's desk phone rang. He was in the middle of eating lunch. He swallowed the mouthful of taco and answered the phone.

"Marshal Dillon."

"Dillon, Emily down in Tech. You want to come down? I got something for you."

"Be right there," he said and hung up.

"Suel, Emily just called, and she's got something with the facial recognition on those images I sent her. You want to check it out?"

Suel nodded with a mouthful of food. He took another large bite of his sandwich and followed Dillon out of the office. They took the elevator down to the first floor, made their way through the halls, and finally pressed the buzzer at the Tech Lab door.

"Yes?" Emily answered.

"Hi, Emily. Dillon and Suel."

The door buzzed, and they pushed it open. The lab had four long counters with computers and tables filled with everything from blood-stained clothing to a small hatchet in a plastic evidence bag.

"Back here, Dillon," Emily called. She was running her fingers across a keyboard while staring at a large screen attached to the wall. The three images taken from the security tape at The Quays pub were on the screen. The images had been enlarged, and just like Emily said, they were blurry. Suddenly, the image of a nice-looking dark-haired man Dillon recognized as the driver of the Kia Sorento appeared in the upper right corner of the screen.

"There's your guy, Dillon. Dessie Phalen, age twenty-five. Arrested for two counts of burglary in 2018 and 2019. Nothing on him since, well until this."

"Yeah, I didn't pick up on it earlier, but that's him. Damn it."

"Yeah. The image registered at ninety-nine point nine percent positive. The other guy, blonde, nothing from our files, but I'm beginning to search the EU file, and then we have some US files I can go through, too."

"He's been described as having a Russian or possibly a Polish accent."

"Mmm-mmm, we don't have access to any Russian files, I'm afraid."

"Okay, but the dark-haired guy is definitely Dessie Phalen."

"Yeah, without a doubt."

"Can you email me the file? He might be involved in another incident, and I'll need to contact people."

"I'll have it up to you in ten or fifteen minutes."

"Thanks, Emily, much appreciated."

"Always my pleasure, Dillon."

They took the elevator back up to the third floor. Suel studied Dillon for a moment and said, "I can see you're thinking of something, Dillon."

"You think we got a strong case on nailing him for raping Kate Cullen?"

"Yeah, those images were from the security tape at The Quays. Even if the blonde guy can't be identified, there's a good chance you can turn this douchebag, and he'll give the Russian up. We can nail their asses to the wall. With any luck, we could have both of them locked up and behind bars before the end of the day. It would be a blessing to get these two worthless fecks off the street."

"Yeah," Dillon said.

When he was back at his desk, he phoned Dennis DaVanni.

"No, Dillon, I haven't gotten a response on the tracking devices yet. For God's sake, we only discussed this forty minutes ago."

"Yeah, well, something else has come up since then."

"Oh?"

Dillon went on to tell him about the positive identification of Dessie Phalen. "You saw the images. These two fools are lacing the woman's drink with a roofie. She was beaten and raped. Rohypnol was found in her system. Even if we don't get the Russian guy, folks will be chomping at the bit to arrest Phalen."

"Shit," DaVanni said. "Any way you can slow this up?"

"No way. It's going to be looked at as getting him and possibly the other guy off the street. They've assaulted four women that we know of. Drugged one, beat her up so bad they may have left her for dead. I want to help you, Dennis, but I can't slow this down, and to be honest, I don't want to. I want these bastards off the street as much, if not more, than anyone else."

"Okay, you're going to have to get an arrest warrant, aren't you?"

"Yeah, but we'll have that this afternoon. We'll be heading into McCabe's office to give him the update in the next fifteen minutes. I'm just waiting for an email from our Tech Lab confirming the identification."

"I hear you. Let me get moving on this end," DaVanni said and disconnected.

Ten minutes later, Dillon's computer signaled an email arriving. He clicked on the file and saw it was from Emily. He sent the attached file to the printer, requested four copies of the file to be printed, and called over to Suel. "I just got the email from Emily. It's at the printer. You ready to see the boss?"

"Be with you in a second," Suel said and stuffed the last of his sandwich into his mouth.

Dillon walked over to the printer and gathered the first five pages from Emily's file. He glanced through them to make sure it was complete and stapled them together. He did the same with the next three copies and then walked back to Suel's desk.

"All set?" Suel asked.

"Yeah, let's run it past DCI McCabe."

The door was open, and they knocked on the doorframe.

"Come in, take a seat," McCabe said as he closed a file, placed it on a stack behind him, and pulled the top file from the stack on his desk. "What's up?"

"We've got a definite identification on one of the two individuals attacking women in Temple Bar," Dillon said.

"Excellent, excellent," McCabe said as Dillon handed him the five-page file from the Tech Lab.

McCabe took a moment to scan all five pages. "Dessie Phalen? He's Irish with a previous record? I thought they were both Russian?"

"We believe the second individual, the one who stepped out of the car and physically assaulted the women, is Russian. But Phalen has been identified from security tapes showing them drugging a woman's drink with Rohypnol."

"I'm getting the sense you seem to have a problem with this, Dillon."

"Yes, sir, on a couple of levels." Dillon went on to explain the thought that the Russian partner might be staying at the Phalen house and that he may, in fact, be there as a guarantee that the stolen paintings will eventually arrive. He mentioned that FBI Agent DaVanni felt the paintings could arrive at any moment, and an arrest might sabotage the recovery of the paintings.

"But from what we know, these two, if indeed they are the culprits, have been attacking women in Temple Bar for the past two months. Now you're suggesting that after two months of this Russian individual remaining under the watchful eye of Aidan Phalen, suddenly the paintings will arrive? What if whoever has them decides that, instead of delivering them now, they might make a wonderful Christmas gift?"

Dillon shook his head and said, "I don't know, sir."

"Exactly. Do you have the name of this Russian individual?"

"No, sir, other than an image of him and witness statements, we don't have anything."

"This is what we're going to do. I will coordinate with the Malahide department and Pearce Street Station," McCabe said and quickly fingered through the Rolodex next to his computer screen. "Yes, here we are. You'll be dealing with DCI Patrick Gogan in Malahide. He'll have their Emergency Response Unit involved. I want these two arrested, transferred to our custody, and locked up. Paintings be damned."

TWENTY-SIX

It was after 3:00 when Suel walked over to Dillon's desk. "Just got off the phone with DCI Gogan up in Malahide. They're going to move on Dessie Phalen and the Russian in two hours. We're going to join them and serve the arrest warrants."

"He phoned you?"

"McCabe gave him my name as the point of contact."

Dillon closed his eyes and exhaled. "Jesus Christ," he half-whispered.

"Don't let it get to you, Dillon. Come on. We've got a job to do. Let's get these bastards off the street. Hopefully, the witnesses and the victims can identify both of them, and we can lock them up for five to seven years. Forget about the damn paintings and focus on Kate Cullen getting the shit kicked out of her by these bastards."

Dillon took another deep breath and nodded. "Yeah, you're right. Let's go get them."

"We're in an official vehicle. I'm supposed to drive," Suel said.

"Are you supposed to leave me in the car when we get up to Malahide?"

"I'm just doing what I'm told to do, Dillon."

"Yeah, I get it, but thanks for reminding me, Paddy," Dillon said, and they headed down to the parking area. Suel signed out an unmarked vehicle, although the flashing lights in the rear window, the movable spotlight on the exterior of the driver's door, and the screen between the front and back seats made it pretty obvious they were in a Garda vehicle.

The twenty-five-minute drive up to Malahide was fairly quiet. Neither Suel nor Dillon had much to say. The Malahide Garda Station was a two-story, cream-colored building with white trim located in the center of town on James's Terrace. It was surrounded by a four-foot black wrought iron fence. Suel had to park halfway up the block from the station.

As they climbed out of the car, Suel said, "We best put the vests on here," and he pressed the key fob. The lights flashed, and the boot lid rose six inches. Suel lifted the lid, reached in, and handed Dillon a black bulletproof vest. On the back of the vest was a blue patch with six-inch high white letters that read GARDA. Dillon slipped the vest on and tightened the straps on the side.

They entered the station through the front door. Suel recognized the desk Sergeant and said, "Hi, Kevin. We're meeting up with DCI Gogan."

"It'll be a full house, Paddy," the Sergeant said, then looked at Dillon.

"This is my partner, Marshal Jack Dillon. Kevin Neacey, Dillon. We go back a long way, hurling teams as kids."

"You could always count on Paddy Suel to swing at your head," Neacey said and laughed.

"Yeah, and if I managed to hit your head, Kevin, it would have just broken my hurley."

"Dillon, you're the American I heard about."

"Don't believe everything you hear. I'm actually a pretty nice guy."

They all laughed, and Neacey said, "Let me get someone down here to take you up to the conference room. They've got the Emergency Response Team going in on this."

"Just playing it safe, Kevin. Hopefully, everyone will smile and come along nicely."

"A pair of rapists, I heard. The bastards. I got two daughters. Give 'em a swift kick from me if you get the chance."

"Happy to oblige," Suel said.

Neacey made a quick phone call, and a moment later, a young officer with short dark hair and a black bulletproof vest opened the door and gave a nod. Dillon and Suel followed him up the stairway and down the hall to a crowded conference room. There were eight chairs around the conference table, all occupied, and another ten officers standing in the room.

"Suel?" one of the officers seated at the table called.

"Yes, and Marshal Jack Dillon, attached to Special Branch."

"DCI Gogan, I got the call from McCabe earlier. You have the arrest warrants?"

"I do," Suel said and reached inside his vest, pulled out the warrants, and handed them to Gogan.

Gogan gave a quick glance at the arrest warrants, nodded, and handed them back to Suel. "Same as the copies I got from McCabe. We're going to have a team stationed at the back of the house, and once they're in position, we'll move in. I'd like you next to me when we knock on the door. Hopefully, someone will answer. We'll knock three separate times. If there's no response, I'll make the call for forcible entry. Questions?" he said and looked around the room.

No one responded.

"All right, let's get to it. I'll lead. Emergency Response Unit will follow me. Dolan and team will assume positions in the lot behind the house. Alert me when you're in position, and then we'll move in. Mount up," he said as people began to head out of the room.

Dillon and Suel followed the crowd down the staircase. Everyone stepped out a side door and headed into the parking lot. Dillon and Suel hurried out the front door and jogged to their unmarked car. Suel quickly slid in and started the car. Dillon closed the passenger door as Suel made a U-turn in the middle of the street, sped down to the corner, and made a righthand turn. As it turned out, they didn't need to hurry. Eventually, DCI Gogan pulled out of the parking lot. He was followed by the Emergency Response Team vehicle, a black van with rear doors. The Response Team van was followed by four white Garda cars with lights on the roof and the word 'GARDA' in foot-high blue letters on both sides, plus the front and back of the vehicles.

"So much for a low-key presence," Dillon said as Suel fell in behind the parade.

"At least the flashing lights are off," Suel said. "Say, did you notice Mike O'Halloran in that conference room?"

"I don't think I know who that is."

"He's with Pearce Street Station. He's okay. When we get a chance, I want to ask him about Horace the Whore. Thank God that idiot's not here."

"I can only hope he doesn't know anything about this. I don't want him making a call and tipping Phalen off."

TWENTY-SEVEN

They followed the line of vehicles to The Sycamores street. Two cars turned down the street before The Sycamores to take up positions behind the Phalen house. They waited for almost five minutes before the Emergency Response vehicle headed down the street to number eleven. Suel parked two doors away, and they half-ran to the Emergency Response vehicle. DCI Gogan was standing in front of the vehicle, talking to another officer. Two other uniformed officers were behind Gogan.

Suel nodded at one of the officers and said, "Mike O'Halloran, you come up here just for the fun?" Then Suel shot Dillon a look.

"I'll be glad to get these two off the street. We've had a half-dozen cases reported in the district."

"A half-dozen? That's two more than we know of," Dillon said.

"The last two were fairly recent. I think last Thursday and one over the weekend. Same routine, drugged the woman, and on Thursday night, they were leading her out of the pub when someone stopped them. Sunday, they were in the process of drugging a glass of wine. One of our guys just happened on the scene, the two ran off, and the bartender told him they'd run off without paying. Turned out the wine was laced with Rohypnol."

"You get a description of them?" Dillon asked.

"Dark hair and a blonde mutt. Your blonde knacker had an accent."

"Security tape?" Suel asked.

"DI Tevlin went down there this morning to check it out, The Workman's pub, on Wellington Quay. Apparently, they weren't on the tape."

"Let's go, people. Suel, you're with me. You'll hand the warrants to whoever answers the door, just as long as they're over eighteen," Gogan said and headed up the driveway toward the house.

Suel held the arrest warrants in his hand and was next to Gogan. Dillon was just behind Suel. He glanced over at the holly hedge in front of the white wall. O'Halloran and another officer followed behind Dillon. Six Emergency Response officers, dressed all in black and wearing helmets and holding what looked like HK416 assault rifles, were scattered across the front of the house. One of them stood in front of the garage door.

Dillon noticed that the black Kia Sorento wasn't parked in front. He hoped it might be in the garage, but what were the odds with a single-car garage? A gray Mercedes was parked up against the house in front of a four-panel window. Each panel was filled with diamond-shaped pieces of beveled glass, seventy or eighty pieces on each panel.

Gogan stepped up to the white front door and rapped forcefully four times using the brass door knocker. He appeared to count out his pause and had rapped two more times when the door opened and a man, looking to be in his late fifties or early sixties, answered the door.

"Yes?" Aidan Phalen said. He didn't appear surprised or frightened. Suel handed him the arrest warrants and said, "By order of the court, we're here to arrest Dessie Phalen and a second, unnamed individual."

"Oh, well, please come in. I'm afraid Dessie isn't here at the moment. In fact, I believe he's left the country."

"Your name, sir?" Gogan asked as he stepped into the house. Suel, Dillon, O'Halloran, and another officer followed Gogan into an elegant entryway with two oil paintings in gilt frames hanging from the wall. Both paintings appeared to be portraits of women from back in the 17th century.

"My name is Aidan Phalen. Dessie is my son. Unfortunately, I've no idea when he'll be back in the country. He's on an extended trip across Europe. May I offer you a tea or perhaps a brandy? It's late in the afternoon."

"If you don't mind, we'll search the premises."

"By all means, be my guest. I'll just move to the kitchen, so I'm out of your way."

Gogan directed O'Halloran and the other officer to search the first floor. He nodded at Suel and Dillon, and they followed him up the elaborately carved staircase to the second floor. They stepped into the first bedroom.

There was a king-sized bed and two antique chests of drawers in the room. A bedside table with a lamp was on either side of the bed. The oak floor was covered by a large red and blue oriental rug.

"Someone alerted these bastards," Gogan said as he shook his head.

"My money's on DI Tevlin at Pearce Street Station," Suel said.

"You think O'Halloran gave him the word?"

Suel shook his head. "No, O'Halloran's good. I'd say Tevlin found out reading the email McCabe sent to Pearce Street or from overhearing a conversation. They probably left hours ago before we even had the warrants. Whether they're actually out of the country remains to be seen."

"Let me call Special Branch and have them issue an alert on Phalen's Kia Sorento," Dillon said.

"I'll get everyone in here to help conduct the search," Gogan said. "You two may as well start in this room."

Dillon called in an alert on Phalen's Kia Sorento. It took little more than an hour with fifteen officers to search the place from top to bottom. Aidan Phalen offered them a glass of wine, thanked them for not creating a mess, and smiled as they left. Dillon and Suel followed everyone back to the Malahide station, and they reassembled in the conference room. DCI Gogan was brief and to the point.

"I want to thank you all for your time and effort this afternoon. Unfortunately, word was clearly leaked to Phalen, allowing his son and the accomplice to disappear. I have a hard time believing they left the country, and we'll be checking to verify that fact. Should you learn or hear anything, please don't hesitate to contact me. Thank you for your time. That's all."

Gogan walked out of the room and down the hallway to his office. He slammed the door behind him, shouted, "Son of a bitch," and followed up with more colorful phrases.

"What do you think?" Suel said.

"I think a pint back in Dublin might help. You mind if I call DaVanni, the FBI guy?"

Suel seemed to think for a moment and said, "Any chance he might have spilled the beans? Warned these two bastards to take off?"

"There's always a chance, but I can't see him doing it. Despite his polite response, he's got to be wondering if this doesn't sink his ship on the paintings."

"How so?"

"Well, for starters, if you were going to be delivering these paintings to Phalen and suddenly there we are searching his house, what would you think? Even if they've got the handoff scheduled for somewhere else, would you feel comfortable dealing with the guy now? And the Russian guy who was probably staying with them, once they make the tradeoff, is he going to be able to get out of here? No, more than Dessie's arrest got screwed up today."

"You're making that pint sound better and better. Yeah, go ahead and call what's his name."

"DaVanni, Dennis DaVanni."

TWENTY-EIGHT

Dennis DaVanni met Suel and Dillon at the Hole in the Wall, a pub alongside Phoenix Park on Blackhorse Avenue, not too far from the Special Branch office. It was a pleasant, early fall evening, and they were seated at a table outside on the patio.

Dillon gave a wave as DaVanni stepped out of his Volkswagen Golf and looked around. "Get you guys something?" DaVanni asked when he saw their nearly empty pint glasses.

"I'll take another Guinness," Dillon said.

"Same, and thank you," Suel replied.

DaVanni placed the order and was back at the table. "It cost extra, but I'm having them delivered," he said as he took a seat.

Suel laughed and said, "Yeah, right."

"Dennis, you remember Paddy Suel," Dillon said.

DaVanni and Suel shook hands. "So you said things didn't go exactly as planned this afternoon."

"That's an understatement," Dillon said and went on to give a more in-depth explanation.

When he had finished, DaVanni was quiet for a moment. He took a couple swallows of Guinness and then said, "Where do you think the leak came from?"

Suel looked at Dillon and nodded. Dillon went on to explain their suspicions regarding DI Horace Tevlin. He finished with, "I'm not sure what this is going to do as far as the delivery of the stolen artwork."

"I'm not sure either, so let's take the best scenario," DaVanni said.

"You mean there is one, a best one?" Suel said.

DaVanni nodded. "Whoever or however they got these paintings, there's been an awful lot of time and probably money involved. I still think Russians, specifically this Pavel Krupin person, is involved. I expect information on him sometime soon. But here's the deal. Money, and lots of it, will change hands when the artwork is delivered. Also, the young Russian man who's been with Aidan's son will be free to leave."

"Except that there's an alert out on him," Dillon said.

"Believe me. They can deal with that. A boat, a helicopter, a private plane across the channel to Scotland, and he's essentially free. What this has done is ensure that the arrival of the Rothko paintings is not going to occur at the Phalen home. It will be somewhere else, and if we can follow Phalen, I believe he'll eventually lead us to the paintings and to the two criminals who escaped arrest earlier today."

"What are you thinking, we have a stake out at the end of the street, and when Aidan Phalen drives off, we follow him?"

"That's one way, or we could place one of these on his car and track him," DaVanni said and pulled a small brown paper bag from his pocket. He reached in and took out three small black plastic boxes. Each one an inch by an inch-and-a-half. "Here you go, magnetic, good for one-hundred-and-eighty-six hours before they need to be recharged. You can attach it to the exterior, in a wheel well or to the chassis, and you can track the vehicle using your cellphone."

"Where'd you get these?" Dillon asked.

DaVanni smiled and said, "I ordered them online."

Dillon bought the next round, and they discussed how to gain access to Aidan Phalen's car.

"You mentioned Pavel Krupin," Dillon said. "You find anything out about him?"

"He did some time in Russia. He was linked to the theft of an Aivazovsky painting. He was a 19th-century artist. The painting was stolen from some bigwig's home in Moscow, who was supposedly keeping the painting safe for the State Tretyakov Gallery in Moscow. It's the premier art museum in the city. Anyway, Krupin was sentenced to ten years, but after three years, the painting was returned, Krupin was released, and the Moscow big-wig disappeared."

"And Krupin lives here now, in Tallaght?" Dillon said.

"At least for the moment. Did anyone mention him in relation to Aidan Phalen?"

Both Dillon and Suel shook their head. "No, the focus was strictly on Dessie Phalen and the supposed Russian. We didn't arrest either of them," Suel said.

"Might be a good idea to check Krupin out. My sense is he could serve as a safe house for Phalen's son and the Russian. Based on his reputation, he's not the sort of person you'd want to mess with, and he'd probably be pretty good at keeping those two on a very short leash."

"Perhaps that's where the paintings will be delivered," Dillon said.

DaVanni shook his head. "Could be, but he strikes me as the type of guy who would prefer to have that happen at some neutral location. A park, an alley, a warehouse. He wouldn't want anything linked to him or his property."

"So are you thinking of putting these tracking devices on their cars?" Dillon said.

"In a word, no. First of all, we can speculate where the Phalen kid is, but that's all it is, speculation. Even if I could get these tracking devices on all three of these vehicles, it would be impossible for me, or anyone else, to track all three of these people at any one time."

"So you're suggesting we help," Suel said.

"Here's the deal," DaVanni said. "I'm convinced this is going down in the next forty-eight hours if for no other reason than Phalen's house was just filled with a couple dozen officers conducting a search. I'm pretty damn sure Dessie Phalen and his accomplice are being kept under the watchful eye of Pavel Krupin. Everyone is anxious to get this done. It won't happen at Phalen's home, and it won't happen at Krupin's. It will occur somewhere where they will all be present. The paintings will be exchanged for the Russian, and everyone will disappear."

"Disappear?" Dillon said.

"They'll vanish for a period of at least five years. With the money involved, they can go anywhere, under whatever name they choose, and it will be almost impossible to find them."

"But how do you know that? They could—"

"This is what they do, and the only thing that today's search did was convince them they have to act quickly. Phalen isn't going to hold onto the paintings. He's a middleman. Krupin wants to get paid and get as far away from Phalen as possible. Someone is going to take possession of the Rothko paintings. An individual where money is no object. He may have buyers already lined up. He may even hold onto one or possibly two of the paintings. But after today, this is all going to happen and happen fast."

"What about Horace Tevlin?" Suel asked.

DaVanni shook his head. "He's a minor player. If he, in fact, warned them about the pending arrests, I'm sure they're grateful. But he's small time. They have a lot of time, effort, and money tied up in this, and the crooked cop, Tevlin, is on the sidelines. He'll keep his ear to the ground at the station, but that's about it. To be honest, he won't be thinking this way, but he's probably in danger of being silenced at some point."

"Silenced? You mean killed?" Suel said.

"Exactly, depending on what he knows or thinks he knows. Something happens to Tevlin, and that's a sign things are about to go down. Who's up for another pint?" DaVanni asked.

Both Dillon and Suel shook their head.

"Hope I didn't put a damper on the party."

"No, it's just been a long day," Suel said. "And from the sound of it, we may be busy over the next couple of days."

"One can always hope," DaVanni said.

"I'll see you in the morning, Dillon. Dennis, nice to see you again, and thanks for bringing us up to date," Suel said and stood. He shook hands with DaVanni, patted Dillon on the shoulder, and headed out the door.

"Apparently, he's not that interested," DaVanni said once the door closed behind Suel.

"Things get tough, he'll be there, and you can count on him to watch your back."

"What are you thinking?" DaVanni said.

"I'm thinking you should grab one of those trackers and figure out a way to get it onto Aidan Phalen's Mercedes. I'll take these other two and see if I can attach it to Pavel Krupin's BMW Coupe and, God forbid, Dessie's Kia Sorento."

"Thanks, Dillon. Much appreciated," DaVanni said and picked up one of the tracking devices from the table.

"Hopefully, this will happen sooner rather than later," Dillon said.

TWENTY-NINE

Dillon was home just before 8:00. He let Lucifer out, then set the two tracking devices on the kitchen counter and opened up the refrigerator in search of something for dinner. There was a tray with half a meal of chicken curry from the Red Torch, his favorite Thai restaurant, a package of smoked salmon, half a bowl of pasta, a baked chicken thigh, and a cheese and sausage pizza from Aldi. He wasn't all that hungry after the Guinness, and nothing really appealed to him anyway, so he closed the refrigerator.

He pulled out his phone and called Nessa, thinking an evening with her might be just the thing. After two rings, he was dumped into her voicemail. "Hi Nessa, checking in. Wondered if you'd like to get together for a late dinner or a glass of wine while I pay very personal attention to you. Give me a call back."

He figured she was probably on the phone with some girlfriend, which led him to think it could be another ninety minutes before she got off the line. He headed upstairs and grabbed a quick shower, put on some cleaner casual clothes, refilled Lucifer's water dish, and coaxed him back inside with a biscuit.

He glanced at the digital clock on the stove. The Grape Vine, his local wine store, was open for another fifteen minutes. He climbed into his car and hurried over. He was able to park right in front and, once inside, headed straight for the cooler and grabbed a chilled bottle of Sauvignon Blanc.

"You want a bag for that?" the woman asked after she rang him up.

"No, thanks, but not necessary." He drove down Ballymun Road, where it turned into St. Mobhi Road, which turned into Botanic Road. After a half-mile, he turned left onto Lindsay Road and pulled to a stop across the street from Nessa's home. He grabbed the chilled bottle of wine off the passenger seat and hurried across the street. A red BMW with County Meath license plates was parked in front of Nessa's, and he had to step around the car to get to the front gate.

The front drapes were pulled, but the lights were on in the sitting room, and a light was on in her bedroom upstairs, so she was probably home. Dillon stepped onto the front stoop and rang the doorbell. He checked out his reflection in the front door window and adjusted his shirt slightly. He rang the doorbell again. This time, holding it just a little longer. Still no answer.

He rang it once more, pushing the doorbell for a good thirty seconds. He could hear the thing chiming inside, not that it did any good. Finally, he gave up. He debated leaving the wine bottle at the front door but then decided some knacker walking past would probably grab it, so he headed back to his car.

He slid in behind the wheel, set the bottle on the passenger seat, and gave a quick glance up to the second floor and Nessa's bedroom window. Was the curtain moving? Dillon stared for a long moment, debated going back to the front door, and then decided against it. Could be she'd been asleep in bed. Perhaps she wasn't feeling well, or what if he'd just been mistaken?

He turned the engine on, pulled away from the curb, and drove home. He set the wine bottle on the shelf of the refrigerator door. Placed the chicken curry dish in the microwave and settled in front of the TV with his dinner. He finished eating in little more than ten minutes and called Nessa again. He disconnected as soon as he was dumped into her voicemail.

He watched a movie of no redeeming social value, went to bed, and woke just before six the following morning. He let Lucifer out into the front garden and cooked up two fried eggs and four slices of bacon. Lucifer was already settled into his pillow in the sitting room when Dillon left for Special Branch. Suel wasn't in yet, and rather than torture himself with coffee from the break room, Dillon headed out to the food truck in Phoenix Park, got a large black coffee and a sweet roll, and went back to the office.

He'd finished the sweet roll and the coffee, and Suel still wasn't in the office, so Dillon left him a note.

Heading down to Tallaght to check on the Pavel Krupin address. Should be back by half-past ten. D

It took him twenty minutes driving the M50 and then the N81 to get down to Tallaght. Krupin lived at 21 Newtown Park. Dillon's GPS gave perfect directions, and as soon as he turned onto the street, the GPS announced that he had arrived at his destination.

Krupin's house was the end unit of four attached homes. Each unit looked to be twice the size of Dillon's place. At no surprise, all the homes were white-stucco, two-story units that appeared to have similar floor plans. The front door was centered on the unit, with apparently two large rooms on either side of the door. A three-foot-high white stucco wall ran across the front of every lot. Each home had a black wrought iron gate in front of the sidewalk leading up to the front door. Krupin's house was the only place with a driveway. Dillon drove down the street for two blocks, turned around, and then drove back past Krupin's a second time. The driveway ran along the end of the unit and led into the back garden, which, at a quick glance, appeared to be paved.

Krupin's black BMW was parked in the driveway next to the house, effectively blocking any vehicle or, for that matter, any person walking out of the back garden and into the front. That seemed to Dillon to be the perfect setup to keep Dessie Phalen's car from any prying eyes. The back garden was surrounded by a six-foot-high concrete block wall.

Dillon drove two streets away, parked, and walked back to Krupin's. He had the two tracking devices in his pocket, but he didn't expect to be able to attach them to any vehicles at the moment.

The grass was long in the front garden, and the area was devoid of flowers, bushes, or trees. Dillon wondered if that suggested there wasn't a woman living on the premises. He made a mental note to check to see who the owner of the property was. It would make sense if Pavel Krupin was simply renting the place. He headed up the street and made his way back to his car.

When he returned to Special Branch, Suel was on his phone at his desk. He gave Dillon a wave as Dillon settled into his desk chair. Once he hung up, Suel walked over.

"You find anything out on the Russian?"

"Yeah, he lives in a fairly large place, about twice the size of mine. Certainly big enough to handle two guests for an extended period of time. He's got a drive-way along the side of the house leading into the back garden. It would be the perfect place for Dessie Phalen to keep his car, and no one would ever be able to see the thing. I'm just looking up the property record now to see if he owns it or is renting."

"I was on the line with O'Halloran over at Pearce Street Station. He's going to check on Tevlin and see if he actually went to the Workman's pub to view their se-curity tape." Dillon glanced at the clock on his computer screen. "I'm thinking it might be nice to grab some lunch at the Workman's. Then while we're there, we can check the security tape. Even if Tevlin went down there and viewed the tape, he can just say he never saw Phalen or the Russian, and no one is going to double-check."

"You actually think they'd be down there knowing that the word is out on them in Temple Bar and everyone is looking for that car?"

"Yeah, I do because this happened before the arrest warrants. This was the place they were drugging the woman's glass of wine, and they took off when a Guard just happened to show up."

"And you want to head down there for lunch? To-day?"

"Yeah. Why you got something else going on?"

Suel shook his head. "No, at least nothing that can't wait. Yeah, let's do it. Head out in about forty-five minutes?"

"Yeah, I'll call down there and get things lined up so we can view the tapes."

Suel headed back to his desk. Dillon logged onto the property records site for Dublin County and input Krupin's address. It turned out the property was owned by a company called Brown Rentals. Dillon phoned the number listed on the property record.

"Brown Rentals, how may I help you?" a woman answered.

"Hi, I'm interested in renting one of your proper-ties."

"One moment, please, and I'll connect you to Gemma Brown."

"Thank you," Dillon said, but the woman had already transferred his call.

A woman picked up after three rings. "Gemma Brown, how may I help you?"

"Hi, thanks for taking my call. I'm interested in renting one of your properties. A neighbor mentioned it to me."

"Oh, wonderful. Would you happen to have an address, and I can check on it for you?"

"Yes, it's in Tallaght, on Newtown Park, number twenty-one."

"Let me just check," she said, and Dillon could hear her clicking the keyboard. "Mmm, unfortunately, that's rented at the moment, but just for three months, so this might work. It looks like it will be available in twenty-three days. Now, I do have someone else interested in that unit. If you'd like to give me your name, I can keep you appraised of the situation."

"Oh, thanks, but I'll need it sooner than that. Thanks for your—"

"We have a number of other properties available. I'd be glad to send you a list, and you could take a look. I'm sure we have something that would fit your needs."

"Thanks, I'll think about it," Dillon said and hung up.

He phoned Dennis DaVanni next.

"Hello?" was how he answered.

"Jack Dillon, Dennis. I went past Pavel Krupin's place this morning."

"That big place on the corner, right?" DaVanni said.

"Yeah, you've been past it?"

"No, just checked it out online."

"Well, it's certainly large enough to accommodate two guests. Plus, there's a driveway that runs along the side of the house, and the back garden appears to be paved. It looks like the perfect place to park Dessie Phalen's Kia, and no one would be able to see it. Krupin's car was parked next to the corner of the house, so if there's another car in the back garden, it's not getting out unless Krupin moves his car."

"Interesting. Were you able to check it out?"

"The back garden? No, and I didn't want to alert them that I was looking around. I drove past twice and walked past once. That was earlier this morning. I'm thinking of going back sometime after midnight and at least place the tracking device onto Krupin's BMW, and then I'll take a look and figure the best way to get into the back garden."

"That sounds good. I've been sitting out here on the crossroad to Aidan Phalen's place for the last four hours, waiting for him to drive past. It hasn't happened yet."

"I'm heading down to the Workman's pub in a bit to check out their security tape and see if Dessie and that other idiot show up. This is the place they were drugging some woman's glass of wine. A Garda officer came in, and they took off."

"Anyone happen to check the glass for fingerprints?"

"Not even sure they got the glass, but I'll call O'Halloran at Pearce Street and see."

"Another thing I'm wondering about does—Oh shit,
there goes Phalen. God, finally. Talk to you later," Da-
Vanni said and disconnected.

Dillon phoned the Workman's pub. He talked to a
manager and set up an appointment to view the security
tapes from Saturday night. He found it interesting that
the manager never mentioned an officer being there earlier, which suggested that DI Tevlin never went in there
to look at the tapes.

THIRTY

Dillon drove them to the Workman's pub over on Wellington Quay a little before noon. They checked in with the manager, a guy named Brandon McDonald, who looked all of fifteen years old.

"Look, I know I said I'd dial it up, but we're in the midst of our midday peak. I'm not going to be able to get on this for at least another forty-five minutes. I'm really sorry. I thought I mentioned it on the phone."

"You probably did, Brandon. Not a problem. We just wanted to let you know we're here. We're going to order some lunch, and then when things calm down, we'll take a look at the Saturday night tapes. That sound okay?"

"That sounds perfect. Thanks. Hey, drinks on the house. You's gonna have a pint with lunch?"

"Thanks, but we're on duty, so we better not."

"Oh, yeah, of course. Sandwiches are up on the rooftop terrace. I'll come find yas when things slow down," Brandon said and hurried off.

"That kid is the manager? He doesn't look old enough to drink," Suel said.

"Let's see what the menu looks like," Dillon suggested, and they headed up to the rooftop terrace. The room had a blue tile floor and bright yellow stools arranged around raised round yellow tables with purple trim. The walls were painted a deep purple except for the kitchen area, which was decorated with wide red and yellow stripes. The sandwich menu was attached to the wall above the kitchen counter. They ordered sandwiches. Suel ordered tea, Dillon got a coffee, and they grabbed a seat at one of the raised yellow tables just as three people left.

Neither one spoke for the better part of ten minutes as they looked around the place. The roof had been rolled back, and fortunately, it was a pleasant day, and the sun was shining in. Their sandwiches arrived, pulled pork for Suel, BBQ chicken for Dillon, and they dug in. Dillon told Suel about DaVanni following Aidan Phalen.

"Be interesting to see if he gets the tracking device attached," Suel said.

"I hope so. I told him I'm going back to Krupin's place in Tallaght late tonight and hopefully attach a tracker to his car. I'd love to get into that back garden and see if the Kia is back there. You interested in coming with me?"

"I think I better, just to make sure you don't screw something up."

"Thanks, I'm thinking sometime after midnight."

"This is going to sound awful, but you know what might be better?"

"I don't want to wait around for him to drive to a store or someplace."

"No, as long as you're talking after midnight, might as well wait until about 4:00 in the morning. Chances are, whoever is in the place will be sound asleep. I'm thinking if you can get into that back garden, there's a good chance you could be dealing with motion detector lights. People are most often in their deepest sleep around 4:00."

"How 'bout I pick you up about 3:30?"

"Yeah, that should work. Send me a text when you're leaving your place. If I don't reply, call me."

"Thanks, Paddy," Dillon said just as Brandon, the manager, stepped onto the terrace. Dillon gave him a wave, and he headed toward them. The place had definitely cleared out. Now they were one of only three tables occupied.

"How was lunch?" Brandon asked.

"Very good, thanks," Dillon said.

"You ready to take a look at the tape? I think I've got it set right before those two took off. It was just a few minutes before eight last Saturday night."

"Let's take a look," Suel said, and they headed down to Brandon's office.

A computer screen and keyboard were set up on a table just opposite Brandon's desk. Two metal folding chairs were pushed in against the table. Dillon and Suel took up seats, and Brandon gave them a quick rundown on how to navigate the tape. Unlike the images at the

Quays pub that shifted every four or five seconds, the tape at the Workman's was a constant thread, so there was no jerky movement.

Much like Kate Cullen's situation, a woman was seated on a bar stool with her back against the bar. She appeared to be focused on the stage. She sipped from a wine glass, and they watched her for close to three minutes when, suddenly, Dessie Phalen and his blonde-haired partner appeared.

They stood chatting to one another, and then Phalen said something to the woman. She smiled, nodded, drained her wine glass, and handed it to Phalen. The blonde guy placed the drink order with the barman while Phalen and the woman conversed.

The drinks eventually arrived, two pints of Guinness and the wine glass. You wouldn't have picked up on it unless you were looking for it, but the blonde guy, with his back to the woman, reached into his pocket and dropped something into the wine glass. He picked the glass up, began to swirl it, and suddenly set it down on the bar as a uniformed officer stepped up and apparently said something to the bartender. The blonde tapped Phalen on the shoulder, nodded toward the officer, and they disappeared off camera.

A few minutes later, the bartender said something to the officer, who studied the wine glass and shook his head.

"Jesus Christ, talk about a close call," Suel said.

"You saw it," Brandon said. "Your man's from Pearce Street Station. We'd heard about the problem drugging drinks. The barman poured the wine in a jar and gave it to the officer."

"Yeah, it tested positive for Rohypnol," Dillon said. "That woman is lucky as hell. A glass of that, and she wouldn't be able to tell you her name twenty minutes later."

"Has anyone from Pearce Street Station seen this tape?" Suel asked.

Brandon shook his head. "Funny you should ask that. The officer that night was right on. Left with the wine in a jar and hurried back to the station. I expected to hear from them the next day, then thought it might take a day or two to run the test. Plus, it was the weekend, and now here we are, and you're the first ones to see the tape."

"Can you make a copy of that and email it to me, please?" Dillon said and handed a card to Brandon.

"Yeah, sure, I'll have it in your email before you get back." He glanced at Dillon's card. "You're in that station in Phoenix Park, right?"

"Yeah, that's the one."

"Anything else I can do for you?" Brandon asked.

"No, thanks, you've been a big help," Dillon said.

"Much appreciated, and I loved the pulled pork," Suel said.

"You need to come back and check out our bands. It's crazy every night."

"We'll be sure to do that, Brandon. Thanks again, and thanks for sending me the copy of that tape."

"It'll be waiting for you when you get back."

"Nice kid," Suel commented once they stepped out onto the street.

THIRTY-ONE

Dillon got a call from DaVanni toward the middle of the afternoon.

"Did you get the tracker on his car?" was how he answered.

"Yeah, I followed him to some swanky place out on the coast. He had lunch with a fat guy in a three-piece suit. Interested in who it was?"

"Let me guess, Royce Farley?"

"You got it. The guy must weigh four hundred pounds. He had this white linen napkin tucked in under his chins, and it looked like he'd ordered an entire roast turkey for lunch. No wonder the guy is that big."

"You're sure it was Farley?"

"Yeah, I got his license number. You have a pen nearby?"

"Will my color crayon work?"

"Yeah," DaVanni said and laughed. He gave Dillon the license plate number and then said, "He was driving a white Mercedes Benz G Class."

"I'm not familiar with that model."

"Neither was I, small wonder. I looked it up online, and the thing starts at a hundred-and-fifty-grand and goes up from there, and that's before any VAT Tax is tacked on."

"You gotta be kidding."

"Dillon, I told you this guy was big bucks. Well, plus the fact he's so fat no normal car could probably deal with the weight."

"And he met with Phalen?"

"Yeah, the two of them were laughing away over lunch. I sat at the bar and had two seltzers to the tune of twenty euros. What a rip-off. I can't imagine what their lunch cost. Farley just signed a receipt, and that was it. He must have an account there or something. I never saw a credit card."

"Could be he owns the place."

"Hum-mmm, I never thought of that."

"Did you get the tracking device placed?"

"Yeah, I wish I'd had two. I would have put one on Farley's car, too."

"Where'd you place it on Phalen's?"

"I attached it to the back of the car, just below the trunk and behind the license plate. I tracked him when he left just to be sure it was okay. It was working fine. He headed home, and I just checked. The car has been there ever since. Were you able to put one on Krupin's vehicle?"

"No, not yet. Last I checked, it was parked on the driveway in front of his house. Suel and I will be heading over there after midnight, hopefully get one on his car and with any luck Dessie Phalen's Kia if that's parked in the back garden."

"Have you seen it back there?"

"Phalen's Kia? No, unfortunately, but Krupin's back garden would be the perfect place to hide a car. No one can see back there without climbing a six-foot wall."

"Good luck tonight. These two meeting up for lunch makes me think this is about to happen."

"Give a yell if you get any movement on Phalen's car. I'll text you once we get the tracker on Krupin's."

"Good luck and stay safe," DaVanni said and disconnected.

Dillon worked for the next couple of hours and then stopped at Suel's desk and gave him the update on Phalen's lunch with Farley and DaVanni attaching the tracking device to Phalen's car.

"Perfect. We get that thing on Krupin's car, and if the kid's car is in the back garden, we'll be well taken care of. You heading out?"

"Yeah, I'm going to hit the sack early and hopefully get some decent sleep. I'll send you a text around 3:15 and be at your door shortly after that."

Suel nodded. "I'm still thinking about the possibility of those motion detector lights. This Krupin strikes me as a very careful guy. It wouldn't surprise me. I might have a way to disarm those lights."

"How do you plan to do that?"

"I'm not sure. I'll have to study it a little more tonight. See you this morning at zero-dark-thirty."

"Not quite that early, but yeah," Dillon said and headed out the door. On the drive home, he thought about Suel's comment, *'A way to disarm those lights.'* Suel had never seemed like the type of person to study up on things. Then again, if he had a way, and it worked, that would be great.

Once home, he let Lucifer out, picked up the waste-basket contents scattered around the kitchen floor, and put the pizza in the oven. He watched TV until the news came on, then turned it off and went to bed.

He eventually fell asleep and woke to his digital alarm going off. He dressed quickly in black socks, jeans, and a long sleeve black sweatshirt and sent a text to Suel as he went out to the car. Suel's one-word text reply, *'Shit,'* arrived just as Dillon opened his car door.

THIRTY-TWO

Suel was waiting just outside his front gate when Dillon pulled up. He carried a thermos and a soft black case for a rifle. He opened the back door of the car, placed the rifle case on the floor, and climbed into the front passenger seat.

"I brought some coffee in case you're feeling drowsy," Suel said and held up the thermos.

"Yeah, and what about that rifle? What do you plan on doing with that thing?"

"Relax, it might be a way to put any motion detector lights out of commission, that's all."

"You're going to shoot them?" Dillon said as he drove down the street. "You'll wake up Krupin and every neighbor within a half-mile."

"Calm down and relax. They won't even hear it. It's just a high-powered pellet gun. Think of it as just another way to turn off a light."

"I don't know. It—"

"Let's see what we're dealing with when we get there. If you're still going to act like a petulant child, I won't use it." Dillon glanced over at Suel, shook his head, and smiled. Suel shook his head. "Just double checking, but you did remember the tracking devices, didn't you?"

"Oh, God. I knew there was something I forgot."

Suel looked over again and saw the grin on Dillon's face. "Yeah, okay."

The M1 and the N1 weren't empty, but they had to be the quietest Dillon had ever seen. They made the drive into Tallaght in almost half the time it took previously. Dillon turned onto Newtown Park. As he drove down toward the end of the street, he made a mental note of the fact that all the lights in the homes were off. One unit had a front porch light on, but that was it, and it was three doors away from Krupin's. He slowed as they passed Krupin's house.

"That's his house," he said.

"Yeah, you were right. All these places are big. That's his BMW in the driveway?"

"Yeah, see what I meant about it blocking anyone coming out of the back garden. I'm thinking he parked there on purpose."

"Be interesting to see if the Phalen kid's car is actually in the back garden," Suel said as Dillon turned at the corner.

He pulled up onto the sidewalk at the far end of the wall along Krupin's back garden and climbed out of the car. Once Dillon climbed out, Suel had to ease over the console and slide out of the driver's door because Dillon parked just inches away from the garden wall.

"I'll stay here. No point in both of us drawing attention in the front."

Dillon nodded and hurried along the wall to the front of the house. He was surprised and glad to see that the wrought iron gate on the driveway was open. He did a quick glance up the street. Everything appeared quiet.

Krupin's house was dark, and Dillon quickly made his way up to the BMW. He had hoped to place the tracker behind the rear license plate, but it would have caused the license to not be flush with the car body. Based on Krupin's history, that could be exactly the sort of thing he would notice. Instead, Dillon switched on the tracker and attached it to the inside of the rear chrome bumper. He hurried back down the driveway, around the corner of the wall, and turned on his cellphone. He clicked on the tracker link, enlarged the image a half-dozen times and, suddenly, there was a red dot right where the car would be on the street map.

He walked down to his car at the end of the garden wall just as Suel, holding his pellet gun, was sliding off the hood of Dillon's car. Suel flashed him the 'okay' sign using his thumb and forefinger.

Dillon nodded, climbed onto the hood of his car, and looked over the wall. There were back windows on the first and second floors of the house, but all the windows on the second floor were covered with closed metal blinds. The first-floor windows appeared to have designer shades and cloth drapes.

Dillon hopped up onto the top of the wall, gave another quick look, and dropped to the ground. The back garden was indeed paved. Up next to the back door was a wicker couch, two wicker chairs, and a square, glass-topped table with four chairs. A grill beneath a black canvas cover was up against the house. A car was parked in the far corner of the back garden. The vehicle had a silver cover pulled over it.

Dillon hurried over to the car, thankful that no motion detector lights flashed on. He lifted the front of the cover. The car was black, and there was the Dublin County license plate with 2020 identifying the year, a capital 'D' indicating Dublin County, and the number 1010, meaning the one thousandth and tenth car sold that year. It also meant this was Dessie Phalen's Kia Sorento. Dillon turned on the tracker and attached it to the back of the front bumper. He pulled the silver polyester cover back down, smoothed out any wrinkles, and then hurried over to the corner of the wall.

He jumped up on the wall, hoisted himself up with his arms, half-scurried up along the concrete blocks, turned around, and softly dropped onto the hood of his car.

Suel was already seated in the passenger seat, sipping coffee from the thermos cup. "Any problems?"

"No, and the Kia was back there under a cover."

"Yeah, I saw that. I was pretty sure it was the Phalen kid's car. I took out the motion detector lights. It could well be a week or a month before anyone notices. Hopefully, this will be over long before that."

"Good job," Dillon said and turned on the car. He pulled back onto the street, took a right at the next corner, and stopped.

"What's wrong?"Suel said.

"Nothing, I just want to make sure that tracker is working," Dillon said and pulled out his phone. Just like before, he enlarged the map a half-dozen times then showed the image on his cellphone to Suel.

"Oh, perfect," Suel said.

Dillon drove down the street and said, "You interested in some breakfast?"

"I'm thinking I'd like to go home, shower, and shave. I could meet you somewhere, What about over by the office?"

"Sounds like a plan," Dillon said. He dropped Suel off at home and then headed toward his place. Just for the heck of it, he decided to drive past Nessa's house. It was almost 5:00, and if the lights were on, he might be able to grab a coffee or, if he was really lucky, he might be able to grab Nessa. He turned onto Whitworth Road, then drove around the block on Prospect Road to get onto Botanic Road, and then made a left-hand turn onto Lindsay Road. He began to slow when he could see the lights on up ahead in Nessa's unit, but then the front door to her unit opened and out stepped a dark-haired guy Dillon didn't recognize. It was more than a little early for a painter or a plumber to be making a call. The man got into the red BMW parked in front of Nessa's. The car had a County Meath license plate and drove past Dillon's car without so much as a glance.

Dillon checked the time on his clock, 5:16 am. That didn't seem good. A few minutes later, he pulled onto the drive in front of his house and went inside. Lucifer was still asleep as he took off his clothes and headed into the shower. He was downstairs, dressed, and had just sent an email to Suel asking where he wanted to meet for breakfast when Lucifer came downstairs. Dillon let him outside, then went back on his cellphone and checked the trackers on Krupin and Dessie Phalen's cars. At no surprise, neither car had moved in the last hour and a half. He sent an email to Dennis DaVanni telling him both cars had a tracking device attached, and both devices were working.

Suel replied to the email suggesting they meet at Ryan's for breakfast, which was a good idea since it was the only place open at this early hour. They met a half-hour later. Suel was already seated at a table drinking a steaming tea when Dillon walked in. Not surprisingly, close to half the tables were already occupied with early morning workers.

Dillon settled in across from Suel. "You been here long?"

"No more than ten minutes. After our early morning start, I'm starving."

Dillon glanced at the menu, and a minute later, a waitress stepped over. "What'll it be, lads?"

They ordered full Irish breakfasts. She gathered up the menus and was back with Dillon's coffee a moment later.

"Did you let DaVanni know the trackers are live?" Suel asked and followed up with a loud slurp of tea.

"Yeah, I'm not expecting anything for the better part of the morning. With the Phalen kid under the watchful eye of Krupin, I'm not expecting his car to move at all unless they're going somewhere to exchange the paintings for the Russian rapist."

"You know when they begin to move, we're liable to have very little time to get this organized. Are the arrests supposed to be our responsibility or DaVanni's?"

"Excellent point. We'd better get that sorted out now rather than wait, or these guys will meet up for five or ten minutes and disappear."

Dillon glanced over at the clock on the wall. It wasn't quite 6:30, and he decided to wait until 7:00 before he called DaVanni to see what, if any, plans he had made. Breakfast arrived, rashers, hashbrowns, sausage, two fried eggs, mushrooms, tomatoes, baked beans, and black pudding. Dillon passed his black pudding, actually a blood sausage, and his baked beans over to Suel.

"You don't know what you're missing, Dillon."

"Actually, I do, and you're welcome to both items."

THIRTY-THREE

They were almost, but not quite, the first ones in the office. Dillon placed a call to Dennis DaVanni on his desk phone.

"DaVanni," was how he answered.

"Hi, Dennis. Any movement on your man Aidan Phalen?"

"Hi, Dillon, and no, nothing. My limited experience suggests he'll stay put until around eleven, then he either runs a couple of errands or meets up with someone. What about Krupin?"

"Nothing. It will be interesting to see if he sets any type of pattern. He strikes me as the type who keeps his car turned off for days at a time. Based on how the Kia was literally kept under wraps in his back garden, I'd be surprised if that moved at all. I wanted to check with you on the plans. If we get an indication that something is about to happen, do you have a team assembled? Are we supposed to alert an Emergency Response Team?"

"Thanks for asking, and no, you don't need to alert the ERT. We've got our own group waiting patiently."

"I'm thinking there's a possibility the exchange of the paintings for the Russian blonde guy and cash could be done literally in a matter of seconds. So, I don't want to take any chances."

"Well, first of all, given whatever the cash payment is, it will be done in advance. Funds will probably be electronically transferred to an account somewhere, clearly not in the States or the EU. I'm guessing Grand Cayman, Panama, or even Columbia."

"You're talking a hundred and fifty million, right?" Dillon said.

"That's what the paintings are valued at, but payment will be something less, possibly substantially less, than that figure. Obviously, Phalen, Krupin, and Farley are involved, along with perhaps one or two others we're not even aware of at this stage. They'll be taking a cut of the funds. Rest assured, everyone is anxious to get things moving. The mere fact that Dessie Phalen's car has been put under wraps suggests that things will be happening, and soon. I'll give you a call the moment I see any movement with Phalen's car, even if he ends up at the grocery store. Please do the same for me."

"You can count on it, Dennis."

DCI McCabe arrived thirty minutes later. Dillon gave him fifteen minutes to settle in and then knocked on his doorframe.

"Come in, Dillon. Any news on this painting situation?"

"The FBI agent, Dennis DaVanni, expects it to happen sooner rather than later. We have tracking devices on three of the suspects' vehicles. DaVanni has a team waiting to move as soon as we determine it's happening."

"Is this the Emergency Response Team from Pearce Street Station?"

"No sir, in speaking with DaVanni, he mentioned, and I quote, 'We've got our own group waiting patiently.'"

"Meaning they're Americans, here, in Ireland?"

"He didn't actually say that, but that's my thought. He did mention that there is a possibility that, once this is taking place, it could actually happen in a matter of just a few minutes."

"No doubt," McCabe said and shook his head. "There's a part of me that's very glad they're not depending on our Emergency Response Team. I'm guessing this is some American FBI group. They're welcome to the problem. I'm presuming you and Suel will be involved."

"That's my understanding, and we've got tracking devices on two of the individuals' vehicles. Theoretically, once things start to happen, we'll be in communication, if for no other reason than providing updates on where the two are headed. At some point, everyone has to end up meeting, even if it's just for a minute or two."

McCabe shook his head again. "And the two responsible for the assaults on the women in the Temple Bar area, we'll have them in our custody?"

"I believe so, sir. They are one of the two vehicles we will be tracking. Currently, that car is parked in the back garden of a home in Tallaght. The car is hidden under a silver polyester cover in the back garden of the Russian man's house. His name is Pavel Krupin."

"I recognize the name from your report. No chance of them escaping in the car?"

"The back garden is surrounded by a six-foot concrete block wall. The driveway leading out of the back garden is blocked by Krupin's car parked next to the house. The fact that Phalen's son, Dessie, is essentially being held in the house suggests things are about to happen."

"Not soon enough for my tastes. All right. Please keep me informed and stay safe, Dillon. Thank you," McCabe said, essentially dismissing Dillon.

"Thank you, sir," Dillon said, pushing the chair back and heading out of McCabe's office. As he walked toward his desk, Suel looked over and gave him a look, suggesting, *'What's up?'*

Dillon flashed him the okay sign.

Dillon and Suel basically treaded water for the rest of the day, waiting for something to happen. Nothing changed. Neither car moved. Dillon checked in with Dennis DaVanni toward the end of the day.

"Wish I had some news for you," DaVanni said, "but based on his car, Aidan Phalen never left the house today."

"They could be meeting up tonight."

"Possibly. It might be a good idea to have a low-key evening and wait. Things have to be happening, and soon. I can just feel it."

"I'll be at home watching my cellphone. If anything happens, I'll give you a call."

"Same goes for me," DaVanni said and disconnected.

Dillon had the chicken thigh and the smoked salmon from his refrigerator for dinner. He kept thinking about the trackers, checked his phone a half-dozen times, and neither vehicle had moved. He hooked the leash onto Lucifer's collar, placed him in the back seat of the car, and drove down to Tallaght. He pulled onto Krupin's street and parked a block away from his house. He got Lucifer out of the back seat, clipped on the leash, and led him down the footpath, past the house. Krupin's BMW was parked in the driveway in exactly the same position as it had been at 4:00 this morning. Tonight the drapes in one of the front windows were open, and Dillon could see a large flat screen TV mounted on the wall. What looked like a soccer game was currently on the TV. They walked around the block, back to the car, and then drove past Krupin's house. Nothing had changed.

Back home, Dillon left Lucifer in the front garden and checked the trackers once more with his cellphone, nothing. He stepped inside and settled in front of the TV. Lucifer's scratching at the front door reminded him that the dog was still outside, and he let him in the house. They both nodded off in front of the boring movie that was playing. Dillon woke, checked the trackers once more, and got the same result, nothing happening.

He woke Lucifer, and they headed up to bed. Dillon plugged in his phone and placed it next to his pillow. He checked it a half-dozen times over the course of the night, but nothing ever changed. When Lucifer woke him, it was almost 8:00 in the morning.

He hurried downstairs, let Lucifer out, then ran upstairs to shave and shower. He filled the food and water dishes, skipped breakfast, and coaxed Lucifer back in with a biscuit.

He was already late, and he figured, at this stage, ten more minutes wouldn't make a difference, so he drove past Nessa's. Fortunately, he didn't see the red BMW with the County Meath plates, but then, based on yesterday morning, your man would have left over three hours ago.

Suel was already at his desk when Dillon finally arrived in Special Branch. As Dillon walked past, Suel said, "Good Lord, were you with Nessa last night? You look exhausted, Dillon."

"God, I only wish. No, I sat around checking my cellphone every thirty minutes and then woke up every hour on the hour to check again. Safe to say, no one left in their car."

"You ever think they might be wise to this, the tracking devices? Did you check with DaVanni?"

"No, not yet."

"Might be a good idea to give him a call. Just a thought, but what if they're wise to this, and they just called a taxi or walked to a bus stop?"

"Oh man, I don't even want to think about that," he said. But of course, he was thinking about it. He pulled out his cellphone and called DaVanni.

"Relax, Dillon, nothing's happening," was how he answered.

"I think I checked every fifteen minutes last night. I feel like I slept for about an hour, total, and not all at one time."

"Dillon, if the car moves, the tracker will send you a signal, so calm down."

"Well, here's a thought for you, what if they take a taxi or even a bus?"

There was a long pause before DaVanni said, "I'm counting on them not doing that. Besides, I can't see them placing eight rolled canvases in a taxi."

"Well, if they're rolled, what if they're just in a box?"

"Let's stick to the plan, Dillon," DaVanni said and then disconnected.

Suel laughed at Dillon and said, "Feel any better?"

THIRTY-FOUR

At the end of the day, Suel wandered over to Dillon's desk and said, "I'm thinking of stopping for one pint. You up for it?"

Dillon thought for a moment and said, "I can do one. You want to meet at the Autobahn?"

Suel nodded. "Give me a couple of minutes to finish up, and I'll see you there."

"I'll head out now," Dillon said. He cleared off his desk, locked it up, and headed out. Since Suel was finishing up whatever he was involved in, Dillon stopped at home and let Lucifer into the front garden. Amazingly, there was no mess to clean up.

Dillon debated calling Nessa, decided against it, and drove over to the Autobahn. A car was pulling out just as he drove into the parking area, and he parked right next to the front door. Once inside, he glanced around but didn't see Suel, so he grabbed a table in the corner and settled onto the more comfortable upholstered bench.

Dillon had just finished ordering two pints of Guinness and was checking the tracking devices when Suel arrived. "I just ordered for us," he said as Suel settled onto the wooden chair.

"Hopefully, there won't be any movement over the next forty-five minutes, and we can enjoy our drinks."

"I'm getting to the point where I'm wondering if this is even going to happen."

Suel nodded. "To be honest, I'm glad your man Da-Vanni is here to worry about this. All we have to do is follow directions, and whether or not anything goes down, we did our job."

"I still want to nail those two punks who were attacking the women."

"There might be a resisting arrest situation, and they'll have to be subdued," Suel said just as their pints of Guinness arrived.

"Can I get you anything else?" the server offered and flashed a pretty smile.

"Just the check when you have a moment," Dillon said.

"You weren't kidding on just one," Suel said and took a healthy sip from his glass.

"I just want to get this thing behind us. Although I have to say, after talking to DaVanni earlier and him saying whatever they pay is going to be far less than the estimated value, I'm curious how much money is going to be involved."

"Eight paintings, I'd guess at least ten million," Dillon said.

"Be interesting to see if Royce Farley is actually involved."

"He's a rich guy with a ton of money. He probably thinks he's entitled to these paintings. If for no other reason than he'll take care of them properly and won't keep them rolled up for the next twenty years. Once we get them, I'd like to give Melanie Brussard a viewing before DaVanni hurries them back to the US."

"I wonder if he'd ever consider displaying them at Dublin's National Art Museum?"

"That would be something. The senator could add some pressure. There'd be some news stories regarding the recovery of the paintings, and he could get some free publicity. I could see the story going onto news stations and papers all over the US and especially in their hometown of New Orleans."

Dillon's phone suddenly beeped. He took a quick sip and said, "Now what?" He pulled out his phone and stared. "They're moving, Paddy. Both vehicles." He was about to call DaVanni when his phone rang. DaVanni was calling Dillon.

"You got movement?" Dillon said.

"Yeah, Aidan Phalen is turning around in his driveway as we speak."

"Krupin and the Kia are moving. I was just about to call you."

"I've alerted our team. Once we get an idea of where they're headed, I'll get back to you."

"I'm with Suel at the moment. We're in Glasnevin. We're heading to the car now," Dillon said, but DaVanni had already disconnected.

Suel lifted his pint glass and took three healthy swallows. He shook his head as he set the glass down and got out of his chair. Dillon slipped around the table and stood. He placed a twenty euro note on the table, took a final swig, and headed for the door.

"I'll drive," Suel said as they stepped outside. "You can watch your screen and tell me where they're headed."

Dillon checked his screen as they hurried over to Suel's car parked out on Glasnevin Avenue. Suel clicked the fob on his key, the lights flashed, and the locks made an audible sound as they released. Dillon opened the passenger door just as Suel started the car.

"You might as well hold on for a second, Paddy. Let's see where they're going. It looks like they're heading toward the N1."

"Both cars?"

"Yeah, looks like they're going to move in our direction."

Suel turned the engine off and gave a sigh. "I've never in me life left close to a half-pint of Guinness in a glass and walked out of a pub."

"Oh gee, sorry, a new low in your life. Let's see where they go."

"Probably got word you were buying pints, and they're headed up here."

Dillon watched as the two cars made their way onto the N1 heading east toward the M50. His phone rang, and he was about to send the call into voicemail until he noticed it was from DaVanni.

"Yeah, Dennis, what's happening with Phalen?"

"Looks like he's pulled into a petrol station on Church Road in Malahide, and he's probably filling up. What's with your two?"

"They're heading east on the N1. Could be they're going to turn onto the M1 or even head into the city center. Dessie Phalen is following Krupin. I'm thinking this is it."

As Dillon said that, Suel nodded and climbed out of the car. He opened the boot, pulled out two protective vests, placed them in the back seat, and climbed back in behind the wheel.

"Keep us posted," Dillon said and disconnected.

"So, what's the news?"

"You heard Phalen's gassing up. DaVanni's moving into the city center, and he's going to wait there depending on where Krupin goes." Dillon checked his phone again. "They're a couple miles from the M1, we'll see if they get on it."

Two minutes later, Dillon said, "They're on the M1, heading north toward us."

Suel started the car, checked his side-view mirror, and pulled away from the curb.

Dillon called DaVanni. "Dennis, they just turned onto the M1, heading north. We're going to move up by the entrance and wait. We'll be able to pull onto the M1 heading either North or South. Whichever way they decide to go."

"I'll stay in position here just over the Liffey by the Customs House. Let me know if they pass Palmers Town, and I'll move up by Fairview Park."

Dillon went back to watching the two vehicles. Suel took a left at the light onto Ballymun Road. They drove past the Ballymun library, the Setanta GAA club, a Garda Station, and a number of shops, then waited for the light to change at Santry Avenue.

"They still heading North on the M1?" Suel asked.

"Slowly but surely," Dillon said. He pressed the call button on his phone, and when DaVanni answered, Dillon said, "They just passed Palmers Town still on the M1."

"Okay, Phalen is heading south on Malahide Road."

Suel jumped in. "You know where I'm thinking? Howth. And there's a yacht club there. A boat could dock, and no one would be the wiser. They'd pay a fee to stay for a few hours or even a day and head back to wherever they came from."

Dillon couldn't disagree. He thought about sending the information to DaVanni and immediately decided against it. The light changed, and Suel pulled forward toward the roundabout. He drove up over the curb and parked on the grass. The driver behind them leaned on the horn as he sped past.

"We can go either way from here. Let's just sit and wait. If they're coming this way, they should pass us in about ten minutes."

"Good idea," Dillon said, then called DaVanni and gave him the information.

"Okay, I'm going to wait a couple of minutes and then start heading up Howth Road," DaVanni said. "Any change, let me know. Phalen is still heading down Malahide Road, just coming up to St. Doolaghs. He seems to be in no particular hurry."

"Same with Krupin and Dessie. They're just driving the speed limit, not attracting any attention."

Five minutes later, Dillon watched on his phone as Krupin and Dessie Phalen drove past the roundabout where Dillon and Suel were waiting. "They just passed us," Dillon said.

Suel turned on the car, waited for a car to pass, then pulled onto the road. Three-quarters of the way around the roundabout, he took the entrance onto the M50.

A moment later, Dillon said, "There they are up ahead in the left lane. It's the Kia, and Krupin should be just ahead of them."

Suel increased his speed slightly, keeping a car between him and Dessie Phalen's Kia.

"He's got his left blinker on," Dillon said.

"Yeah, I see it. This is the exit going to Howth. I'm still thinking that damn Marina out there."

DaVanni suddenly called. "Phalen is turning onto the R139, heading toward Howth. I'm four or five minutes behind him."

"We're doing the same," Dillon said as they took the exit off the M50 and followed, making a half-circle over the M50 and onto the R139 heading toward Howth.

THIRTY-FIVE

They drove on the R139 for another ten minutes. It was still bright out, and Suel didn't have the headlights on. Most of the time, he was able to keep another vehicle in front of them all the way to Baldoyle, a small town on the coast. They took a right onto the R106 for a couple of miles and then turned left onto Burrow Road. They drove past Burrow Beach. The Howth Yacht club was just a mile or two ahead.

Dillon phoned DaVanni and asked, "Where are you?"

"Just passed the Aldi store and heading into Baldoyle. I'm hanging back. There's no one but Phalen ahead of me."

"We're on Howth Road, coming up to the yacht club. They're slowing and heading into the yacht club parking lot. Burrow eventually turns into Claremont Road. Once it changes names, take the next right. That will bring you onto Howth Road. Follow the signs to the yacht club. We're sitting in the parking lot of Crabby Jo's seafood. It's a white building with dark blue trim. Suel's car has the flashers on," Dillon said and nodded at Suel.

"See you in a couple of minutes," DaVanni said.

Sure enough, three minutes later, he pulled in next to their car and lowered his window.

Dillon lowered his window and said, "They pulled into the Yacht Club. There's a large parking lot where he'll have to park and then walk to the boat, wherever that is. There have to be at least two hundred slips. You got any idea what we're looking for?"

"It's a sailboat," DaVanni said. "Any idea what your guys are wearing."

Dillon shook his head and said, "No. What about your backup team? Where are they?"

"On their way. They should be here shortly."

"Follow us. We're going to park at the yacht club," Suel said. He started the car and backed out of the parking place. He stopped at the exit, glanced both ways, and then sped across the street toward the parking lot. "The backup team should be here shortly. Jesus Christ, are you kidding? They should be here now. We've no idea where in the hell these fools are meeting up. A sailboat, for God's sake, there are over two hundred slips, and by the way, they're all sailboats, and now we're somehow supposed to find these knackers?"

"Yeah, a little bit odd," Dillon said as they pulled into the yacht club parking lot.

Suel glanced around and then drove down a lane and parked next to a black Kia Sorento. Krupin's black BMW coupe was parked just four spaces away.

Suel looked around, checking the parking lot, then opened the backdoor and pulled out a black protective vest. He quickly took off his shirt, slipped the vest on, tightened the straps, and pulled his shirt back over the vest. Dillon was in the process of doing the same thing when DaVanni walked over. Dillon was about to ask him if he had a vest but then noticed he had one on beneath his shirt.

"You guys armed?" DaVanni asked.

Both Dillon and Suel nodded. "What about your response team?" Dillon asked.

"We should see them any minute. They're hoping we'll have a sighting of the boat these guys are on," DaVanni said.

Suel shook his head, swore, and said, "Well, we're not going to find it standing around in the parking lot. Let's go," he said and hurried around the blue and white striped yacht club building, past three porta-potties and over to the harbor. Dillon and DaVanni followed. There was a long pier that led across the harbor. Five docks led off the lefthand side of the pier. Each dock had fifty slips, twenty-five on either side of the dock. Virtually all but a half-dozen slips had a boat moored. The bad news was they were looking for a sailboat, and every boat in the harbor had a main mast. They were all sailboats.

DaVanni's phone rang, and he answered. "Yeah. Okay. No, not yet. We're in the harbor trying to find them now. Okay," he said and hung up. "Let's split up, and each take a dock. We're just guys looking at boats.

You see something get in touch. You have my number, Suel?"

"Yeah, I do."

"Okay, then, let's get started. I'll take this one. You two take the middle one and the end one. Let's go," Davanni said and began to stroll down the dock.

"Jesus Christ, and this passes for organization," Suel mumbled. "Why don't you take that third dock, and I'll check out the last one. I don't see anyone, so if they're here, they're down below. Keep an eye peeled."

"You do the same, Paddy," Dillon said. Suel headed down the pier to the last dock while Dillon strolled down the third dock. He didn't know much about boats in general and even less about sailboats. He did know one thing. There was an awful lot of money invested in each and every one of these vessels. A number of the doors to the cabins had locks and chains on them, which suggested to Dillon there have been a problem with people breaking in or possibly even taking up residence for a day or two.

He was walking past a sailboat at least thirty-five feet in length. It was white with dark wood trim that looked like mahogany. On the back hung a rack with a smaller motorized dingy attached. Dillon heard some noise coming from below. Something bumping and voices, but was it people down there or just a radio? The door to the galley suddenly opened, and a young blonde woman in a very small light-blue bikini stepped up onto the deck. She stretched for a moment and moved her head from side to side, then turned around and got a surprised look on her face when she saw Dillon.

Dillon studied her lovely figure for a long moment and said, "Good evening."

She nodded and said, "Same to you," just as a gray-haired guy stepped onto the deck. He had red scratch marks up and down the back of his shoulders.

He turned and looked at Dillon. "Can I help you?" he said in a tone that suggested anything but wanting to help.

Dillon was tempted to tell him he had a lovely daughter but decided against it. "Just admiring your boat, very nice. Have a pleasant evening," Dillon said and continued along the dock. He walked to the far end and then turned and headed back to the pier. Only the crabby old guy was visible. The gorgeous young blonde had apparently gone below.

He walked back to the pier, over to the fourth dock, and repeated the exercise. He glanced over and saw Suel heading back up the pier.

Suel looked over and shook his head.

Dillon glanced over to the first pier and saw DaVanni on his phone. Had he seen something and was calling his response team? Dillon stopped. He attempted to get DaVanni's attention without any luck, so he continued on his walk along the dock.

He passed a guy in a swimsuit and a t-shirt attaching a window to the cabin. The man looked over at Dillon, smiled, nodded, but didn't say anything and went back to work. Dillon walked to the end of the dock and looked around the harbor. Just across the way was a cabin cruiser. Navy blue with a white top. It appeared to be tied up to the harbor wall.

There was a young guy seated behind the wheel of the cabin cruiser, drinking from a mug. Dillon guessed it might be tea or possibly coffee. He was tanned and somewhat muscular in shorts and a strappy t-shirt. He wore flip-flops and seemed focused on his cellphone.

What really caught Dillon's attention was the small inflatable dingy with an outboard motor tied to the ladder at the back of the cabin cruiser. Dillon studied the dingy for a long moment, then turned his back to the cruiser and stretched, hoping to give the impression of someone in no hurry. He headed back up the dock, ducked between two larger sailboats, and placed a call to DaVanni.

"Dillon."

"Yeah, Dennis, you spot anything?"

"Unfortunately not. I'm wondering if they may have gone into the clubhouse."

"I think I saw something, not sure, but it could be what we're looking for. There's a cabin cruiser, dark blue hull, white upper cabin tied to the harbor wall. A young guy is just sitting behind the wheel, muscular, tan, dressed like you would on a boat. Thing is, there's a dingy with an outboard tied to the ladder at the back of the cruiser. The kind of dingy you'd take to pull along-side and climb aboard. Otherwise, with the exception of a blonde in a bikini, I didn't see anything."

"Stay on the line. Let me walk down and check it out. Did you spot a name on the cabin cruiser?"

"No, if it's on the back, I'm not in a position to see it. I'm on the fourth dock. I'm not sure going over to the fifth would give me a better angle."

"Okay. Yeah, I see it now. Hold on, let me check something. Shit. Tell you what, I'll call you back," he said and disconnected.

Dillon waited for what felt like close to an hour. It was actually just a few minutes when his phone rang.

"What'd you find out?"

"They're thinking that could be it. Here's the thing, if it is, they're going to put people in that dingy tied to the back, and they'll head for shore. The cruiser will want to get out of here, so they'll make their way to the harbor entrance and head into open water. The team will grab them, and we'll take care of the little dingy, bringing the Phalen's and, or, Krupin back to shore."

"Where do you want Suel and me?"

"Make your way into the yacht club, one at a time. Don't walk together. Take up a position at one of the windows and watch. If they're in the cruiser, I think they'll be leaving sooner rather than later. We'd want to wait until they're out of the dingy, on land, and carrying the Rothko paintings."

"Is your team going to be able to stop that cruiser?"

"Yeah, they know what they're doing."

THIRTY-SIX

Dillon phoned Suel and gave him the news about the cruiser. "No Kidding? I didn't even see that thing," Suel said.

"Not to worry, it's easy to miss. Where are you now?"

"I'm on the pier heading toward land. I can be in the yacht club in about two minutes."

"Okay. Go inside and call me when you're there. I'll be a couple of minutes behind you. While you're in there, look around and see if you can find a pair of binoculars."

"Yeah, okay. See you in a bit," Suel said and disconnected. He sent Dillon a text message a minute later. *'In the yacht club.'*

Dillon waited two more minutes and then took what he hoped looked like a leisurely stroll along the pier and into the yacht club. Suel was standing in front of a window, looking out on the harbor. "Anything happening?"

Dillon shook his head and said, "Not yet."

"There's a shop upstairs. I'll run up and see if they have any binoculars. Text me if something happens. I'll be right back," Suel said and hurried over to a flight of stairs.

Dillon watched the cruiser tied to the harbor wall, hoping Suel would hurry up and get back. A few minutes later, the guy behind the steering wheel on the cruiser suddenly stood and shoved his cellphone into his pocket. A moment later, someone stepped out of the galley. From this distance, it could quite possibly be the blonde-haired Russian with the tattooed fingers on his left hand, but Dillon wasn't sure and wished to hell Suel would get back.

"Got them," Suel suddenly called as he hurried down the staircase with a blue paper bag labeled 'Yacht Club' in yellow letters. He reached into the bag and handed the binoculars to Dillon.

Dillon put the binoculars up against his eyes and focused them on the blonde-haired figure just as someone stepped in the way. Dillon moved slightly and focused on Dessie Phalen. The two shook hands, hugged, and Dessie went over the side and climbed down the ladder. Aidan Phalen suddenly appeared, holding the handles on a metal case that looked six feet long. He shook hands with the blonde Russian and then turned and shook hands with an older gentleman Dillon recognized as Pavel Krupin. He'd studied Krupin's photo online.

Phalen handed the metal case over the side to his son. He waited a moment, then gave a final wave and proceeded to climb down the ladder. Eventually, they pushed off from the back of the cruiser. Aidan Phalen gave two pulls on the outboard, and they headed for shore, steering directly toward the clubhouse.

Dillon and Suel waited inside as the Phalen's drew closer to shore.

Dillon glanced over at the cruiser. The young man who had been sitting in the driver's seat was now standing on the bow of the boat, untying a rope. Someone else Dillon didn't recognize was doing the same thing at the back of the boat. Once he was finished, they both pushed against the harbor wall, and the cruiser drifted away from the wall. The man Dillon didn't recognize settled into the driver's seat, fired up the cruiser, and slowly began to make their way out of the harbor.

"What in the hell? Those bastards are getting away," Suel said.

"Let them go. The guys we want, at least this jackass Dessie Phalen, are heading for shore. That cruiser is DaVanni's problem, not ours."

They waited for the inflatable dingy to pull into a spot at the first dock. Dessie jumped out and tied the dingy to the dock. He took the metal case his father handed to him and placed it on the dock, and then extended a hand to help his father out of the dingy.

Aidan said something, and they both laughed. He placed his arm around his son, gave him a hug, then picked up the metal case and stepped off the dock and onto the pier.

"Wait for it. Wait," Dillon said as the father and son team headed up the sidewalk. Just in front of the door, they turned toward the parking lot. "Now," Dillon said as Suel ripped the door open, almost tearing it off its hinges.

"Hold it right there, stop," Dillon shouted.

Both Phalen's looked over their shoulder. Dessie Phalen began to reach beneath his shirt as his father started to run.

Dennis DaVanni suddenly appeared around the corner of the building with his gun drawn. "Stop right there. Stop, damn it," he shouted just as Dessie Phalen turned, squinted into the setting sun, and fired a round at Dillon.

Dillon and Suel both returned fire. Dessie appeared to take a half-step back, dropped his pistol, and fell to the ground.

Aidan Phalen had glanced over his shoulder and shouted something just as Dillon and Suel fired. When Dessie fell, Aidan dropped the metal case and ran toward his son.

"Hold your fire. Hold your fire," DaVanni shouted as he followed Phalen with his gun drawn. Dillon and Suel had spread apart and approached with their weapons aimed at Phalen.

"Dessie, Dessie," Phalen shouted. He was on his knees with his arms wrapped around his son.

Suel kicked the son's pistol off to the side and then slapped a handcuff on Phalen's wrist. He pulled his arm behind his back and cuffed his other arm.

"No, no, Dessie? Dessie? He needs a doctor. Call an ambulance. Call a damn ambulance," Phalen shouted.

Dillon looked at the son groaning on the ground with blood seeping from his right shoulder and arm. He pulled Dessie's belt off his jeans and fashioned a tourniquet around his upper arm. Then took a plastic baggie from a pocket of his vest, laid it over the shoulder wound, and placed pressure on the wound to slow the bleeding. Dessie's eyes closed, but he continued to breathe. Suel was already on the phone with emergency services.

"No. No. No." Aidan Phalen sobbed just as a low-flying helicopter raced across the harbor. A man in a camouflaged protective vest sat on the floor of the chopper. His feet were dangling out the door. He held what looked like an MP5 submachine gun.

"Watch him for a moment," DaVanni said. He walked over to the metal case, turned it over, clicked both latches open, lifted the lid, nodded, and lowered the lid.

The distant sound of automatic weapons fire came from somewhere outside the harbor, and then a voice on a loudspeaker said, "Drop your weapon and raise your hands. Raise your hands. Do it now."

Dessie Phalen was transported to St. James's hospital. Aidan, his father, was hauled to Special Branch. As they were being taken away, the cabin cruiser reentered the harbor. Two armed men, wearing camouflaged protective vests, stood on the deck, holding submachine guns. Apparently, three men were sitting on the deck of the cruiser, but Dillon could only make out the tops of their heads. The cruiser headed into a slip on the second dock where four armed officers were waiting.

Once it was secured in the slip, the three men were helped off the cruiser and led into the rear of a black Garda van that had backed into a parking place next to the Yacht Club. A small crowd of approximately a dozen people, workers and yacht club members, were watching from the terrace on the second floor as the handcuffed men were led into the back of the van.

Dillon recognized the young man wearing shorts and flip-flops he'd seen focused on his cellphone on the boat, and then there was Pavel Krupin and the blonde Russian guy. As they were led past, Dillon saw the tattoos on the blonde Russian's left hand cuffed behind his back. It was a safe bet none of the three were happy.

DaVanni turned over the metal case to two individuals wearing suits and ties and then walked over to Dillon and Suel. "I want to thank you both for your help today. We couldn't have pulled this off without you. In fact, it probably would have been me being taken to the hospital instead of Phalen's kid."

"Yeah, we had him. He should have just surrendered," Dillon said.

Suel shook his head and said, "Young and dumb, too many movies."

THIRTY-SEVEN

Suel drove Dillon down to the Autobahn to get his car. They were back in Special Branch just before 10:00 p.m., and they'd been going through the standard post-operation interviews. There were a few pats on the back and 'Glad you're okay' comments from Special Branch members. At the moment, Dillon, Suel, and DaVanni were in DCI McCabe's office. There was also another FBI man named Wilson, who, apparently, DaVanni reported to. He was one of the two men Da-Vanni had handed the metal case to. The case was resting on the floor in front of him.

"Here's the problem as I see it. Even though the news trucks and reporters were kept at a distance, you are going to have to hold a news conference. Clearly, someone was shot. Five people were arrested and led away, one of whom was shot twice. If we can withhold names of the arrested individuals, as well as the individual wounded for forty-eight hours, we might be able to get the person who orchestrated this event."

"Any idea who that might be?" McCabe asked.

"We're thinking, and have always thought, he's an Irish national by the name of Royce Farley. We've had him under surveillance for the past eight days. He's met twice with your man Phalen. He has the financial capability to put this together, and last but not least, he funded Phalen's week-long trip to the States visiting Martin Lane prior to Lane's death two years ago."

"And you know this how?'"

"We've watched Phalen for a few years. We played a tangent role in his arrest in Italy. Farley's company paid not only for Phalen's flight but for his accommodations as well. We kept an eye on Mr. Phalen from the time he was released until he got back on the plane to Dublin."

"I'm still not following. How do you intend to get Farley involved?"

"You make an offer to Phalen. He and his son are going to be facing a long stretch behind bars. The son was wounded. Offer to give him some special care, a few years off, or offer Phalen something. Could be that, after the way today turned out, he just might like to see Farley pay a price. You can instill some interest in Mr. Farley with this," Wilson said and pushed the empty aluminum case toward Dillon using his foot.

Two hours later, Dillon, Suel, and DaVanni were studying Aidan Phalen, sitting in Interview Room Two. He was attached to the table by a metal chain wrapped around his waist. "You ready?" Dillon asked.

"I will be in a minute. Let me just make a call," DaVanni said. "I want to give him an update on his son."

"They'll probably have him sedated. The wound on the arm went through the bicep. I don't think the bone was damaged. Hopefully, that upper chest wound missed any arteries."

"We'll find out in just a—Yeah, Tommy, Dennis DaVanni. We're about to try and garner information from Aidan Phalen. He's the father of your hospital patient. What's his status? Mmm-hmm. How long ago? Recovery time? Is he secure? Oh, that's too bad. Drink plenty of coffee. All right, thank you. Anything develops, let me know. Yeah, good luck to you, too."

"That didn't sound too good," Suel said.

"Oh, no, that was more a comment on him having to pull a double shift. No, the patient is doing well under the circumstances. You were right. He's sedated. Staff is checking him hourly. The surgery was successful. He's cuffed to the bedrail, so he's not going anywhere. He will begin a prescribed diet of more or less solid food beginning with breakfast tomorrow morning. Security, in the form of Agent Tunney, will be just outside the door until 8:00 tomorrow morning, at which time, Tunney will be relieved by another agent."

"Let's see what we can learn from Mr. Phalen," Dillon said, and they headed out of the viewing room and over to Interview Room Two. Dillon glanced at Suel and DaVanni and then gave a polite knock on the metal door as he opened it.

"Hi, Mr. Phalen. We'd like to ask you a few questions," Dillon said. "I'm US Marshal Jack Dillon. This is DI Paddy Suel. We're both assigned to An Garda Síochána, Special Branch, here in Dublin. This gentleman standing behind us is FBI Agent Dennis DaVanni. Before we get started, can I get you anything? A tea or a glass of water?"

"Thanks, I'm fine."

"Need a run to the loo? We can get you an escort."

"No, thanks. Let's just get this over with. Okay? It hasn't been my best day."

"I hear you," Dillon said as he and Suel sat down across from Phalen. DaVanni leaned back against the wall, three feet away and behind Dillon and Suel.

Dillon turned on the laptop, hit record, and went through the standard routine, getting a verbal okay from Phalen that he was there and talking with them of his own free will. Once he was finished with the necessary procedure, Dillon said, "First, let me give you an update on your son, Dessie. He's doing fine. The surgery was a success. He's been given a sedative to enhance recovery, allowing him to relax, basically sleep, and let the body begin to heal."

"You didn't have to shoot him. He—"

"Actually, Aidan. If you'll recall, he shot first. We simply returned fire, which, if someone has ever shot at you, you'll understand is a necessary and automatic response. I don't mean this unkindly, and I know it's horrific to experience, but the situation that you placed him in led to his getting shot as one of the logical consequences."

"Are you aware of the rape and attempted murder charges pending against your son and that blonde Russian knacker with the tattoos on his left hand?" Suel asked.

"Rape and attempted murder? Who are you trying to kid? My son—"

"Pardon me for interrupting," Suel said as he held up his hand, "but your son, along with the blonde-haired Russian who stayed in your home, is on security tapes drugging women's drinks. The two of them raped a woman down in Killinardin Park in Tallaght. They beat the shit out of her and left her for dead. Only she survived. They've been identified by a number of women who fought them off, along with a half-dozen witnesses who can identify them. Dessie's 2020 black Kia Sorento has been identified as the vehicle they used."

Phalen shook his head. "I don't believe a word of what you're saying."

"Well, I think you'd better start," Dillon said. "A number of assaults, rape, attempted murder, his attempt to murder the two of us this afternoon. There's a good possibility your son isn't going to see the light of a free day ever again."

"But, but he's a—"

"He's a rapist and a thief. He attempted to shoot two An Garda Síochána officers just today. No, let me be honest here, Mr. Phalen. Your son is in deep trouble, and he's going down, big time, as are you. You will not be released before your trial. After the trial, you will be escorted from the courtroom and begin serving time. Given the charges, you're both liable to spend the rest of your days behind bars. We're meeting with you now, strictly as a courtesy. But let me be very clear. This will be your one and only chance to convince us there might be some benefit to allowing a little leeway on your sentence. After this meeting, all bets are off. It's your choice."

Phalen seemed to think for a long moment. Eventually, he gave a slight nod and then said, "All right, all right. What would you like to know?"

"Be nice to start at the beginning. Remember, we're taping this conversation," Dillon said.

THIRTY-EIGHT

It took the better part of two-and-a-half hours, but Aidan Phalen went into detail. It turned out he was aware of the original robbery from the Patrick Kincannon Abstract Art Museum in New Orleans within twenty-four hours of it happening. He'd received a phone call from an American the following day informing him of the burglary. That led to Aidan phoning Royce Farley forty-eight hours later, knowing Farley had an insatiable interest in Rothko paintings. They met, discussed what was known of the burglary, and that was pretty much it until nineteen years later when Phalen received word that Martin Lane, the surviving suspect in the robbery, was in poor health.

Phalen flew to New Orleans, met Lane, and visited him every ninety days for the remaining two years of his life. It turned out Lane was pretty much a loner. No family, no real friends, and still in possession of eight stolen paintings. The unanswered question was where, exactly, were the paintings? As Lane lay dying in his bed during the final week of his life, Aidan Phalen ransacked his house and finally found the paintings hidden in the wall behind the bedroom dresser.

He left Lane to die and contacted Pavel Krupin to work out the specifics of getting the eight Rothko canvases into Ireland. The canvases were kept in a storage locker not more than two blocks from the Kincannon Art Museum for over a year before Krupin began the process of transporting them into the Republic of Ireland. They were flown by commercial air to Portugal. A private vehicle drove them across the EU and into the UK. From the UK, Scotland actually, they traveled in a private cabin cruiser along the Irish coast and into the Malahide Yacht Club. Were it not for the pressure created by the search of Phalen's home, the Rothko paintings would probably have been placed in the hands of Royce Farley earlier in the evening.

"Were you going to take the paintings to Farley?" DaVanni asked.

Phalen nodded. "I was going to send him a text. He gave me the number. It's a burner phone. I have a burner I'm supposed to use to send the text to him. We established a four-day window when I would contact him. After that, we would have to reestablish contact procedures. Once I contacted him and received a reply, I would deliver the paintings."

"And he knows what you look like? He can identify you?"

"Yes, we've met at least a half-dozen times."

"You were going to deliver these paintings to his home?"

"Close to his home, in Phoenix Park, actually. At the top of the Papal Cross hill. That way, we could both make sure we weren't being followed."

"And he would pay you in cash?"

"Good Lord, no. He would send payment to an overseas account in the Cayman Islands. Once I received notice of the payment, I would hand over the paintings to Farley."

"It seems there could be a number of ways Farley would be able to take advantage of you and, by the same token, you of him."

Phalen nodded and said, "Yes, and with the contacts I have, he would also be aware he wouldn't live to see another sunset. It's just a way to do business, provide an incentive."

"Where is that burner phone now?"

"The burner? It's in my home."

The room was quiet for a moment. Phalen's "offer" was on the table.

Finally, Dillon said, "And what are you hoping for?"

"I'd like the charges dropped on both me and my son, Dessie. If you can do that, we'll leave the country and never return."

Dillon shook his head. "I'm afraid that's not going to happen. First of all, as we mentioned, your son is facing a series of charges unrelated to this specific situation, and he will be charged. We may be interested in reducing some time served for you, but I must stress the word 'may.' We have the paintings. We have you. We have your son, and we have Pavel Krupin. Other than Royce Farley, are we missing anyone?"

A smile slowly spread across Phalen's face. "The Garda Officer who kept us informed of what you were doing up until today. He slowed the investigation of my son and his accomplice, and he provided us with information regarding your interest in my particular business venture. Unfortunately, it appears he was woefully wrong. Still, he is a member of your department and more than willing to make information available for a price."

"So you would testify against DI Horace Tevlin?" Dillon said.

Phalen appeared more than a little surprised at Tevlin's name, then quickly recovered. "Umm, yes, of course, I would testify."

Dillon glanced over at Suel. Suel pulled out a business card, wrote on the back of the card, and pushed it over to Dillon.

Sentence 5 yrs. They serve 2.5 and leave country.

"We'll see what we can do. Found guilty, you'll be looking at five years. You'll serve half that and then leave the country. Never to return," Dillon said.

"That's for both me and Dessie."

"Yes, regarding involvement with the paintings. As far as the other charges against your son, we're not involved in that aspect, and there's nothing we can do, especially with the assault of a number of women."

"No, this has to cover Dessie or the deal is off."

Dillon looked at Phalen for a long moment and then said. "Well, okay, if that's the way you want it, we've nothing else to say. Enjoy your stay, Mr. Phalen." He stood, nodded at Suel and DaVanni, and they headed for the door. He said a quick prayer on the way, hoping Phalen would change his mind.

They had actually opened the door when Phalen called, "Okay, okay. Yeah. I'll do two-and-a-half years and leave the country. Dessie will have to deal with the results of his other activities."

Suel's back was to Phalen, and he gave Dillon a quick wink and followed him back to the table.

"You made the right decision, Mr. Phalen. I'll draw up a contractual agreement and be back. I'd like to contact Royce Farley on the burner phone as soon as possible."

"Once I see the agreement in writing," Phalen said.

"Trust me. You'll get it. It's after midnight, and I'd like to contact Farley as soon—"

"I'm sorry, but I have to see the agreement."

Dillon turned to Suel and said, "Would you and Agent DaVanni mind keeping Mr. Phalen company while I run up and type this agreement out?"

"My pleasure," Suel said.

DaVanni simply nodded. Dillon hurried out of the interview room and entered the Special Branch office a minute or two later. He hurried to his desk, turned on the computer, and typed out the agreement. He emailed a copy to DCI McCabe, then printed off four copies. He grabbed some pens from the desk next to his and hurried back to the interview room. He stopped at the door, took two deep breaths, and stepped inside.

Suel looked up and nodded as Dillon walked over to the table. "Here it is. I printed off four copies. Each of us will sign all four copies. Questions?"

Everyone shook their head. Dillon handed the pens to Suel and DaVanni. "I'm afraid you're going to have to wait a moment, Mr. Phalen. Once we've signed these, you can sign all four sheets and keep a copy. I'll let the guards know you have a sheet of paper."

Suel signed each sheet and passed them to DaVanni, who signed even though he really didn't have any say in the matter. Still, an FBI signature might just carry some weight. Dillon took all four copies and handed them along with a pen to Phalen.

Phalen took his time reading each copy, even though they were identical, and then signed and handed them back to Dillon.

"Thank you, now, entrance to your home along with the code and phone number to send Farley."

"The code to turn on the phone is 20012022, the year the paintings were taken from the New Orleans Museum, and this year, the year they'll theoretically arrive in Farley's hands," Phalen said and then smiled.

"How do we get into your home?"

"There's a large flowerpot with red geraniums next to the front door. A key to the house is buried just below the surface at the back of the pot. A plastic insert from the geraniums is inserted on top of the key. Once you know it's there, you can't miss it. Now, my alarm is set. So, once you step inside, punch in the code, 1791. That's the year I was born, 1971, backwards. You'll find the burner phone in the top drawer of the cabinet in the front hall. The code to send Farley is the phrase, 'ready and waiting.' All one word, no space between the words, and no capital letters. Farley will respond with a time. My advice is to be in Phoenix Park when you send your text message. He lives nearby. He's anxious, and he just might rush over. He's only a matter of a few minutes away."

"Will he ask any questions? Want some sort of re-ply?"

Phalen shook his head. "He's not supposed to."

"Paddy. Why don't you stay here? Just in case Far-ley asks a question or wants some sort of confirmation, I can send it to you, and you can show it to Mr. Phalen."

"Yeah, okay, just mind yourself," Suel said.

"You kidding? I'll have the FBI watching over me."

They called the guard, who arrived a few minutes later. Suel followed them out and down to Phalen's cell. Dillon and DaVanni hurried out to Dillon's car and headed up to Malahide. Dillon turned his flashing lights on, not that there was much traffic on the road at that hour. They made the drive to Malahide in record time.

THIRTY-NINE

They pulled onto The Sycamores and drove down to the end of the street and the Phalen home. Dillon noted that all the front porch lights along the street were still on. He compared the difference between here, in a very elite and high-priced neighborhood of unattached homes, and the middle-class Tallaght neighborhood where Pavel Krupin lived. The gate was open to the brick drive leading up to the house. Dillon pulled in and parked in front of the four-panel window made up of diamond-shaped pieces of beveled glass. They climbed out of the car and headed toward the front door.

The large pot of red geraniums was just as Phalen had described. The little plastic tag with the image of red geraniums was inserted at the back of the pot. DaVanni reached down, placed his index finger in the soil, and pulled out the house key. As he stepped toward the door, he gave a wave.

"What are you doing?" Dillon asked.

"It's a wireless doorbell. The thing has a camera, and somewhere, probably on Phalen's cellphone, is the monitor." He inserted the key in the lock, turned it, and then glanced over at Dillon. "Are you ready?"

"I've got the code here on my phone, 1-7-9-1," Dillon said. "The year Phalen was born, input backwards."

"Okay, let's hope it works," DaVanni said as he turned the doorknob and opened the door.

An alarm immediately began chirping a warning. The keypad was just next to the door, and Dillon quickly entered 1-7-9-1. The alarm stopped a second later. DaVanni was already pulling open the top drawer on the mahogany cabinet in the front hall.

"Just like he told us," Davanni said and held up the burner phone.

"Let's not text anything until we're down in Phoenix Park. If Farley is all worked up about the paintings, he's liable to drive into the park as soon as the code comes across."

"As long as we're in here, do you want to take a look around?"

Dillon shook his head. "I just want to get this over and done with. The sooner, the better. Let's go, lock the door behind us, and hang onto the key."

He headed out the door. DaVanni took a moment to look around the entry before he followed Dillon out the door. Dillon had the car started by the time DaVanni climbed in. He backed out of the driveway, put the flashing blue lights on, and hurried back to Dublin. They pulled into Phoenix Park eighteen minutes later.

"Is it safe to open my eyes now?" DaVanni asked. "You must have been doing eighty miles an hour."

"Closer to a hundred, but who's counting?" Dillon said as they drove up Chesterfield Avenue in the center of Phoenix Park. He took the roundabout to Acres Road, which led to the Papal Cross parking lot. The Papal Cross is a simple white cross, 116 feet high, and made of steel. It was built to honor the Papal visit of Pope John Paul II back in September of 1979. It stands on a hill with granite steps leading up to the Cross.

There was absolutely no traffic at this hour. Dillon thought there might be someone, somewhere, sleeping in a car or even a tent, but nothing like that was apparent. He pulled to the front of the parking lot and stopped. They both climbed out of the car. Dillon opened the trunk, removed the shiny aluminum case, and then handed a protective vest to DaVanni. He pulled a second vest out of the trunk, took off his sports shirt, put the vest on, and then worked his shirt back over the vest. He reached into the trunk and grabbed a black stocking cap.

"What are you thinking of doing?" DaVanni asked.

"I'm thinking we send Farley a text message. I'll stand up on top of the hill with the case. Once Farley pulls in and gets out of his car, you can drive up and block the entrance. I'm afraid he's liable to have someone with him, possibly more than one person, so be prepared. I've got this stocking cap to hopefully disguise myself and with any luck make him think I might be Phalen."

DaVanni nodded and said, "Well, at least worth a try. You ready?"

"As ready as I'll ever be. Let's see if you get a response."

DaVanni took out the burner phone and input the code 20012022. The phone chimed, and the screen lit up. "Okay, time to text him 'readyandwaiting,'" DaVanni said and began tapping on a small keyboard.

"Remember, it's all one word," Dillon said. "No spaces."

"Yeah, I know. All set?" DaVanni turned the cellphone toward Dillon.

"Yeah, perfect. Send it, Dennis."

DaVanni tapped the screen, and a moment later, the cellphone sounded a ding. "I guess now we just wait for a response."

"Just in case he's already here, I'm going up the hill. When you hear from him, send me a text from your phone. I'll be out of sight until he's parked and climbs out of his car," Dillon said.

DaVanni took Dillon's car keys and pulled out of the parking lot. Dillon took the stairs halfway up the hill. He stopped and watched the taillights on his car turn onto the roundabout and then back onto Chesterfield Avenue. Once the taillights disappeared, Dillon continued his climb to the top of the hill and looked around. It would be dark for at least another hour, or an hour and a half. From where he stood on the hill, he would be able to spot any vehicle approaching. He pulled out his cellphone and checked the time, 4:07 am. Now all he had to do was wait.

He checked the time on his cellphone for the third time, 4:32 am. Twenty-five minutes and still no answer. Apparently, Farley was sound asleep and unaware the message had even been sent.

Dillon glanced around for the umpteenth time. The only traffic he saw was a city bus driving down Chapelizod Road with the illuminated banner that said, "Not In Service," where the route number would normally be displayed. He checked the time once more, 5:03 am. He felt as if he'd been on his feet for seventy-two hours straight. When he closed his eyes for a moment, they actually burned. At least it wasn't raining. Off to the east, there were hints of a gray sky signaling a sunrise not too far in the future. He was wondering if Farley had possibly learned of the arrests at the Malahide Yacht Club last night and was possibly on his way to a relaxing week in Paris or even Spain. It would make sense because—Dillon suddenly spotted a distant pair of headlights on Chesterfield Avenue, heading in his general direction. They were coming from the opposite direction he'd taken to enter the park, which would be in line with the location of Farley's home.

He sent DaVanni a text. *'Headlights coming down Chesterfield from Farley's direction.'*

He didn't receive a response, but then he didn't really expect one. Two minutes later, the headlights approached the roundabout and went almost completely around before taking the exit for Acres Road and heading toward the entrance to the Papal Cross parking lot. He sent DaVanni a short text. 'On Acres Road.'

Dillon watched as the vehicle stopped too far away to be identified. He thought he may have heard a car door slam but couldn't be sure. A minute later, the car slowed at the entrance to the parking lot. The vehicle fit the description DaVanni had given him of Farley's white Mercedes G Class. It slowly drove up the short lane to the parking lot and then, very slowly, turned in a half-circle illuminating the area with the lights on high beam. The vehicle leaned slightly to the right, and Dillon suspected that could be due to Farley's weight.

He sent a text to DaVanni, *'large white car in lot.'*
Finally, he got a response, *'coming.'*

FORTY

The car remained at the entrance. Dillon turned on the flashlight on his cellphone and pointed it in the direction of the car. He placed his hand over the screen and then removed it a number of times, hoping the flashing light would serve as a signal to Farley.

Apparently, it did because the headlights suddenly flashed, and the car headed across the parking lot toward the Papal Cross. Once the car parked and was turned off, Dillon used the flashlight to illuminate the shiny aluminum case at his feet.

The sky, although still gray, was beginning to lighten up ever so slightly, and as the driver's door to the Mercedes opened, the massive figure of Royce Farley slid out of the driver's seat. The Mercedes rocked back and forth. It looked like a military off-road vehicle with what appeared to be a support platform over the grill to push other vehicles. Farley closed the driver's door, appeared to take a couple of deep breaths, and waddled toward the asphalt path leading to the staircase. Dillon ran his phone back and forth to illuminate the shiny aluminum case at his feet.

Farley eventually made it to the base of the staircase. He stopped, leaned against the granite wall with the handrail, and attempted to catch his breath. He eventually started up the steps. After five or six steps, his heavy breathing became audible.

Dillon picked up the case and slowly made his way to the staircase as Farley continued to climb, hanging onto the stair rail and slowly taking one step at a time. Dillon could now clearly hear the occasional groan along with Farley's heavy breathing. He started down the staircase in no apparent hurry. His head was lowered and focused on his feet in an effort to hide his face.

Farley stopped for a long moment in an effort to catch his breath. He looked up toward Dillon and called, "Jesus Christ, Aidan, how in the hell did you make it all the way up there?"

"You's can do it, Royce," Dillon called, hoping he sounded somewhat like Phalen.

It must have worked because Farley shook his head, took a deep breath, and started to climb the stairs again. As they drew closer, Dillon set the case on a step, quickly opened the lid, and lifted the case up, holding it in such a way that it hid his face from Farley. "You're going to love these, lad. Gorgeous, absolutely gorgeous."

"Careful, Aidan, be a shame to drop them now after all we've been through. Oh, God, but it's a long way up. Bring them down to me, will you? I can't make it any further," Farley said, sounding completely exhausted after having made it no more than a quarter of the way up the steps.

Dillon continued moving down the stairs, keeping the open top of the shiny aluminum case in front of his face. He glanced from side to side every other step, checking for someone sneaking up, but didn't see anyone.

He was just four steps away from Farley, who was in the process of clearing his throat, spitting, and gasping for air, when a voice from behind Dillon suddenly said, "That's far enough. Put the case down, nice and easy like." Dillon began to turn, but whoever it was shoved a pistol against his back and said, "I wouldn't do that if I were you. Just keep on looking straight ahead."

Dillon set the case down, closed the lid, and said to Farley, "Take it, sir, and look inside. See that they're all there."

Farley took a deep breath, hurried as best he could up the four steps, and spun the case around. He appeared so anxious that he never gave Dillon a look, at least until he opened the case and stepped back.

"Aidan, where the hell are the—Wait a minute. You're not Aidan Phalen. Who the hell are you, and where are my Rothko paintings?"

"I'm just an emissary," Dillon said. "Aidan has everything up at the top of the hill just like he promised."

"What the hell? He's supposed to be alone," Farley groaned.

"As are you, sir. But, as we can see . . ."

Farley shook his head and said, "Follow him up to the top and get the damn paintings. I'll die of a heart attack if I go much further." Based on his flushed face, he was probably right.

Dillon raised his hands in surrender and said, "I'm going to turn around and head up the stairs. Okay?"

"Just don't do anything stupid."

Dillon turned and slowly headed up the stairs. The man with the gun was average-sized and looked to be forty. None of which mattered because he had a gun pointed at Dillon. As Dillon turned, the man had stepped off to the side and against the granite wall on the opposite side of the staircase. He'd be able to pull the trigger more than once before Dillon could come close to reaching him.

They headed up the stairs with Dillon wondering where in the hell DaVanni was. He literally had seconds to formulate a plan since the top of the hill consisted of the steel cross surrounded by a white wrought iron fence. Other than the cross and fence on a granite platform, there was nothing.

They reached the top of the stairs, and the man with the gun said, "Where the hell is he? What are you trying to—" Thunk.

Dillon turned as the man dropped to the granite-flagged platform, and DaVanni stood over him, holding his pistol by the barrel.

"Thank God. I was running out of options," Dillon said. "Cuff him. I'll go after Farley," he said and nodded toward Farley, attempting to waddle down the staircase, holding onto the handrail.

"Looks like you can take your time," DaVanni said as he slapped a handcuff around the man's wrist, then raised his arm and attached the cuff to the handrail on the granite wall. "I'll text backup for you."

Dillon was already heading down the stairs with his pistol drawn, taking the steps quickly. Farley's heavy breathing and coughing grew louder as Dillon approached. "You might as well stop, Royce. You're not going to make it," Dillon called. He'd just passed the aluminum case lying on the step and was only a few feet behind Farley.

"Agh, uff, agh," Farley gasped as Dillon closed the gap to just a foot or two.

"Royce, will you stop, for God's sake? It's over," Dillon said as red flashing lights suddenly appeared, speeding down Acres Road toward the parking lot. "You're not going anywhere."

"I…I didn't do anything. I was just trying to recover the paintings. Honest, I was going to hand them over, do the good deed."

Dillon had slowed to almost a walk alongside Farley at this point. He reached up, grabbed him by the sweaty collar, and leaned him up against the granite wall along the stairs. Red-faced, Farley bent forward with his hands on his knees, gasping and coughing.

"You can tell that to the judge," Dillon said as he took hold of Farley's right arm and slapped a handcuff onto his wrist. He gave Farley another minute or two before he tried to pull his left arm behind his back and attach the cuff to his wrist. Farley was so fat Dillon was afraid he'd cause his shoulder to pop out of the socket cuffing him behind his back. Instead, he cuffed his hands in front of him.

Three vehicles with lights still flashing were parked around Farley's Mercedes. The officers were walking up the asphalt path toward the granite staircase. DaVanni must have contacted them because they didn't appear to be in any hurry.

Farley glanced down at the handcuffs on his wrists and then looked at the half-dozen uniformed officers heading their way. "Please take these off me and tell them I was on your side. Please. I can make it very worth your while. I promise."

"Come on, Farley. I'll help you down the stairs. You're going to have plenty of time to rest up."

FORTY-ONE

After getting five hours of well-deserved sleep, Dillon, Suel, and DaVanni were back in Special Branch just after the noon hour. They spent a couple of hours relating specifics of the incident to the Garda Board and reviewing the arrest procedures. In the meantime, Royce Farley had secured legal representation for himself and Damien O'Mara, his sidekick with the gun.

At the moment, the three of them, Dillon, Suel, and DaVanni, were watching Farley and two solicitors, a gentleman by the name of Andrew Higgins and an associate named Conor Devine. They were viewing on a screen as Farley and his solicitors sat in Interview Room One discussing the few options they had. They could watch the three of them, but there was no sound. The conversation appeared calm. Dillon found it interesting that Farley was clothed in a light-blue hospital gown because there were no jumpsuits large enough to fit him.

There was a knock on the door, and DCI McCabe stepped into the viewing room. "They're ready, gentleman. Take your time. Farley strikes me as someone who won't say a word unless his legal team approves it in advance. So be prepared."

They entered Interview Room One in a prearranged manner, moving directly to the three chairs opposite Farley, with Higgins and Devine seated on either side of him. Farley was seated in a chair and took up more than half the space on the other side of the table. His body oozed over both sides of the chair, and Dillon wondered two things. First, how in the world could the chair support that massive weight? Second, how in God's name could anyone allow themselves to grow to that size? Farley was a lot of things, but stupid wasn't one of them. With your weight adding on an ounce at a time, at what point do you stop and do something about it? Apparently, Royce Farley hadn't reached that point yet.

The plan was to move right into business. Dispense with offering a tea or a trip to the restroom. Farley had two solicitors, more than enough to offer objections to anything Dillon and company presented.

Dillon began reading the standard opening lines. The interview would be taped. He had all six people in the room state their names and occupation. Once the standard legal statements were read, and all present stated that they had heard and understood them, Dillon read off the charges facing Farley.

"Mr. Farley, do you have an opening statement you would care to make?"

"Only that I was there, just like any other morning, preparing to say my prayers and begin the day."

"So you were there to pray and knew nothing about the Rothko paintings?"

"Yes, that's it exactly."

"And how many times a week or a month are you there to pray?"

Farley looked at his solicitors. They attempted to lean in and whisper in his ear, but he was so fat they couldn't get close enough, and so they had to stand and whisper.

A moment later, Farley said, "I'm there as often as possible. As you might imagine, my schedule is rather full, and so I find it oftentimes difficult to be there."

"And when you are able to pray, is it always in the early morning?"

"No anytime, day or night, whatever I can fit in. It's one of the advantages of living close to Phoenix Park."

"So when you received the text 'Ready and Waiting,' did you think that was from someone who wanted to join you in prayer?"

"My thought was—"

Higgins placed his hand on Farley's arm, stood, and whispered into his ear.

"I've no comment," Farley said.

"Were you going to pray with Damien O'Mara?"

"I'm not sure who you're referring to."

"He is the gentleman who had the gun. The gentleman you told to follow me up the stairs. He's the gentleman you've arranged legal representation for."

"I'm sorry, but I have no memory of that."

"Do you know a gentleman by the name of Aidan Phalen?"

Higgins stood and whispered in Farley's ear.

"I believe he may be a client in one of my businesses, and I may have met him at some point. Unfortunately, I can't seem to recall where or when. I've been experiencing some memory loss after you struck me in the back of my head."

"For the record," Dillon said. "I did not, nor have I ever struck Royce Farley in the back of his head or anywhere else for that matter."

The conversation went on like that for another twenty minutes, at which point Dillon got the nod from Suel and DaVanni. "Gentlemen, based on the information you are providing, or rather, the lack of information, we will close this and see you in court. Do you have a final statement you wish to offer?"

Farley looked over at Higgins, who shook his head, then said, "I wish to state for the record that my client, Mr. Royce Farley, is completely innocent of these nefarious charges. You are prosecuting a man whose only crime was praying for those who need help."

"Nice chatting with you, Mr. Farley. See you in court," Dillon said as he stood, gathered up his file, and they left the room.

"What a complete waste of time," Suel said once they were down the hall.

"What'd you think?" Dillon asked DaVanni.

"Typical, it's like when you catch a politician doing something illegal, and they rant about how innocent they are and why you aren't after someone in their opposing party. At the end of the day, I think it tells us that your friend Mr. Farley has little or no wiggle room, and he knows it. You've got Phalen, who said he'd testify. You might even have text messages or emails that correspond to the relationship. There's a good chance someone as old as Farley is more or less oblivious to the potential for damaging evidence on cellphones and computers. You might also want to invest in a search warrant for his property. If you had a list of missing artwork, he'd be a logical suspect."

Both Dillon and Suel nodded. "How long are you in town?" Dillon asked.

"It's going to take at least another week to arrange transport of the artwork back to the States. I'd like to meet again with Melanie Brussard. You've got the Rothko paintings in a vault somewhere. You think you might arrange a time when we could show her the paintings? The old man is a senator, might be a nice way of stepping up a positive effort of returning those paintings and adding a little more heat to Farley's fat ass."

"Oh, please, I don't even want to think about that," Suel said, and they all laughed.

FORTY-TWO

For the first time in what felt like a month, Dillon was home at a decent hour. He let Lucifer out into the front garden and picked up the bits of two styrofoam trays that had held pork chops and chicken breasts. He grabbed the leash, clicked it onto Lucifer's collar, and headed over to Albert Park for a long walk. They did three laps of the park, for a total of three-and-a-half miles, and then walked home.

For no particular reason, Dillon decided a salad was all he wanted for dinner. Could be that was the logical reaction after dealing with someone the size and shape of Royce Farley. Anyway, the salad wasn't too bad. He poured himself a glass of wine and thought about Aidan Phalen, his son Dessie, Pavel Krupin, Damien O'Mara, and Royce Farley. They were all going to pay a hell of a price. He had a second glass of wine, read three chapters in a mystery book about a gang of female bank robbers, and went to bed.

He took the longer route to Special Branch the following morning and drove by Nessa's home. He wasn't actually on Lindsay Road, but he slowed as he passed her street and glanced down toward her place. There was no sign of a red BMW, but then, whoever that guy had been, he seemed to leave around 5:00 in the morning.

He made it to Special Branch, trying not to think of Nessa, and ran into Suel in the break room.

"Working up the courage to risk your life on the coffee in here?" Suel asked.

"Actually, that's what I was planning to do, but based on the way you put it, I think I'll head out to one of the trucks and pay for a cup."

"Can't say as I blame you. What are you working on today? Trials for Phalen, Farley, and the rest of those knackers won't be for months. I think Farley will be able to post bail, and probably Aidan Phalen as well. Not sure about the others. Given the estimated value on the paintings, they could be cooling their heels compliments of the state for quite some time."

Dillon shook his head and said, "I was thinking about it last night, and I'm now of the mindset that they'll get what they deserve. Which reminds me, I'm going to try to line up a meeting with DaVanni and Melanie Brussard. Are you interested in joining us?"

"No offense, but no, thanks all the same. Nice folks, but they're going to be talking about the art world, and it's just not my thing. So, if you don't mind, I think I'll take a pass."

"Not a problem. Well, I'll be back in ten minutes, just running to get a coffee," Dillon said. He walked out of the building and headed toward the truck with coffee and sweet rolls. "Yeah, hi. I'll take a medium-sized coffee, black, and I'd better have one of those caramel rolls."

"Good choice," the woman said. "The rolls are fresh, still warm from the oven. They just came in not ten minutes ago."

Dillon smiled, thought for half a second, and said, "Better give me two."

He headed back into the building and up to Special Branch. Coffee in one hand, a bag of caramel rolls in the other. He set the coffee and the bag on his desk, took one of the caramel rolls over to Suel, and placed it on his desk. "Careful, it's sticky," he said and licked his fingers.

"Oh, thanks, I owe you, lad."

Dillon went back to reviewing the paperwork regarding yesterday's arrests. At 10:00, he placed a call to Dennis DaVanni.

"Dillon," was how DaVanni answered the phone.

"Hi, Dennis. I was going to try to reach Melanie Brussard. What's your schedule look like?"

"I'll adjust to whatever time works for her. I was thinking it would be fun if we could actually show her the paintings. But the more I thought about that, the worse the idea seemed. These things have been rolled up and apparently hidden behind a wall in the Louisiana heat for the better part of twenty years. There's a good chance they won't be in prime condition. We're putting out calls to a couple of restoration teams as I speak."

"What if we meet her in the art studio at Trinity?"

"That sounds like the better idea. Let me know the time, and I'll be there."

"I'll call her now," Dillon said.

They disconnected, and Dillon placed a call to Melanie Brussard. She answered on the second ring. "Hello, Melanie, Jack Dillon with Special Branch."

"Oh, yes, I saw it on the news last night. They didn't say it was the Rothko paintings, but I've had my fingers crossed ever since. Please, tell me you have them."

"Yes, we do, all of them. I've seen them, well, I've seen the canvases. They were all rolled up. They're currently in a vault, and Dennis DaVanni, he's the FBI Agent. He—"

"Yes, I remember him, very nice. He's on the Art Theft Crime Team, isn't he?"

"Yeah, he is. We were wondering if we could stop over and see you. Not sure of his schedule, but Dennis will be heading back to the States at some point. Would you have any time available? We could meet you in the art studio."

"Well, I'm just heading to my 11:00 class. What if we met at, say, 1:00? This will be so great. I'm working on another Rothko, and I'd love to have him take a look. Oh, and you too, of course."

Dillon smiled at that last line. "Let's plan on 1:00. If something comes up, just let me know."

"Okay, thanks, see you this afternoon," she said and disconnected.

Dillon phoned DaVanni again, told him the time, and promised to pick him up.

He pulled in front of DaVanni's place on Havelock Square ninety minutes later. Davanni was in the process of locking the pink front door. He gave Dillon a wave and hurried over to the car.

"Oh, thanks for setting this up, Dillon. I really enjoyed talking to her the last time we were there."

"She's all excited, told me she's working on another Rothko."

"No kidding? I'd like to see that."

It was a short drive to Trinity. Dillon pulled into the only available parking spot in the Staff Lot. He placed the sheet with the An Garda Síochána logo on his dashboard, and they climbed out of the car.

When they arrived, Melanie was painting in the back corner of the Art Studio. Her painting today was black with purplish rectangles. Dillon was unimpressed.

DaVanni, on the other hand, was all excited. "Oh, Melanie, don't tell me. Rothko's *Black on Maroon*, it's gorgeous."

She turned and grinned. "Hey, you guys. Thanks for coming over, and congratulations on getting those paintings back. I was on the phone with my dad last night after the news. I was hoping he would have more information, but he didn't know a thing about it. I can't tell you what a thrill it is to know something before he does."

Dillon gradually wandered around the studio, looking at various paintings, four pottery bowls, and some sort of a metal sculpture about three feet high that had assorted copper pipes sticking out of a tree stump in a number of different directions. He eventually settled into a chair and checked his phone for messages. He debated calling Nessa and decided that might be a bad idea with DaVanni and Brussard as an audience. She'd be at the office, and he thought it might be a good idea to be private just in case things headed down the wrong road.

It was at least forty-five minutes later when Da-Vanni said, "I suppose I'd better wake up Dillon and get him back to work."

"I'm awake, Agent DaVanni," Dillon said and opened his eyes. "Oh, say, Melanie, a little icing on the cake. I don't know if Dennis mentioned this, but two of the individuals arrested yesterday are being charged for assaults and rape on women in the Temple Bar district. You should be contacted shortly. The Garda will want your testimony to help lock those two up for a long time."

Brussard didn't say anything for a long moment. She just stood staring at Dillon with her mouth half-open and a stunned look on her face. "They, they caught them. Are you sure?"

"Oh yeah. We've got them on a security tape drugging a woman's glass of wine. Their car and license number have been identified. They've both been arrested, and I think it's a pretty sure bet they'll be going to jail for a long time. You'll be one of a number of witnesses."

"Oh, you've no idea how you just made my day. I'd like nothing better than to testify against them. Thank you. Thank you. If only they had the death penalty here."

Melanie and DaVanni promised to stay in touch. She gave DaVanni a hug, waved at Dillon, blew him a kiss, and they headed back to the car. Dillon and DaVanni shook hands when Dillon pulled to a stop in front of the house with the pink door.

"Any idea how long you're going to be in Dublin?" Dillon asked.

DaVanni shook his head and said, "I thought it might be longer but it's no more than a couple of days. I think we've got a restoration team lined up. They're going to send someone over and get the items secured. The Kincannon Art Museum is sending a private jet over so we won't have to deal with commercial airlines. It's all coming to a nice end for a change."

"It's been a pleasure working with you, Dennis. Really, it has. Thanks for being up at the top of the hill yesterday."

DaVanni shook his head. "My pleasure. Given the characters involved, it's amazing they got as far as they did."

"Never fails to amaze me," Dillon said.

FORTY-THREE

It was late afternoon in the office when Dillon's desk phone rang. "Marshal Dillon," was how he answered.

"Hi, Dillon. DI Quinn over at Pearce Street Station. How's your day going?"

"Pretty well, Seamus. How are things going on your end?"

"Been an interesting day."

"Oh?" Dillon said, wondering what had gone wrong.

"Based on the information we received regarding your arrests of this art theft group, it sounds as if two of them are quite possibly the Temple Bar pair that have been attacking women. The same pair who assaulted and raped the Cullen woman."

"There's no 'possibly' about it. They're the two. You've seen the security tape?"

"From The Workman's Pub? Oh yeah. We also picked up information from this Phalen character. Apparently, it's his son and a Russian thug they're associated with, although Phalen claims no knowledge."

"Aidan Phalen, yeah, sounds as though he served as a middleman for Royce Farley. Not surprisingly, that didn't work out very well."

Quinn chuckled. "I'm sure they'll both have plenty of time to reevaluate their decisions. Not to mention the trouble Phalen's son is about to find himself in when the rape and assault cases are filed. That said, the real reason I'm calling is DI Horace Tevlin. Thought you might be interested in an update."

"I've heard him referred to as 'Horace the Whore,'" Dillon said.

"That's what he's known as over here in Pearce Street Station. Apparently, Aidan Phalen identified him as our leak. He's been providing inside information on a variety of cases, including our effort to catch these two bastards who've been assaulting women in Temple Bar, as well as whatever the plans were on this artwork business."

"Yeah, we got hold of Dessie Phalen's car license, and he'd been identified on the security tape from the Workman's. At no surprise, he was missing in action when we arrived at Phalen's to make the arrest. But it turned out to be a small world, and we were able to arrest both of those rapist deadbeats when the artwork changed hands yesterday. No thanks to 'Horace the Whore.' Are you guys going after him, or do you want us to do it?"

"Already taken care of, in a manner of speaking."

"I guess I'm not quite following," Dillon said.

"We were waiting for him this morning. He was late coming in. He didn't answer our phone calls. We went over to his apartment with our ERT unit. To be honest, we were afraid he'd left town."

"That's what I was just thinking, but it sounds like he didn't leave. Did he go along quietly with you?"

"In a manner of speaking. We had to get a key from the manager of the building. Found him at the kitchen table, dead."

"Dead? Someone killed him?"

"I would guess the list is long of people who would have loved the opportunity, but typical of Tevlin, he grabbed the credit for himself."

"I'm not following," Dillon said.

"The plonker committed suicide. Blew out what little brains he had using the department's nine millimeter."

"Really? God, Seamus, I would usually say I'm sorry to hear that, but in Tevlin's case, I think I'll just say well done. That's gotta save a lot of paperwork and time for your station."

"You're not the first person to tell me that. Just thought you should know, Dillon. Probably the most decent thing the man has done in years."

"Thanks for the call, Seamus. I'll pass the word."

"We're all meeting at the Palace pub tonight to celebrate with a pint. You're welcome to join us."

"I'll keep it in mind. Raise a glass on my behalf," Dillon said, and Seamus Quinn hung up.

He met Suel at the Autobahn for a pint, which ended up being three pints each. They raised a glass to Tevlin, or as Suel said, "Here's to 'Horace the Whore' and the best decision he ever made." They went their separate ways after the third pint. Thankfully, Dillon only had two blocks to drive. He'd settled onto the couch, ready to read more of his mystery book, when his phone rang. Amazingly, the call was from Nessa.

"Hey, how are you doing? I was just thinking about you. You up for a glass or two of wine?"

"No, I'm not," she said in a tone that suggested he was about to learn more.

"Okay, what seems to be the prob—"

"What's the problem? Honest to God, that's the problem. It's like you're out to lunch. We haven't seen one another for days. I haven't heard from you. You could have sent me an email. God, you could have sent me a written letter, it's been so long, but no, you didn't do anything. Apparently, I'm just on call, and when you feel like it, well, we just meet up in the bedroom. This just isn't working. It's just not working."

Dillon was tempted to ask about the red BMW parked in front of her house or the guy stepping out of the place just after 5:00 in the morning. Instead, he said, "I'm sorry, I've been working on a big case. Actually, two, and they ended up being closely related. If you caught it on the news, there were a series of attempted abduct—"

"I don't care about that. All I care about is that you're going to do this again and again, and I guess I'm just supposed to sit around and wait for a phone call."

"No, that's not it at all. I, or rather we, were working on a very complex couple of cases. There was this art heist and—"

"Oh, well, why didn't you say so? That makes all the difference in the world. Not!"

"Nessa, I'm just trying to tell you what happened, and you keep cutting me off."

"Yes, because I don't want to hear it. You're all concerned about yourself and whatever the Garda have going on. Well, let me help. Don't ever call me again." Click.

Dillon thought for a half-second about driving over to her house and almost immediately shook his head. She was obviously clearing the decks for whoever the guy was driving the red BMW. No point in going over there. If the BMW was there, he'd want to slit the tires.

He opened his book, read a few chapters, and went up to bed. He woke the next morning, let Lucifer out, and was in the office before almost everyone else. Suel arrived an hour later with a smile on his face and the same clothes he'd had on yesterday.

"What? Did you sleep in your car last night?" Dillon asked.

"Well, If you must know, I ended up spending a wonderful night with Kira, who gave me up close and very personal attention."

"Oh, that's great news. Good for you."

"What's up with Nessa?"

"Oh, I think she's got something going that's keeping her busy."

Suel nodded in a way that suggested he'd read between the lines.

Later that morning, an envelope was dropped on Dillon's desk. Dillon looked at the envelope with a return address in County Wicklow. He opened the envelope and pulled out a card.

MR. AND MRS. KEVIN CULLEN
REQUEST THE PLEASURE OF YOUR
COMPANY
AT THE MARRIAGE OF THEIR DAUGHTER
KATHLEEN GEMMA CULLEN
TO
THOMAS J. DAUGHERTY
SON OF MR. AND MRS. CORMAC
DAUGHERTY

Dillon stared at the wedding invitation to Kate Cullen's wedding just a week from now, then quickly replied to the handwritten email address at the bottom of the invitation.

EPILOGUE

A week later, Dillon pulled in front of Suel's house. He grabbed the bag of dog food, two metal dishes, and dog biscuits, and then opened the back door and took hold of Lucifer's leash. They walked up to the front door. The fact that a white Honda Accord, exactly the same type of car that Kira owned, was parked in front of Suel's house wasn't lost on Dillon.

He had to pull on Lucifer's leash and get him to move closer so Dillon could reach the doorbell. Dillon rang the doorbell three times before Suel finally answered.

"What in the hell do you think—Oh Dillon, is it this week? The wedding? I thought it was next weekend." Suel was wearing flip-flops and red plaid boxer shorts when he answered the door.

"No, it's this afternoon, down in Wicklow. Thanks for offering to watch Lucifer for me. I was planning to leave him with my neighbor Tara, but she said she would be out of town. I got everything you're gonna need. His dishes, dog food, and biscuits to coax him into doing anything you want him to do. Now he's on a schedule. Let him out first thing in the morning and—"

"Paddy, are you coming on back to bed? Or should I start without you?" A woman's voice called from up on the second floor.

"Oh, well, sorry to interrupt. Hey, not to worry, Lucifer likes to watch," Dillon said and handed the armload of supplies and the leash to Suel.

"Hurry back," Suel said, then groaned and hip-checked the door to close it.

Dillon hurried to his car and drove off before Suel had a chance to change his mind. He was down in Wicklow ninety minutes later and had checked into the hotel where the reception would be held. He shaved, showered, dressed in a dark suit, and headed to St. Patrick's Church, where the wedding was.

He was seated in the back of the crowded church as guests were being escorted up the center aisle to be seated. The first three pews on either side of the center aisle were marked with a bouquets of white roses, signaling seating for the bride and groom's family.

Dillon was watching the people moving up the aisle when a voice from behind him said, "Excuse me, Officer Dillon?"

Dillon turned and looked at the man in the classic black tuxedo with tails. He had close-cropped white hair and sparkling blue eyes that, at the moment, looked ready to cry.

"Yes," Dillon said.

"My name is Kevin Cullen. My daughter Kate was hoping it was you. She'd like to see you, please. We all would. If you'd follow me."

Dillon stepped out of the pew and followed him to a room just off the vestibule of the church. There were four girls in long blue gowns, three women, probably a mother and two aunts, and then in a long white gown, Kate Cullen, the gorgeous bride.

The room immediately grew silent as Dillon entered.

"Here he is, Kate," her father said and wiped a tear from his cheek.

Kate Cullen stood in a gorgeous long bridal gown, staring as Dillon approached. Her face had healed, the cast was off her arm, and the missing tooth had been replaced. Her eyes began to water, and she bit her lower lip.

"No, darling, no tears. We don't have time to redo your makeup," one of the women said as she stepped forward with a Kleenex in her hand.

"Okay, okay, Mam. I promise I won't. Detective Dillon, I just wanted to thank you. I, I wouldn't be here today if it weren't for, for—"

"No Kate, no tears, honey," her mother said.

"You look gorgeous, Kate. We'll talk after the wedding," Dillon said.

She suddenly stepped forward, kissed him on the cheek, and whispered, "Thank you."

Dillon nodded and followed her father out of the room and back into the church. They walked past the pew where Dillon had sat, and Kevin Cullen led him up to the pews marked with the white roses. "You're part of our family today, sir. Thank you," Cullen said. He shook hands with Dillon, and wiped another tear from his face.

Dillon settled into the pew. A few minutes later, Terrence and Cara Greely, the couple who let Kate into their home and called the police, settled in next to Dillon. They exchanged smiles and handshakes, and suddenly the pews were filled with family members, each one smiling and giving the nod to the Greely's and Dillon as they entered.

The wedding ceremony was lovely, exactly fifty-five minutes, and Dillon was back in his car following the parade of vehicles to the reception.

Dillon chatted with the Greely's, sat next to them for dinner, and clapped as the bride and groom had their first dance. After dancing with her father, the bride approached Dillon and led him out to the dance floor, where he successfully avoided stepping on her bridal gown. "I can't thank you enough," she said and gave him another kiss on the cheek. "Come on and let me introduce you to my Tommy."

It was getting toward the end of the evening. Most of the guests were feeling little, if any, pain, and Dillon decided it was time to head up to his room.

"Well, if it isn't the guest of honor," a voice behind him said.

He turned to look. "Tara, what are you doing here?"

"I'm a first cousin to the groom's mother. You, umm, wouldn't happen to be staying down here, would you?"

"Yes, I have a room up on the fifth floor. What about you?"

"Well, I was planning to leave an hour ago and drive back home. Then I got talking to people I haven't seen since forever, and, well, you know how that goes."

"I do," Dillon said. "Need a place to stay?"

"I don't know how much sleep we'll get."

"I'm thinking I'm okay with that," Dillon said.

THE END

Thanks for taking the time to read <u>The Heist</u>. If you enjoyed the read please consider leaving a review, it really helps.

Don't miss the sample of <u>Jewels to Kill For</u>, the next book in the Jack Dillon Dublin Tales series.

JEWELS TO KILL FOR

PROLOGUE

Suel groaned as he slid out of his car. It wasn't quite 8:00 on a Monday morning, and he happened to park next to Dillon. "Oh, for God's sake, it's fecking freezing out. Of course, it wouldn't be Irish weather without some rain to make it completely miserable," he said as he hurried into the building.

Dillon grew up in Minnesota. He'd checked the weather report over there this morning like he did every day. The forecasted high temperature for this February day was fifteen degrees below zero on the Fahrenheit scale. That was minus twenty-six in Celsius, not to mention the three feet of snow on the Minnesota ground, with more on the way. He looked around the parking lot and glanced up at the gray sky. There was a light drizzle, but it wasn't lashing rain. *Yeah, it's a hell of a lot better than Minnesota at the moment*, he thought and followed Suel into the building.

"I don't know how you can stand it. There's something wrong with you, Dillon. The more miserable the weather, the more you like it," Suel said as they stepped onto the elevator.

"What can I tell you? I grew up in worse. It would get so cold I've seen dogs lifting their legs and getting stuck to fire hydrants."

"Really?" Suel asked. He gave Dillon a look and shook his head. They stepped out of the elevator and headed down the hall to Special Branch. Dillon input the code on the keypad next to the door. The door buzzed.

Suel pushed it open and headed for the breakroom. "I'm grabbing a hot tea. You want anything?"

"I'll see you in there," Dillon said.

The door to DCI McCabe's office suddenly opened, and McCabe stepped out. "Oh, Dillon, Suel, perfect. A moment of your time, please. Might as well leave your jackets on."

Suel waited until McCabe stepped back into his office and then looked over at Dillon and mouthed a rather foul invective. When they stepped into the office, McCabe was standing at the printer behind his desk. He took the two pages coming out of the printer, tapped them twice on the credenza, stapled them together, and handed them to Suel.

"This just came across from Finglas Station. Another shooting. The third in as many days. Victim is a male, no ID yet."

"Was he homeless, someone living on the street?" Suel asked.

"Slim chance. He was found in the driver's seat of a Mercedes parked in front of a council housing residence in Finglas."

"Did they think to run the license plate?"

"I'm presuming they have by now. The request came through around four a.m. Anyway, he was apparently shot sometime in the early morning hours. Finglas Station is asking for help. It's their third shooting in as many days. They're seeing a pattern and hoping to stop a gang war before it gets any worse. They're still on site. I'd like you to check it out and let me know. Any questions?"

Dillon shook his head. Suel said, "We're on it, sir."

"Good, close the door on your way out," McCabe said.

They headed out of the office. Suel gave a longing look at the breakroom as they made their way back to the elevator. "I'll drive," Dillon said.

Suel didn't respond. Once back in the car, he sat in the passenger seat with his arms crossed and looking anything but happy. Dillon input the Finglas address into the GPS and then pulled out of the parking lot. Instead of following the GPS directions and turning left to head out of Phoenix Park, he turned right and headed up Chesterfield Avenue, the main road in the park. He took the second turn in the roundabout and then pulled into the parking lot at the Phoenix Park Tea Room. "You stay here and see if you can find a smile. I'll grab a tea and a coffee."

Suel gave a slight nod. Dillon left the car running and hurried up the asphalt path to the Tea Room, a white octagonal structure surrounded by picnic tables. Given the weather, no one was seated outside. When he stepped inside, there were only four customers in the place, all quietly sipping tea. Dillon ordered tea, black coffee, and two chocolate brownies. He was back at the car four minutes later. He knocked on Suel's window, handed him the tea and the bag of brownies, and hurried over to the driver's side. He settled in behind the wheel, took a sip of his coffee, and set his cup in the console.

"You didn't have to do this, Dillon. Thanks. Sorry if I'm a bit of a pain this morning."

"You're not a bit of a bit of a pain, Paddy. You're a major pain in the ass. What's up? And before you say anything, let me just guess, Kira, again?"

"She said she didn't want to see me any more. Said it just wasn't working out."

Dillon had a number of different comments on the tip of his tongue. Not the least of which was this wasn't the first time Kira had expressed her unhappiness. Instead, he just said, "I'm sorry to hear that. Been there a number of times, and it's not fun. If there's anything I can do to help, let me know. I got us each a brownie in that bag. Figured you could use some sweetening."

Suel smiled and said, "Thanks. I take back some of the things the lads have been saying about you."

"That's more like it," Dillon said. They headed out of Phoenix Park and up to the Finglas section of Dublin.

ONE

They were headed over to Plunkett Avenue in Finglas. The crime scene was in the front parking lot of a two-story council housing structure, probably built in the mid to late 50s or early 60s. There were twenty attached units in the brick building, all with an outside entrance and a set of exposed stairs leading to the ten units on the second floor. A parking lot was at the front of the building where, at the moment, there were three Gardaí vehicles and a van from Dublin City Mortuary.

Dillon parked out on the street since both entrances to the parking lot were taped off by white plastic tape with blue letters that read '**GARDA NO ENTRY**' and then below that in smaller letters **CONFIDENTIAL TEL NO** with the **1 800 666111** number to report any information one might have. Two officers in raincoats and looking very cold stood at entrances on either end of the parking lot in the event someone decided the 'No Entry' didn't apply to them.

Dillon and Suel climbed out of the car and walked over to the nearest entry. Their IDs dangled from lanyards around their necks. The officer at the entrance took one look and nodded in the direction of the squad cars, then sneezed and sniffled. Dillon and Suel headed toward the black Mercedes surrounded by the squad cars. As they approached, Suel asked, "Who's in charge?"

"That would be me, DI Suel, and it's about damn time. How are you doing?" a voice called from the front of the Mercedes.

Suel glanced over the roof of the car and said, "God deliver me, Tully Egan. Who did you piss off to be put in charge of this investigation?"

"The list is long, Paddy, very long. It's good to have you with us. We've been more than a little busy," Egan said as he walked to the rear of the Mercedes and shook hands with Suel. "We can use all the help we can get, even if it's from the likes of you."

"Before you go too far down that road, I don't believe you've met my partner, US Marshal Jack Dillon."

Egan held out his hand and shook with Dillon. "No, we've not met, but I've heard about you and always wanted to meet the legend. You've been with Special Branch for a bit. You were involved in that situation out at Terminal Two a few years back, weren't you?"

Dillon nodded and said, "We heard you've been busy. Unfortunately, DCI McCabe mentioned this isn't the first incident."

Egan shook his head. "The third in as many days. No ID on your man, but I'm guessing it's somehow related to the other two. We're thinking maybe there's a bit of a flare-up between some locals and perhaps a Russian group."

"No idea who your man is? Have you thought about running the car license?" Suel said.

"Well, now, there you go. Why didn't we think of that? Great advice from Special Branch. Dillon, my condolences. You've got a lot of work to do bringing your partner up to speed, but you probably know that already. Yeah, Paddy, we've been waiting on the information. A new system, and if you can believe it, it's temporarily down. Take a look at him. I'm guessing mid to late thirties. No billfold. The insurance and license information was torn off the windscreen. It's beyond strange. We'll find out who he is soon enough. You can see where they tore the holder off the inside of the windshield."

Dillon glanced over at the passenger side of the car. In Ireland, there was a cardboard strip called a disc holder attached to the inside of the windshield. Usually provided by the insurance company, it has pockets that hold an insurance disc, a tax disc, and an NCT (National Car Testing) disc. Now just the remnants of the strip were stuck to the windshield. *Definitely torn off*, Dillon thought.

"Is there a weapon on your man?" Suel asked just as two men wheeled a gurney over.

Egan shook his head.

Dillon glanced over at the gurney, recognized Noel Leonard from Dublin City Morgue, and said, "Oh, hey, Noel, good to see you."

"Dillon, always a pleasure. How you been keeping?"

"Good, good, thanks for asking. And you?"

"The same, not a bother. Getting up close and personal with DI Egan here over the last few days." Leonard looked over at Egan and said, "Okay with you if we take your man? We've got photographs and stats."

Egan nodded and said, "Yeah, go ahead. We've taken his prints but wouldn't mind if you run them, too."

"Standard procedure," Leonard said.

The body was leaning forward with the right shoulder against the steering wheel, partially holding the man up. The victim's hair was black, cut close on the side and longer on top, partially covering what little of the face Dillon could see. The head was down and turned slightly, with the face more or less hidden either by the long black hair or the console.

Leonard and his partner wore blue latex gloves. They opened the driver's door, lowered the gurney, and quickly stretched out and opened the black plastic body bag.

Leonard took hold of the collar on the victim's jacket and pulled him up and back into a sitting position. As he did so, the long black hair fell away from his face exposing the entry wound on the right side of his skull and the exit wound that was just above the left eye. Leonard reached beneath the arms of the body and began to pull him partially out of the vehicle. As soon as he took a step back, his assistant reached in, grabbed the body by the belt buckle, and then angled the body back and forth, gradually working the legs over the seat and out of the car.

They laid the body on the gurney, and just as they took hold of the sides of the body bag, Suel shouted, "Wait a damn minute. I, I know this knacker."

"Suel, are you sure?" Egan asked and shot a look at Suel.

"Jesus Christ, and no surprise. Neil Kinan. I'm sure of it. I know the family. Grew up with them. Pull the jacket up on his right arm. There should be a tattoo on his forearm, a Celtic cross with the flag draped over it."

Leonard reached down and began to inch up the sleeve of the black leather jacket, and suddenly, there it was, the base of a Celtic cross. He hiked the sleeve up further until both ends of the Irish flag appeared, one side green, the other orange.

"That's good enough for me," Suel said. "I haven't seen him in years. I know he did two or three years in Mountjoy. That was probably six or eight years ago. He was a good kid who took a number of bad turns. Damn it."

"No weapon," Noel Leonard said and then looked up at DI Egan. "Okay to close the bag?"

"Yeah, go ahead." Egan looked over at Suel and Dillon. "Thus far, none of the residents we contacted saw or heard anything. In other words, no one's talking."

"Any idea why he was here?"

Egan shook his head. "Could be anything from meeting someone in the parking lot to paying one of the residents for a night of pleasure. At this stage, no idea, and, like I said, no one is talking, yet."

TWO

As they climed into Dillon's car, Suel said, "I've got the address here." They'd spent the last two hours in the Finglas Police Station, filing reports and reviewing records on Neil Kinan. Suel had been correct. Kinan had been sentenced to four years in Mountjoy Prison for drug trafficking but was released after two years and served the last two years in the community on license, a process that was pretty standard.

The address listed for Kinan turned out to be his mother's home. Suel recognized it because he'd grown up on the next street over. He'd offered to inform the family of Kinan's death, and he read the address off to Dillon, who input it into his GPS, although Suel knew exactly how to get there.

Dillon backed out of the parking place at Finglas Station, and they headed over to 52 Maryfield Cres. Suel had lived nearby at 110 Ardlea Road, in the area of Dublin known as Artane. Along the way, Suel described the Kinan family, five children. Neil was the second oldest and one of two boys. His older brother, Eoin, was a bricklayer and, as far as Suel knew, lived somewhere in Dublin. Of the three girls, Suel could only remember the name of one, Shannon. She was two or three years younger than him, and he lost track of her once he left school.

They drove out of Finglas along Glasnevin Avenue, which eventually turned into Collins Avenue once they entered Glasnevin. They drove all the way to Malahide Road, where they turned left and, a few minutes later, entered Artane and pulled onto Maryfield Cres.

"That's the place up ahead, the third one in, with that red car parked in the drive," Suel said and shook his head. "Amazing. It looks pretty much the same. Well, except that's a nicer car than I recall ever being in the area." The home was one of eight attached, two-story stucco units. The housing was the same up and down the street and no doubt on all the other streets in the area, including the next street over where Suel had grown up.

Dillon had been in enough of the homes to know the floor plan just by looking at the front windows. Three bedrooms upstairs, in this case, one for the parents, one for the boys, and one for the girls. A bathroom would be at the end of the hall on the second floor next to the stair-case and across from the third bedroom. With any luck, the bathroom would now have a shower rather than the original cast iron tub. The bedrooms on either exterior wall would have been built with coal-burning fireplaces for heat, although now all the units would have radiators and gas-fueled furnaces. The first floor would have a sit-ting room with a coal-burning fireplace and a kitchen with a dining area and another larger, coal-burning fire-place originally meant for cooking.

Dillon pulled to a stop in front of number 52 and glanced over at Suel. "You want me to come in with you? Happy to sit in the car and wait if you'd prefer."

"No, come on in. Wouldn't want you to miss out on the fun. Actually, I could use your support. I haven't seen Mrs. Kinan for twenty-plus years. I doubt she'll remember me, and after I tell her what happened, she sure as hell will never want to see me again. Damn it, come on, we might as well get this over with."

They climbed out of the car, walked through the front gate, and headed for the door. A sign just above the mail slot on the front door said, 'Please. No Solicitors.' Suel rang the doorbell, and they heard it chime inside. A moment later, the door opened, and an attractive blonde woman dressed in jeans and a red sweater answered the door.

She looked at the two of them and was about to say something when Suel said, "Shannon? Shannon Kinan?"

"Yes, I'm sorry. Do I know you?"

"Yeah, from a hundred years back, I'm Paddy Suel. I grew up behind you on Ardlea Road."

She seemed to think for a moment and then smiled and said, "Yes, yes, now I remember, and didn't you join An Garda Síochána?"

"Yes, I did. Still there, umm, as a matter of fact, that's why we're here. I'm afraid—"

"Oh, for the love of God. Don't tell me. No, wait, on second thought, do tell me. What stupid thing has my idiot brother Neil done now? Is he back to selling drugs? Did he rob a bank and leave his credit card there?"

"Actually, no. May we come inside and talk to you?"

After standing back to let them enter, Shannon asked again what was going on.

"I'm sorry to tell you this, but he was shot early this morning. Shot in his car."

She just stared for a long minute, trying to process what Suel had just said. "Shot? Where? When? Is he okay? What hospital is he—"

"Shannon, he was killed. We're part of the investigative team. Right now, we're just beginning to look into the situation. Because I knew Neil and your mother, well, and you, I wanted to be the one to tell you this unfortunate news. Is your mother home, and could we talk to her?"

She suddenly looked past Suel and extended her hand. "I'm sorry we've not met. Nothing like a first impression, eh? I'm Shannon Kinan."

Dillon stepped forward and said, "Shannon, it's nice to meet you. I'm sorry it's under this circumstance. And I—"

"No. You know what. In a way, this is good news, and it's not a surprise. This was bound to happen sooner or later. Neil just never caught on. You'd think his two years in the Joy would wake him up, but as soon as they let him out, he was back with the same crowd, doing the same dumb ass things. Oh my God, what a waste. What a stupid, stupid—" Tears started running down both cheeks, and she brought her hands up to her face as she cried, "Neil. Oh, Neil, why? Why?"

Dillon wasn't sure what to do, and he automatically wrapped his arms around her. She leaned into him and sobbed on his shoulder for a good long minute before she pulled back and wiped the tears from her face as best she could. "Oh, look at me. Sorry. We've some tea going in the kitchen and—"

"Shannon? Shannon?" An older voice suddenly called from the kitchen.

They followed Shannon into the kitchen. Lizzy Kinan was seated at an oak table with a mug of tea and a plate with a half-dozen chocolate-covered biscuits in front of her.

"Mum, you remember Paddy Suel. He grew up behind us on Ardlea Road."

"Suel? Paddy Suel? Are you the lad that broke the neighbor's window playing hurling in the back garden?" she laughed.

Suel hung his head and said, "Aw, Mrs. Kinan, I was hoping you'd forget that day."

"Forget it? Hardly, I loved it. They were dreadful neighbors."

"I'll get yous both a tea," Shannon said.

"And some more biscuits," Mrs. Kinan said. "You lads would eat an entire package."

"Mrs. Kinan, this is my partner, US Marshal Jack Dillon. He's attached to An Garda Síochána."

"Oh, so you're with the Guards, are you?"

"Yes, ma'am, we are," Suel said as they each took a chair opposite Mrs. Kinan. Once they were settled in, Shannon arrived with two mugs of tea. She set a mug in front of Suel and Dillon and then took a seat opposite them and next to her mother. Suel took a spoonful of sugar from the bowl on the table and stirred it into his tea. Dillon took a long sip and tried not to make a face.

"I'm afraid I have some bad news, ma'am," Suel said.

She looked at him and shook her head. "And you're with the Guards, so I would guess this is about Neil. God save us. What has he done this time?"

"I'm afraid he was killed earlier this morning over in Finglas."

"What? Killed? Neil? But how? What happened?"

"We don't have much information at this stage, just that he was killed in his car, and he—"

"Oh, that fancy black thing. Why am I not surprised? Was it a car crash? I suppose he was on the piss and driving too fast."

"Actually, no, ma'am. He was parked in front of a council house, and he was shot. Apparently, he died instantly. So, he didn't feel any pain."

"Shot? Did you say shot?"

"Yes, ma'am."

She took a deep breath and shook her head. "Good lord, the work we've done. The time we've spent, and he just never ever copped on. I gave him a room here. Can you imagine? He's thirty-five years old and—"

"Thirty-six, mum," Shannon said.

"Oh, even better, thirty-six and still living here. Never had a job he could hold for more than ninety days. Always going for the next big idea, which never, ever seemed to work. Honest to God," she said and shook her head. "Well, if you'll excuse me. I'm going to take some quiet time," she said as she got up from the table and left the room.

"Shannon, I'm sorry. I didn't mean to—"

Shannon raised a hand. "Don't say another word. In many ways, it's the logical end. He just never, ever copped on to life. Always with a plan to be a millionaire. Always knew more than anyone else. Thought he knew more than everyone who worked hard. And now this. I've no doubt whatever he was doing there, he was up to no good. Damn it. So much to offer, and he just always threw it away and messed up. Thirty-six years old, still living with his mum, and never even offered to pay a bill."

"We'll leave you to it, and we should probably get going," Suel said. "Your mother will be contacted by Finglas Station in the next day or two. They'll want to go through his belongings, looking for clues and—"

"The two of yas are not going anywhere until you finish your tea and eat a couple of those biscuits," she said.

THREE

They chatted with Shannon for another forty minutes, exchanged phone numbers, and promised to stay in touch. On their way out the door, they looked in on Mrs. Kinan. She was seated in a wingback chair in the sitting room, quietly saying the rosary. Suel didn't want to interrupt, and after they both said yet another 'goodbye' to Shannon, they headed out to the car.

Once in the car, Suel lifted the bag with the remaining brownie and said, "You going to eat this thing?"

Dillon shook his head and said, "No, you go ahead."

Suel crammed half the brownie into his mouth and said, "I'm thinking of calling Tully Egan at Finglas Station and volunteering the two of us to search through Neil's room and anything else he may have. It might make it easier on Mrs. Kinan if we showed up rather than someone she didn't know."

"Yeah, that's probably a good idea. I found it interesting that although they were both upset, I mean, who wouldn't be, but at the end of the day, they didn't seem to be all that surprised. It was like his death was the logical outcome of the life he led, and if it hadn't happened now, well, then it probably would next month or the month after."

"You think they may know what, exactly, he was up to?"

Dillon shook his head. "I didn't get that feeling. I just had the sense they weren't completely surprised because he was always involved with other idiots doing stupid things."

"Just incredible," Suel said and shoved the rest of the brownie into his mouth.

Once back in the office, Dillon met with DCI McCabe and brought him up to date. Suel phoned DI Tully Egan and suggested he and Dillon search Neil Kinan's personal items looking for something that might lead to a clue to whoever shot him. Egan thanked him and said he expected the warrant to arrive later that afternoon.

Dillon and Suel were having lunch in the breakroom when Suel got a call.

"Tully?" was how he answered. "Mmm, okay. Yeah, about thirty or forty-five minutes," he said and then disconnected.

"Did the warrant arrive?" Dillon asked.

Suel took a bite of his sandwich, nodded, and said, "Yeah."

This time, Suel drove to Finglas Station, a contemporary building on Mellows Road. They pulled into the parking lot and entered the front lobby. As they approached the front desk, the sergeant seated behind the counter looked up. "DI Suel?"

Suel nodded.

"I have an envelope for you, and I'll need a signature." He handed a form to Suel.

Suel signed the form and handed it back to the sergeant, then opened the envelope and checked the warrant. "Yeah, this will do. Thank you," he said, and they headed back to the car.

As they pulled out of the parking lot, Dillon was on his cell phone, placing a call to Shannon Kinan. She answered on the fourth ring. "Hello?"

"Hi Shannon, this is Jack Dillon."

"Oh, hi, umm, is everything okay?"

"Yes, it is. Say, we were able to get in touch with the powers that be over at Finglas Garda Station. They were going to do a search of Neil's personal items at your mother's house. We took the search warrant. Paddy and I would like to do the search ourselves, just to keep things a little more private, if that would be okay with you."

Suel looked over and shook his head.

"So, they're going to go through mom's house?"

"No, they won't because we told them we could do it, and that way, we can keep things focused just on Neil's things."

"When were you thinking of coming over?"

"Well, we could do it today if that works for you. The sooner we get it done, the less problem I think it will be for you and your mum."

"Would you be able to come over right now? That would work the best. My mum is at church talking to the priest, and she's liable to be there for a while. It would be wonderful if you could do this while she's gone."

"We'll head over right now. Thanks, Shannon, see you shortly."

"Smooth, Dillon, very smooth," Suel said and chuckled.

"This will work. Mrs. Kinan is up at the church visiting the priest. Hopefully, we can get in and out before she's back. I don't want to stress her out any more than she already is. At the end of the day, even though he was an idiot, she lost a son to a violent event."

"Yeah, I hear you."

Suel pulled in front of the Kinan house ten minutes later. Shannon opened the front door as they stepped through the gate. "Oh, thanks for coming right away. Mum will be at the church for another hour or two. They've arranged a prayer service, and Father White will be distributing communion."

"Thanks for helping out, Shannon," Suel said. "I felt so sorry for your mum and you this morning. There's just no easy way to let a family know what happened, and at the end of the day, it's a heartbreak for everyone."

Shannon nodded and said, "Come in and follow me upstairs. I'll show you Neil's room."

"Did he keep things anywhere else besides his room?"

She shook her head and said, "Not that I'm aware of. We have a garden shed in the back, and you could certainly take a look. I don't think he was ever in there. One of us had to cut the grass here. Neil was always too busy," she said and rolled her eyes. "Mick, our older brother, was ready to kill him. Oh, God, I probably shouldn't have said that," she said as they climbed the stairs.

"Not to worry," Suel replied.

She walked down the hall and opened the door to the third bedroom, just across from the bathroom. "Here it is, would yous like a tea or anything?"

"No, thank you. We'll be just fine," Suel said.

"All right then, I'll leave you to it," she said and headed back downstairs.

They stepped into the bedroom. A small fireplace, originally coal-burning, was on the wall to the left. A potted plastic plant was centered in the fireplace, and a wooden armoire of stained pine was next to it. A single bed was up against the radiator on the back wall, just below the windows looking out over the back garden. There was a sleeping bag on the bed, no sheets, and a very thin pillow. A worn wooden dresser with four drawers and the initials 'MK' carved on top of the dresser was next to the bed. A framed mirror with a crack running across the bottom was hanging above the dresser.

Dillon opened the door on the armoire. Four wrinkled shirts were on hangers, along with three pairs of jeans. Two pairs of scuffed shoes, both needing a shine, and a pair of well-worn walking boots were on the floor of the armoire. A cardboard box for a case of wine was filled with a stack of papers and envelopes in the back, just behind the walking boots. "I'm getting the feeling his mother didn't want to make things too comfortable for him," Dillon said.

"Who could blame her?" Suel said and pulled the top drawer open on the dresser.

Dillon took out his cell phone and took two photographs of the armoire. He ran his hand over the wrinkled shirts and checked the pockets on the jeans in case there might be something hidden. He stepped over to the bed, unzipped and opened the sleeping bag. A few long blonde hairs lay inside. An apparently used prophylactic was down towards the bottom of the sleeping bag. Dillon took two more pictures and then partially rolled up the sleeping bag, clearing the lower half of the single bed. He reached into the armoire, pulled out the wine box with the papers and envelopes, and set them on the bed.

"Hey, Paddy, take pictures of the drawers just to cover our ass in case we come up with something."

"You finding anything?" Suel asked.

"Not so far, but I'll start on this stack of mail and papers now."

Suel looked over, shook his head, and then pulled his cell phone out and took a photograph of the top drawer.

Dillon started going through the envelopes and papers. After a couple of minutes, he pulled up the disc holder that had apparently been on the inside of the windshield of the Mercedes Neil Kinan was found in. He pulled out the vehicle title. The name on the title for the 2021 Mercedes was listed as a gentleman named Robert O'Shea.

"What do you think about this?" Dillon asked and passed the title over to Suel.

Suel read through the title and looked up at Dillon. "My first thought is that Kinan didn't own the car he was found in, followed by the thought that he probably stole it."

"All this information was in the disc holder that was torn off the windshield of that Mercedes. The car had Dublin plates. I wonder if they were legit or if they'd been taken from another vehicle and placed on the Mercedes."

"Probably one of a number of scams we're liable to find here. All those papers are Kinan's?"

Dillon shook his head. "They're just in his possession, or rather were. A fair amount of mail from different homes on the street. It's like he was going through people's mailboxes looking for information. Well, plus the disc holder from the Mercedes. The guy had no legal source of income, at least that we know of. For the love of God, he was still living in his mother's house. Sleeping in a sleeping bag. Oh, by the way, evidence of a friend joining him in the sleeping bag."

"What? Don't tell me you found a thong."

"No, a prophylactic."

"You mean a used rubber? For God's sake, go wash your hands."

"Relax, I didn't touch it," Dillon said and started to wipe his hand on Suel's shirt until Suel slapped it away.

It took the better part of an hour, at which point Dillon had gone through the wine box full of papers and envelopes from various neighborhood addresses, plus the documents for the Mercedes. Suel had added a Christmas card from the dresser with the photo of a naked blonde woman wearing a Santa hat and a pleasant smile. The card was signed with the name Gemma, and below the name, a heart was drawn with an arrow through it. They headed downstairs, spoke to Shannon in the kitchen for a few minutes, and then left.

FOUR

As Suel pulled around the corner and headed back to Finglas Station, Dillon asked, "You think she was glad to see us go?"

Suel shook his head. "That might be too strong a term. I think she was just happy to have us out of there before her mother returned. It's gotta be tough. Regardless of what a worthless piece of shite her brother was, in the end, he was still the woman's son and Shannon's brother. I'm sure his mother is probably thinking back and wondering what she could or should have done differently."

"Was the father in the picture?"

Suel nodded and said, "Oh, yeah. Nice enough lad, if I remember. Died some years ago. Worked for Dublin County in the parks department. I think he died of a heart attack in his early fifties, but don't hold me to that."

"Do you like Shannon?"

Suel glanced over. "Shannon? Yeah, she seemed very nice. But if you're asking would I like to bed her? I got enough trouble on my hands just trying to get Kira back to being the lovely thing she was when we first met.

The last thing I need to do is bring another woman into the picture. Help yourself if that's what you're asking."

"Thanks, I just might do that."

Suel pulled into the Finglas Station parking lot, and they headed into the building. Dillon carried the wine box filled with papers. They set the box on DI Egan's desk and explained what they thought they might have found, which, with the exception of the Mercedes information, wasn't all that much.

Egan closely examined the photo of the naked woman on the Christmas card and set it off to the side. "Interesting info on the Mercedes. We finally got the response on the license plates a couple of hours ago. The Department of Transport's system is back up and running. The license plates on the Mercedes are actually for a 2020 Volkswagen Golf. I'm guessing Kinan was worried about having the Mercedes spotted and hoping the different license plate might stop him from getting pulled over."

"Yeah, unless they ran a check on that license plate and found it was for a Volkswagen instead of a Mercedes."

"And if the department's system was up and running," Egan said.

"There is that. So, what do you want us to do with all these envelopes and papers obviously taken from neighbors' mailboxes?" Suel said.

"Did you find anything in there like bank statements or insurance papers?"

Dillon shook his head and said, "Nothing like that, but my sense is that's the sort of thing Kinan was looking for. You think this could have been an attempt to find a way into people's accounts? You know, the way someone who isn't necessarily tech-savvy would go about it. Or, did he just gather this information up, the names and addresses, and pass it on to someone who was a lot more tech-savvy?"

"Based on what you have in the box, it would seem technology was not his strong suit," Egan said.

"Yeah, his sister told us not only did he not have a computer, but he hated the things and would do almost anything to avoid having to use one."

"I know the feeling," Egan said. "Okay, I'll pass this on to some underlings. In the meantime, try and find out who Kinan was in contact with. He had to be up to something. Just driving around in that stolen Mercedes seems to point to more than one individual. See if you can find out how, exactly, he acquired that vehicle."

"I'll start by giving this Robert O'Shea a call," Dillon said.

"Good, and Paddy," Egan said, "with any luck, we'll have a number of names from the fingerprints we recovered from the Mercedes. There's an outside chance our shooter may be among them. See if you can find that needle in the haystack."

By the time they were back in Special Branch, it was almost five. They got a couple things organized for the morning and left the office together. "You got plans for tonight?" Dillon asked.

"Herself canceled them. What about you?"

"I'm planning on taking Lucifer for a walk, grabbing a leftover meal from the refrigerator, and going to bed at a decent hour."

"You interested in stopping for a pint?" Suel asked.

"Yeah, I could probably do that. But one's my limit, and I'll buy."

That brought a smile to Suel's face, and he said, "How 'bout we stop at the Autobahn?"

"That would be perfect. I'll see you there," Dillon said. Since they had parked next to each other, Dillon followed Suel all the way to the Autobahn pub. He parked just behind Suel on Collins Avenue, and they headed into the pub together.

"See if you can search out a table, and I'll get the pints. You having a Guinness?"

"Do bears shite in the woods?" Suel replied and looked around for a table.

Dillon happened to catch the barman in between groups and ordered two pints of Guinness. The barman poured the pints, then topped them up after the prescribed two minutes, and shoved the glasses across the bar to Dillon.

Dillon caught Suel's wave from a table in the back of the pub. He took a healthy sip from one of the glasses so it wouldn't spill as he headed for their table. Once he arrived, he set his glass on the table.

"Well, done, you didn't spill so much as a drop," Suel said.

"That's because I took a big sip from both glasses," Dillon said and then took a sip from Suel's glass before he set it down in front of him.

"Oh, Jaysus, but you're a right plonker, Dillon," Suel said as he laughed and raised his glass across the table. They clinked glasses, and each took a big gulp. "Oh, just what the doctor ordered," Suel said. He took another large sip and looked around the place. "Pretty crowded for a Monday night. I guess everyone's in need of some relaxation."

"Yeah, I guess. Hey, you don't have to go into any detail, but I hope things work out for the best with you and Kira, whichever way it goes."

Suel took another sip and nodded. "Yeah, I'm start-ing to get to that place where I'm thinking I can only do so much, and if it's not making her happy, there's feck all I can do to change things."

"Well, believe me, I know how that works. Anyway, I hope things work out. If there's anything I can do, let me know."

"Thanks. Oh, and by the way, I'd say Shannon Ki-nan seemed to have a bit of an eye for you today."

"Shannon? Oh, thanks, do you really think so? She was too—"

"Dillon, you weren't paying attention, again. She was offering you tea and biscuits while we were looking through that depressing jail cell her brother lived in. She wasn't the least bit interested in the likes of me."

"What?"

"Did you notice how she was looking at you? Studying you?"

"No, I guess I didn't pick up on that."

"Typical. You were too interested in going through the contents of your man's Mercedes disc holder."

"Yeah, Robert O'Shea. Say, I wonder if Finglas Station ever contacted him to let him know his car has been recovered."

"Yeah, recovered with a body in it. I'd guess, right now, it's probably being put through the paces in the Tech Department. They'll be getting fingerprints, hair samples, the works. It could be weeks before your man gets it back. Then I don't know, if you're well-heeled enough to drive a Mercedes, would you want one that someone was murdered in?"

Dillon thought for a moment and said, "I think the world is just crazy enough that there's some nut case out there who would pay extra to have a car someone had been murdered in."

Suel thought for a moment and slowly nodded. A waitress stopped at the table and said, "Can I get yous another round?"

"Yes, please, two pints of Guinness," Suel said and pulled a twenty euro note from his pocket.

"Oh, I don't know, Paddy. I should—"

"That's right, Dillon, you don't know. So shut your trap and let me buy. We'll take the two pints, love," Suel said, and the waitress headed toward the bar.

They'd finished the second round, and Dillon said, "Thanks, Paddy. Much appreciated. I'll see you in the morning."

"Thanks for the warning, Dillon. Hopefully, I can get one of those wretched cups of tea from the break-room tomorrow before we head off tracking down another murder."

"With any luck, tonight will be a quiet night in Finglas," Dillon said, and they walked out together.

TO BE CONTINUED . . .

Thank you for taking the time to check out the sample of <u>Jewels To Kill For</u>, the next book in the Jack Dillon Dublin Tales series. As far as a quiet night in Finglas goes, well, better grab a copy and check things out. Thank you!

Don't miss the list of books by Mike Faricy.

Books by Mike Faricy
Crime Fiction Firsts

A boxset of the first four books in four crime fiction series:
Russian Roulette; Dev Haskell series
Welcome; Jack Dillon Dublin Tales series
Corridor Man; Corridor Man series
Reduced Ransom! Hot Shot series

The following titles comprise the Dev Haskell series:
Russian Roulette: Case 1
Mr. Swirlee: Case 2
Bite Me: Case 3
Bombshell: Case 4
Tutti Frutti: Case 5
Last Shot: Case 6
Ting-A-Ling: Case 7
Crickett: Case 8
Bulldog: Case 9
Double Trouble: Case 10
Yellow Ribbon: Case 11
Dog Gone: Case 12
Scam Man: Case 13
Foiled: Case 14
What Happens in Vegas… Case 15
Art Hound: Case 16

The Office: Case 17
Star Struck: Case 18
International Incident: Case 19
Guest From Hell: Case 20
Art Attack: Case 21
Mystery Man: Case 22
Bow-Wow Rescue: Case 23
Cold Case: Case 24
Cash Up Front: Case 25
Dream House: Case 26
Alley Katz: Case 27
The Big Gamble: Case 28
Bad to the Bone: Case 29
Silencio!: Case 30
Surprise, Surprise: Case 31
Hit & Run: Case 32
Suspect Santa: Case 33
P.I. Apprentice: Case 34
Rebel Without a Clue: Case 35
Puppy Love: Case 36

The following titles are Dev Haskell novellas:
Dollhouse
The Dance
Pixie
Fore!
Twinkle Toes
(*a Dev Haskell short story*)

The following are Dev Haskell Boxsets:

Dev Haskell Boxset 1-3
Dev Haskell Boxset 4-6
Dev Haskell Boxset 7-9
Dev Haskell Boxset 10-12
Dev Haskell Boxset 13-15
Dev Haskell Boxset 16-18
Dev Haskell Boxset 19-21
Dev Haskell Boxset 22-24
Dev Haskell Boxset 25-27
Dev Haskell Boxset 28-30
Dev Haskell Boxset 1-7
Dev Haskell Boxset 8-14
Dev Haskell Boxset 15-19
Dev Haskell Boxset 20-24
Dev Haskell Boxset 25-29

The following titles comprise the Jack Dillon Dublin Tales series:

Welcome
Jack Dillon Dublin Tale 1
Sweet Dreams
Jack Dillon Dublin Tale 2
Mirror Mirror
Jack Dillon Dublin Tale 3
Silver Bullet
Jack Dillon Dublin Tale 4
Fair City Blues
Jack Dillon Dublin Tale 5

Spade Work
Jack Dillon Dublin Tale 6
Madeline Missing
Jack Dillon Dublin Tale 7
Mistaken Identity
Jack Dillon Dublin Tale 8
Picture Perfect
Jack Dillon Dublin Tale 9
Dublin Moon
Jack Dillon Dublin Tale 10
Mystery Woman
Jack Dillon Dublin Tale 11
Second Chance
Jack Dillon Dublin Tale 12
Payback Brother
Jack Dillon Dublin Tale 13
The Heist
Jack Dillon Dublin Tale 14
Jewels To Kill For
Jack Dillon Dublin Tale 15
Retirement Scheme
Jack Dillon Dublin Tale 16
The Collector
Jack Dillon Dublin Tale 17

Jack Dillon Dublin Tales Boxsets:
Jack Dillon Dublin Tales 1-3
Jack Dillon Dublin Tales 4-6
Jack Dillon Dublin Tales 1-5

Jack Dillon Dublin Tales 1-7
Jack Dillon Dublin Tales 6-10

The following titles comprise the Hotshot series;
Reduced Ransom! Second Edition
Finders Keepers! Second Edition
Bankers Hours Second Edition
Chow Down Second Edition
Moonlight Dance Academy Second Edition
Irish Dukes (Fight Card Series)
written under the pseudonym Jack Tunney

The following titles comprise the Corridor Man series:
Corridor Man
Corridor Man 2: Opportunity knocks
Corridor Man 3: The Dungeon
Corridor Man 4: Dead End
Corridor Man 5: Finger
Corridor Man 6: Exit Strategy
Corridor Man 7: Trunk Music
Corridor Man 8: Birthday Boy
Corridor Man 9: Boss Man
Corridor Man 10: Bye Bye Bobby

Corridor Man novellas:
Corridor Man: Valentine
Corridor Man: Auditor
Corridor Man: Howling

Corridor Man: Spa Day

The following are Corridor Man Boxsets:
Corridor Man Boxset 1-3
Corridor Man Boxset 1-5
Corridor Man Boxset 6-9

THANK YOU!

Contact the author:
- Email: mikefaricyauthor@gmail.com
- Twitter: @Mikefaricybooks
- Facebook: Mike Faricy Author
- Website: http://www.mikefaricybooks.com

Published by

MJF Publishing

www.ingramcontent.com/pod-product-compliance
Lightning Source LLC
Chambersburg PA
CBHW070508310726
48976CB00002BA/381